GOLDEN NIGHT

"The ride wasn't so bad, was it?" He asked.

"It was fantastic."

Pulling off the helmet, she handed it to him, shaking out her hair. After tucking the helmets away, Cornell closed the distance between them.

"Didn't your grandmother warn you about guys like me?"

He smelled of leather, the wind, and the sea breeze. "You know she did," Gabrielle said, feeling reckless.

He moved closer. "And are you naughty or nice?" There was something mysterious in his eyes, and her insides quivered.

"Depends," she said in a voice unlike her own.

"On what?"

She never got the chance to respond before his lips captured hers in a breathtaking kiss.

Also by Candice Poarch from Dafina Romance

DISCARDED PROMISES
BITTERSWEET

Golden Night

CANDICE POARCH

Dafina
BOOKS

Kensington Publishing Corp.
http://www.kensingtonbooks.com

DAFINA BOOKS are published by

Kensington Publishing Corp.
850 Third Avenue
New York, NY 10022

All Kensington Titles, Imprints, and Distributed Lines are available at special quantity discounts for bulk purchases for sales promotions, premiums, fund-raising, and educational or institutional use. Special book excerpts or customized printings can also be created to fit specific needs. For details, write or phone the office of the Kensington special sales manager: Kensington Publishing Corp., 850 Third Avenue, New York, NY 10022, attn: Special Sales Department, Phone: 1-800-221-2647.

Dafina and the Dafina logo Reg. U.S. Pat. & TM Off.

ISBN-13: 978-0-7582-1977-0
ISBN-10: 0-7582-1977-6

First mass market printing: April 2007

10 9 8 7 6 5 4 3

Printed in the United States of America

ACKNOWLEDGMENTS

My sincere thanks to readers, book clubs, booksellers, and librarians for their continued support. A special thanks to the radio stations that promoted *Discarded Promises* and *Bittersweet*.

As always, profound thanks to my parents, my sister Evangeline who travels with me to promote my books, Sandy Rangel, Kate Duffy, Karen Thomas, and Karen Solem for their unswerving help. Most of all I am deeply grateful for my husband's continued support for my writing. And last but not least, thanks to my writer friends for keeping me sane.

ACKNOWLEDGMENTS

Paradise Island News

Yesterday around four P.M., three children found a late-model black Jeep Cherokee submerged in Heron Lake. An unidentified man was discovered dead inside. The local sheriff said the car must have been there for several months. Due to an unusual dry spell, the water level in the lake has decreased enough so that the roof was visible. . . .

CHAPTER 1

As a child, Gabrielle Long didn't appreciate the beauty of Virginia's Paradise Island. The tall sea grass swaying and bending in the wind, or the feel of hot-pebbled sand under her tiny feet, or the ache, wonder, and peace of the island's solitude. She could spend hours with memories of sinking her toes in the mud while she searched for oysters. Or in wonder over the island's bounty. The musical bird songs, whales bigger than a cottage spouting as they arrived with the warm weather. The dolphins and their acrobatics all so spectacular that technology couldn't begin to duplicate it.

Back then she hadn't appreciated the gathering of family around her or what role each person played in her life.

As a child, she'd enjoyed the beach, playing and swimming with her cousins. She loved Aunt Anna and Grandma's island cooking. If she closed her eyes, she could almost smell Aunt Anna's crabs frying in her cast-iron skillet. She and her cousins had squirmed in their seats waiting for Aunt Anna to place the first bunch of crabs on the layers of newspaper stacked high on the table to gather up the grease, which barely had a chance to touch the paper before the children had reached out, only to snatch their hands back when Aunt Anna warned them to wait while she patted up the excess. By then the crabs would have cooled enough not to burn their fingers.

And that first bite of succulent crabmeat. Oh, my gosh. Nothing on God's green earth could beat that.

Stomach growling, Gabrielle smiled at the memory. But this island was so much more than fun and food, or maybe it was a combination of those things and many other experiences that made it special.

Of one thing she was certain. It would take a lifetime to appreciate all of its bounties. A lifetime because you couldn't see it or appreciate it with your eyes alone. Vision only revealed a fraction of the story. You had to live it—you had to know the old folks to appreciate the rest. Which was almost irony itself. It wasn't until time had passed that wisdom emerged.

Wearing a thick housecoat over her pj's, Gabrielle Long stood outside her kitchen door enjoying her first cup of coffee while listening to the birds' racket outside and gazing at the wash of waves against the shore just a hundred feet from her old bungalow. She might have stood there for tens of minutes or only five. She didn't know which. But finally she turned and made her way inside through the screen door that had holes so large a cat could climb through. Boards on the screened-in back porch badly needed sanding; some also needed replacing and certainly a good coat of paint.

Once inside, she refilled her cup and glanced at the newspaper. A photo of an SUV was prominently displayed on the front page. *Roger Moore drove a black Jeep Cherokee.*

Gabrielle's hand trembled as she read the article. Coffee sloshed over the rim of her cup. Slowly she set it down on the table. He'd been missing since February. February 14, to be exact. Valentine's Day. That night Gabrielle had been feeling sorry for herself. Everyone seemed to be paired off. Her unromantic grandfather had even roused himself enough to spring for the last bunch of bedraggled roses and a box of inexpensive chocolates for her grandmother. Her cousins and friends had gotten roses, gourmet chocolates, diamonds, and whatever—and a man and sex. Sex seemed like something in the distant past for her.

Gabrielle had promoted a special romantic package for Paradise Bed-and-Breakfast—a romantic happy hour with truffles, chocolate-dipped fruit, and wine. A single red rose in each room. The B&B had sold out. But being around all those lovers made her realize how alone she was. She'd drunk wine with her guests, and it only intensified her bleak emotions.

After she left the B&B, she'd gone home to check on her aunt. Aunt Anna had soon gotten sick of her sour disposition and had demanded she go out with some friends. Gabrielle tried not to sink into depression. After all, she was alive, wasn't she? That should count for something.

After putting her aunt to bed, she drove to the bar. She had already downed a couple of Long Island iced teas before Roger joined her. It seemed that every time she drank, something horrible happened. She should have learned her lesson two years ago.

Gabrielle shook her head, casting that night to the back of her mind. All this time, Roger had been dead. And she'd thought he'd run away with her aunt's golden bowl.

Gabrielle nearly jumped out of her skin when the doorbell rang. It was, after all, nearly five in the morning. People didn't visit that early—not unless there was a problem.

Gabrielle padded to the door, and looked through the curtains. Sheriff Harper Porterfield—all six-three of him, dark and huge—stood on her front porch. He wasn't a man you wanted to get on the wrong side of or meet up with in an alley on a bad night. Years ago he had been the star linebacker of his football team. He'd even gotten a college scholarship, but he'd hurt his knees his senior year and never went pro. Defeated, he'd come back to tiny Paradise Island, where there wasn't much work to be had, and joined the local police department. They say he was fifty now and still single. The hair around his temples was turning gray, but that only made him look sexy as heck. Women ran after him as if he were the last breathing male.

Undoing the four locks, Gabrielle opened the door. Her aunt had been paranoid, and although her aunt was dead, Gabrielle still followed her routine before she went to bed, as if a thief couldn't break a window and come right in.

"Morning, Gabrielle," the sheriff's booming voice thundered in the room. "I went by the B and B but no one was stirring."

"I'm running a little late, Sheriff. Come on in."

"I won't take long," he said as he shut the door behind him. For such a large man, he was light on his feet.

"Can I get you some coffee?"

"No, thanks. Have you seen the morning paper?"

"I was just reading the article about the man they pulled from the lake."

He nodded. "The Virginia Beach PD contacted me about a key they found in John Doe's pocket. The key was to room 302 in your B and B. Could you check your records for a customer who may have stayed there in the last few months?" He gave her the license plate number.

"I don't have to check." She took a deep breath. "It was Roger Moore. He stayed there in February—around the time Aunt Anna died. He left a few things in the room. He'd been with us off and on for more than a year, so it wasn't unusual for him to leave things behind. I was wondering why he hadn't been back."

The sheriff took a pen and a small pad from his pocket and scribbled. "You're sure it's him?"

Gabrielle nodded. "He always asks for the same room. Room 302. He likes the privacy, and it's in a secluded area. He also drives a black Jeep Cherokee. I don't remember the license plate number, but I can pull the records as soon as I get to work. It won't take long."

"As soon as you do, call me. In the meantime, I'll send John Aldridge by to pick up his things. Can you have them ready by this afternoon?"

Gabrielle nodded.

The sheriff left, and Gabrielle stood there taking in deep breaths as she slowly closed the door. Heron Lake was her hangout with her cousins when they were teenagers and for summer vacations during her college years. She knew the area around that lake like the back of her hand. Not many people hung out there. It was out of the way, near the Dismal Swamp. People were afraid of all kinds of creatures out there.

Gabrielle had seen Roger in the bar that night. He'd told her he'd give her a bonus if she talked her aunt into selling him her gold heirloom antique bowl; he had even suggested she steal it. With her dementia, her aunt would never remember what had happened, he'd assured her. As if she'd even dream of doing such a thing. Angry enough to wring his neck, Gabrielle had tossed his wine in his face. She'd already told him a thousand times she wasn't going to sell it. It had been in the family since the early 1600s. He'd apologized profusely and told her he respected her integrity, but she didn't trust him one bit.

That night, Gabrielle had had enough of the bar scene. Suddenly, she felt wiped out and had gotten up to leave. As angry as she had been, why had she left the bar with him? No, she hadn't left with him. He'd gone outside at the same time.

After that, her mind was a complete blank.

Now she wondered—had she put thought to action? It was easy to say you wouldn't kill a person. And a golden bowl certainly wasn't just cause, even after being pestered for an entire year. But something had made her blank out. Had she been drugged? Had she seen something too horrendous for her brain to assimilate? Oh, God. Gabrielle rubbed a trembling hand across her brow. What happened between her and Roger on Valentine's night?

Cornell Price was sick and tired of crazy women. He'd gone back to New York to pack up the last of his belongings to ship to Virginia and close up his apartment. But his crazy ex-girlfriend, Angie, had trashed the place. Place had looked like a frigging chicken fight with feathers coating everything.

Ever since *Waiting to Exhale*, when Angela Bassett's character had filled her husband's car with his treasures and burned them, car and all, women started doing even more senseless shit.

But he'd made sure Angie paid. He'd given her an ultimatum. Either she paid for the damages—right then—or he was pressing charges. After a bout of tears and pouting he was totally immune to, she'd marched with him to the bank, but only because with her high-powered corporate position she couldn't afford to have a record. She could also afford to pay for the damages.

His gut roiled with regret. The greatest loss had been his mother's vases. She'd let his brothers and him choose their favorite designs. Angie had smashed every one. She knew they were his prized possessions simply because his mother had made them. They were irreplaceable.

He'd returned from New York the evening before and had spent the night at his parents' place in Norfolk. Now he was on the morning ferry to Paradise Island.

He couldn't count the number of times women had trashed something of his in a fit of anger, and he wasn't taking that crap anymore. Women were devious creatures. It was enough to make a man shake in his boots.

His mother was no better. Well, that wasn't *quite* true. She had enough sense not to damage anything valuable, but she'd do sneaky shit like cut up his dad's favorite pair of briefs or throw away his lucky golf shirt.

Crazy women were the reason he didn't give his key to dates. It had been a mistake giving Angie his keys so she could water his plants while he was away. She'd even killed the plants.

He sighed. Why did the men in his family put up with that crap? One night while he was visiting his Uncle Lucky on the island, he'd put the question to him. The older man, who was courting ninety by then, said he liked women with spice. But Lucky had divorced his spicy woman decades ago—and never got over her.

Cornell shook his head. To calm down, he opened the newspaper and read the article on the car in Heron Lake and wondered who might be in the vehicle.

He chuckled. It wasn't funny, but he wondered if the man's crazy girlfriend had done him in.

He knew one thing. No more spicy women for him. From now on, he was only going for the sweet, malleable ones. There would be no more of this "What about us? I've wasted a whole year on you. And now you decide to move. I can't just pick up and leave. I have a career."

His next woman would say, "Well, honey, when do you want to leave?"

He could already hear the "Oh, pu-leease, I didn't raise my sons to think like fools" coming from his mother's mouth. There was only so much of this madness a man could take. He had the right to protect himself, didn't he?

He wasn't going to be like Uncle Lucky and live down the road from the woman he loved for forty years because he couldn't live *with* her. And damn it, he wasn't going to live in fear of his wife destroying half his stuff whenever she decided to go whacko.

He glanced at the newspaper, thinking of the poor man they'd pulled from the bottom of Heron Lake. He wasn't going to end up like that poor bastard, either.

His dad had once pointed out that because of his sour disposition, he was painting all women with the same brush, but he wasn't willing to acknowledge it right now. He was still pissed off about his broken and smashed possessions, valuable things he'd accumulated over the years. All thrown in the trash because of Angie's uncontrollable temper. He wasn't buying her "I was PMSing," crap, either.

It was time the Price men made some changes. Besides, someone had to set an example for his two younger brothers.

His eyes were barely open when he dialed a number for a residence a few hundred miles away and listened to it ring four times before the receiver was picked up, dropped, and picked up again.

"This had better be good." Jade's voice came across the line sleepy and irritated.

"It is," he said, and proceeded to tell her about what he'd seen on the morning news.

"You think it's Roger?" she asked.

"Who the hell else? He's been missing for months. He's never done that before."

He heard the mattress creak as she sat up in bed. "Do you think he found anything?"

"We talked just before he disappeared, and he told me he hadn't."

"That doesn't mean a thing," she said, exasperated. "He's lied before."

"That backstabbing son of a bitch." Every time he thought about how Roger had cheated them on the last job, he saw red. "He better not have been holding out. Not this time."

"He knew better." Jade was using that calming voice now that grated his nerves. As if she was talking to a nitwit. Roger would cheat his own child if he could get away with it, and they certainly weren't high on his list. "We'll know as soon as the police reveal the contents of his car," Jade continued.

"Look, I didn't work my ass off to end up with nothing. We've been after this longer than any job we've done."

"You got a better suggestion? This will net us enough to get out of the business for good."

He remained silent. They'd been at it for months, and he had nothing to show for it.

"Listen, I have the contacts," Jade went on. "He couldn't have fenced it—not easily, anyway. So my bet is he didn't have it. He told me he searched the old biddy's place and couldn't find it."

"I checked his room when he first disappeared. Didn't find a thing."

"We're going to operate as if he didn't find it. Keep me posted."

He slowly hung up the phone. Easy for her to say. Her butt wasn't on the line. He needed money to finance his fixes, and he didn't have a lot of time to get it. He owed dangerous people a lot of money, people who wouldn't think twice about breaking his legs. So much for a sweet little deal situated in the middle of nowhere. Peace of cake, huh?

This was supposed to be their last job, but from the very beginning, it had been riddled with problems.

Gabrielle quickly dressed and left, but before her engine could warm up, she'd traveled the half-mile to the B&B and parked in the small parking lot in back. She lived close enough to walk if she didn't have to leave during the day to pick up provisions, or if she could wait for daybreak, but two professors were there on an extended stay, and they came down for breakfast at six sharp. They wanted coffee even earlier.

The imposing three-story building never failed to cheer Gabrielle. It sat like a gothic mansion against the backdrop of native trees and impressive gardens that would soon be hosting weddings. Cicadas and tree frogs sang in the background. Against the predawn backdrop, the dark windows lent a ghostly ambiance.

A native of Philly, never in her wildest imaginings had she dreamed that owning a B&B in the middle of nowhere would give her comfort. As she exited the car, she heard the rushing of waves against the shore no more than two hundred feet away.

Instead of starting the coffee, she hurried to the storage room and collected the box of Roger's belongings. She'd gone through his things before and had found nothing. She wanted to make sure she'd checked everything thoroughly before she relinquished the box to John.

She wasn't surprised he'd left nothing useful in his room. A pair of jeans, a couple shirts, some socks, a razor and other toiletries, and a pair of sneakers.

Then she saw a white Post-it note stuck to a sock. It read: *Should have the bowl soon.*

Gabrielle's heart sank. Did he have the bowl? If so, who had he sold it to? The note was obviously meant for another person. Who, other than Roger, was after the bowl? Was someone paying him to steal it? Her family had kept the bowl for nearly four hundred years. She just couldn't lose it on her watch. First she had to find out the contents of Roger's car. If the bowl was there, would she be able to retrieve it?

Gabrielle stuffed everything back into the box and put it back on the shelf.

Now she was running late. In the kitchen, she quickly made the coffee and set two pots in the dining room. Then she took out ingredients in preparation for breakfast.

The B&B held a total of twenty-four rooms on three floors, and all twenty-four of them were occupied due to a small business group meeting. Too bad that when her aunt and uncle first built it in 1940, they hadn't added an elevator.

"Who do you think killed him?" Her cousin, Regina Claxton, burst into the kitchen. With so many relatives on the island, Gabrielle didn't have to hire outside the family.

She glanced up from her chores. "I don't have a clue."

"I could never read him. Seemed nice enough."

"Hmm."

A big flirt, Regina was a whip of a woman around five feet two with a walnut complexion, and she didn't take grief off anybody. She went after her desires with the doggedness of a pit bull.

"Kept worrying you about Aunt Anna's bowl. Have you found it yet?"

"No."

"I wonder where that old bat hid it? She was always hiding things. We could make a small fortune off selling it. They say the whole set of four is worth way over a million dollars. It's been years since I last saw it." Regina poured herself a cup of coffee. "Heard they found one in the Jamestown dig. Wonder how it got there?"

"Haven't got a clue." The last thing Gabrielle wanted to talk about was that damn bowl. She'd lost too many nights of sleep over it.

"You don't think Aunt Anna sold it to someone and forgot, do you? She had terrible dementia the last few years."

"Who knows?" Aunt Anna's dementia was the reason Gabrielle had moved to Paradise Island and taken over the B&B.

"How come you lived in that house with her all that time and don't know? She must have said something about it."

Gabrielle placed several slices of bacon on the grill. "After so many people kept approaching her to buy it, she hid it, and I haven't seen it since."

"Well, it sure is a shame about Roger. He was friendly enough. Got along with everyone. I went out with him once, but all he wanted to do was pump me for information. Must have driven home drunk and forgot where he was. That can happen in the rain and fog. He drank way too much to suit me."

Gabrielle didn't respond. Located far from the beaten path, the lake wasn't a place everyone was familiar with—especially someone who wasn't from the area.

"Well, I started on my garden yesterday," Regina said, changing topics.

"How's it going?"

"It's not. What do I know about gardening? I don't know what kind of grass to plant. Some of the land around my place is sandy, some of it's rich dark dirt. It's a lot of bother."

"Talk to Sam. I'm sure he'll know." A landscape architect, Sam Lyons designed and created the B&B's garden. He owned his own gardening shop—the only one in town.

Regina shook her head. "Do you really think I can get a conversation out of that man? I've been trying to get him to ask me out on a date. Done everything short of dancing on my head. Do you think he's taken notice?"

"Can't help you there," Gabrielle said. Sam was a very private person. You never knew what he was thinking.

Gabrielle heard her cousin Alyssa's motorcycle long before it reached the B&B. "I must have told that woman a million times not to ride that thing here this early in the morning. Some guests like to sleep in."

"But does she ever listen?"

"At least we won't have to worry about her for the next few weeks," Gabrielle said.

A couple of minutes later, the swinging door opened to admit Alyssa.

"You think you can stop gossiping about me long enough to fix my breakfast before I hit the road?"

Alyssa had already poured herself a cup of coffee from the pot in the dining room. She stood in the door with cup in hand—all imposing six feet of her, straight as a beanpole.

"What do you want?" Gabrielle asked.

"The usual. Ham and cheese omelet, and fresh fruit on the side. Could you try not to burn the omelet this time?"

Gabrielle brandished a spatula. "Do you want to eat your breakfast or wear it?"

"Somebody got up on the wrong side of the bed this morning."

"You're getting a free breakfast, so watch what you say."

Alyssa Claxton was the island's only detective.

"If you didn't want the thing so hard on the inside, I wouldn't overcook it." Gabrielle cracked eggs in a bowl. "Aren't you leaving late?"

"It's only quarter to six," Alyssa said. "If you get a move on, I'll catch Melinda before the seven ferry. She's taking me to the airport."

"You be careful in the big city," Regina said.

Alyssa rolled her eyes. "Since when can't I take care of myself?"

"How long will you be gone?" Gabrielle asked, whipping the eggs into a froth.

"Just a few weeks." Alyssa was on her way to Phoenix for a special training class. Gabrielle wanted to talk to her, but there was little her cousin could do on her way out of town. "I stopped by Grandma's on my way over. She wants you to drop by."

Gabrielle glanced over her shoulder. "Did she say why?"

"Nope, and I didn't ask. She's out of sorts with Grandpa, and I'm not about to get in the middle of that."

"Coward. Wonder what he did to upset her this time?"

Regina toasted the bread and spooned strawberries, orange slices, blackberries, and peaches into a bowl while Gabrielle slid the omelet on a plate, added an orange slice, and handed it to Alyssa.

"You want to take over kitchen duties while I chat with Alyssa?" Gabrielle asked Regina. Regina complied, but by the time Gabrielle got to the dining room, the professors were just entering, looking much too cheerful.

"Good morning, ladies," the older man said.

Gabrielle grabbed menus. Approaching them, she started to hand them over, but they waved it away.

"We've memorized it by now," Mitchell Talbot said. He had retired last year and combed long strands of white hair over his bald spot. He was tall and lanky. This morning he wore a soft chambray shirt with jeans.

"I'm serving my grandmother's zucchini muffins for breakfast," Gabrielle said.

"The breakfasts are one of the things I like best about this place." The professor's young assistant, Graham Smith, who looked no older than Gabrielle's twenty-nine, yawned as he sat and snapped open his newspaper. Nothing newsworthy ever happened on the island, if you discounted somebody's dog chasing a neighbor's cat or neighbors bickering over picket fences about some minor infraction. Roger Moore's death was front-page news—his story covered the *entire* front page. The local reporter was a one-woman newspaper office, and she printed the paper weekly.

Graham opened the paper and immediately lost himself in the article.

"We've got big plans today," Mitchell said.

"Oh?"

"After my daughter and her friend leave, we're going to Jamestown. I've set up a meeting with one of their archaeologists. Really looking forward to it."

"Will you be back in time for the meet and greet?"

"Definitely. We should be finished early. Although I wish we'd scheduled it for another day."

"Where is your daughter?"

"Sleeping in. Kelly and June got in late from Virginia Beach last night. I hope they get down here before we leave."

"I'm sure you'll miss Kelly."

"June will be back for the crab feast," Mitchell said. "And Kelly will be here for Founders Day."

"I would appreciate it if you'd save me a piece of the strawberry pie," Graham said, glancing up from his paper. "Just in case we don't make it."

"I'll cut your slice as soon as I set the pies out."

Graham smiled and returned to reading his article.

Gabrielle didn't get a chance to sit with Alyssa, after all. Guests started to pour in for breakfast, and her cousin Lisa came in late for work.

CHAPTER 2

Cornell Price glanced at the twins, Lance and Chance Claxton, who weren't really that young if you thought about it. They were Gabrielle's cousins. Although they were eager to work, they were high school seniors and, at eighteen, were still rough around the edges, even though they thought of themselves as experienced men of the world.

"Explain to me again what happened," Cornell said.

"Well, it went like this, Neil," Lance began. "A couple of steaks were on the countertop. We left the dog outside by the door and told him to stay, but somebody left the door open and he came inside."

"He usually stays put when we tell him," Chance said. "He must have been looking for us."

"He must have been hungry when he ate the steaks," Lance offered. "The smell of food obviously enticed him inside."

"Why didn't you tie him up?" Cornell asked. "Why didn't you leave him in the car? Better yet, why the hell didn't you leave him home?"

"We're only going to be here a little while. We thought we could get some breakfast on our way to school. We have late classes today."

"Sun's bright. Car gets too hot to leave him there," Chance said.

"He's been trained," said Lance.

Cornell rubbed the back of his neck, trying to hold on to his patience. "You should get your money back."

"He's a good dog. We knew he wouldn't run away."

"So he came in here and ate my steaks instead. Can't be too well trained."

"We'll pay for the steaks," Chance offered.

"You can take it out of our paychecks."

"You bet I will."

"We already told the buyer to order extra."

"To replace those Brewster ate," said Chance.

"I trust you sanitized the place?" Cornell hazarded to ask.

"Right away. We know you don't want dog hair on your food."

Cornell closed his eyes briefly. Whatever made him decide to go into business, especially when he was forced to hire these people? What a morning—which started with the fact that Gabrielle intentionally tried to leave as much dust on him as possible when she drove by.

"Get your breakfast," he said. "And never, *ever* bring that dog here again."

"You an animal hater or something?"

"If the health department closes my shop, I don't make money. You're out of a job. Then somebody will have to bail me out of jail after I kill you. Does that answer your question?"

The twins went to get their breakfast.

Cornell escaped to his office, a small room just large enough for a couple of cabinets, a desk, and a chair. The secretary commanded more space.

The building had been a restaurant for more than sixty years. After his uncle's divorce more than fifty years ago, he never remarried and had no children. Uncle Lucky had closed the doors ten years ago when he was too old to run it. Since then, the space had been used for storage and an assortment of things, until about a year ago. When his uncle died, he left it to Cornell.

Cornell spent the last year renovating, doing most of the work himself with help from his father and brothers, who lived in Norfolk. His mother had added a decorating touch.

Cornell didn't want to run a restaurant. A few years ago, he'd seen a show on personal chefs who stocked customers' refrigerators each week with nourishing meals as an alternative to eating out. Many retirees and working parents lived in the Virginia Beach and Norfolk areas, actually most of the Hampton Roads area.

He'd already spent most of the money he'd saved working as a stock trader.

The ads he placed in local papers, including the military papers, were promising. For a month he set up booths in malls offering taste samples. Television spots got the word out. He'd purchased used refrigerated trucks for deliveries. It was even harder finding drivers who could pass the insurance company's tests. But he finally found a couple. So, with two trucks ready to go, his team would begin stocking his customers' refrigerators tomorrow.

Which was great for business. But on a personal note, watching the delectable Gabrielle every day was beginning to wear on his nerves. She reminded him of Halle Berry—classically beautiful with thick, long, black, and what they used to call *good* hair; café au lait complexion; hazel eyes; and she wore five-eight extremely well. He had to remind himself that she wasn't a sweet, malleable woman. None of the Claxton women were.

In a B&B, there were always a million things to do and not enough hours in the day to do them. Gabrielle was so familiar with the place she could tell which employee was approaching just by their footfalls. Now that she knew Lisa was coming, she hoped she would get more towels and not complain. If any other employee complained about working as much as Lisa did, Gabrielle would fire her. But Aunt Anna had doted on Lisa. So she tried to honor the older woman's wishes. Lisa was a great worker when she wasn't complaining.

Gabrielle took a deep breath and waited for Lisa's latest barrage of complaints.

Gabrielle was in the laundry room. She picked up the next towel and folded it.

"I don't understand why I have to clean most of the rooms alone," Lisa Claxton said. Her black hair was secured in a ponytail.

"Until Cornell starts preparing breakfast for us, Regina has to help do it. I thought you said you needed the extra money, anyway." Gabrielle placed the folded burgundy towel on the shelf.

"I can, but I'm due a break."

Gabrielle took in Lisa's sullen look. One that said the world owed her something.

"You work only eight hours. Look, I know you want to work part-time," Gabrielle said, thinking at least until she ran out of money. "I promise you Cornell will take care of the meals soon." Her regular cook had fallen in love with one of the hotel's guests and had left to cook in his restaurant in Florida.

"I need my afternoons off. I don't have a life anymore."

"I don't either right now. I really appreciate your helping out, Lisa. It won't be much longer."

"Humph." She gave Gabrielle a narrow look. "One week, Gabrielle. That's it. By the way, can you give me a small loan until payday?"

"You asked for a loan last week. If you need money, why complain about working a full day?"

"I'm just running a little low, that's all. You don't have to make a federal case out of it. I'll pay you back." Lisa never repaid loans.

"I'll take it out of your check."

"I don't know why you're so damn cheap. Aunt Anna gave you this place."

"Not that I owe you an explanation, but most of the profit goes into paying off the loan." She had a hotel company breathing down her neck to buy out the B&B. She couldn't afford to make late payments. They wanted to extend the B&B into a hundred-room luxury spa. She couldn't picture luxury on the island. It just didn't fit.

Eighteen months ago, Gabrielle had left a high-powered, high-stress job back in Philly. She'd failed to listen to the rules of office etiquette and dated a coworker. He was a nice man, and although they'd dated almost a year, Gabrielle felt herself drifting away from him. She just wasn't feeling it. When she severed the relationship, the working atmosphere grew tense. As long as she was there, he thought he had a chance to patch things up. She knew she'd have to find another job. So when her mother told her Aunt Anna was looking for someone to run the B&B, that no one back home wanted the responsibility, she saw the perfect opportunity to escape.

She thought she'd live in one of the rooms in the B&B, but her aunt's health was declining rapidly. Within a month, she'd moved in to help care for her.

Since Gabrielle's arrival at the island, all the stress from the city had drained from her like water from a shower—until her aunt died. Not that the B&B didn't have its own set of problems. When you dealt with people, there was always something, but most of them paid her exorbitant prices for a low-stress vacation. She made her B&B comfortable and pleasant. She worked long and hard to make their vacation a trip to paradise.

Though her island was only minutes from Virginia Beach, in atmosphere it was miles apart. While the Virginia Beach boardwalk was crowded and noisy, the beaches of Paradise Island were intimate and serene.

The phone rang. Absently, Gabrielle reached for it. She started her greeting spiel, "Good after—"

"Is this Gabrielle?"

"Yes, Grandma."

"I need your help. Come over here right away. Didn't Alyssa give you my message?"

"Yes, but she didn't say it was urgent. Is anything wrong?" Gabrielle asked. Both her grandparents were closing in on eighty.

"I need to talk to you. And don't tell those nosy cousins of yours. They don't know how to keep a secret."

"I'll be there in a few minutes."

Concern had Gabrielle searching for Regina. "I'm leaving. Look after things while I'm gone, please."

"I do, anyway, don't I?"

As Gabrielle drove past Personally Yours, she saw Cornell Price walking toward the front door. Must be nice to start your day late, she thought as she increased her speed. He raised a hand lazily toward her. She waved back but kept going.

"Something on fire?" he hollered after her.

"Not today," she told him as she sped past. He was one fine-looking man. Many mornings Gabrielle saw him jogging along the beach. Long, powerful legs stretched as he kicked up dirt from the soles of his shoes.

It was his company that was going to take over the restaurant duties.

Gabrielle arrived at her grandparents' home, a four-bedroom white Cape Cod. Her grandmother was waiting for her at the kitchen door.

"Your grandfather is in trouble," Naomi Claxton said, easing to the door that separated the kitchen from the family room.

"What kind of trouble?"

Naomi's hair was pulled back into a tight rolled braid pinned to the back of her head. It was so tight it pulled at the deep creases between her eyebrows. It almost hurt Gabrielle to look at her.

"He's been acting strange," Naomi said.

Strange wasn't unusual. Her grandmother always said he was strange when he got on her nerves. Maybe she just needed someone to vent on.

"Granddad's eighty. What kind of trouble can he be in? I know he didn't rob a store. He hasn't been speeding, has he?" The other week, one of her twin cousins almost rear-ended him. "The most he does is hang around Travis' Arts and Crafts store with his cronies."

"He hasn't been himself lately. He and his buddies have been out in the yard whispering all morning." Naomi tended to worry about everything.

Gabrielle sat in a ladder-back chair at the kitchen table. This was going to take a while.

The men—her grandfather, William, Herbert, and Travis— were always plotting and whispering about something. Why did her grandmother think things were different now? "They're probably plotting something to throw the city council meeting off. You know those men. They like to run everything now that they have nothing but time on their hands. Only last year you said Granddad was going down fast sitting around with nothing to do. You even encouraged him to get involved in a hobby. You should be happy he took your advice for a change."

"This is different. I'm telling you, he's up to something, and I want you to find out what it is."

"Me? You sleep next to him every night. Don't married people talk anymore?"

Naomi shook her head. "If he'd tell me, do you think I'd ask you? I may be up in age, but I'm not crazy. He shuts his mouth tight as a clam every time I try to pry it out of him." Naomi sighed. "He didn't sleep well last night—hasn't been for months now. Not since my sister, Anna, died." She whipped her glasses off and rubbed her eyes. "He didn't even like her. When he's not tossing and turning, keeping me awake half the night, he walks the floor or stares at the news channel. He jumps every time a car drives up in the yard. I tell you," she said, picking up her glasses and pointing them at Gabrielle, "those men have done something they've got no business doing. He'll be back in a minute." She nodded toward the connecting door. "Go in there with him. See for yourself." She made a shooing motion with her hands. "Go. Go."

"All right. All right."

Hoyt Claxton came in the front door, letting the storm door slam after him. He headed straight to his recliner. Sitting ramrod straight, he didn't even notice she was there.

"Hi, Grandpa." Gabrielle came farther into the room.

Usually he leaned back in his recliner, kicked up his feet, and crossed his ankles as he watched the news. Today, dark circles rimmed his eyes. For a moment he acted as if he didn't recognize her. Perhaps Naomi was right. Something was going on. But what? Her gentle grandfather getting into trouble? Gabrielle couldn't fathom it. He'd never been in trouble a day in his life.

"Everything okay?" she asked, approaching him.

"Sure, doll baby. I'm just fine."

Gabrielle smiled. He'd called her that since she was a baby.

"Can I get you a cup of coffee or something cool to drink?"

"I'm fine." He pushed the remote button to increase the volume. The morning paper, turned to the article on Robert, lay on the table by his chair. When the reporter on television focused on the car being pulled out of Heron Lake, her grandfather tensed.

Why would he tense? He had no connection to Robert. Was he aware of *her* connection? Had he seen her do something that night? If he had, he would have said something, wouldn't he?

Gabrielle stooped by his chair and rubbed his arm. "Grandpa, is there something you need to talk to me about?"

"No, baby."

"Grandpa, please tell me what you know."

"What would I know? You go on now. Sit a spell with your grandma."

Slowly, Gabrielle stood and regarded him. He was totally engrossed in the story. He watched as the SUV was dragged from the water.

Gabrielle couldn't stand to watch it any longer. She wished she could remember something, anything from that night. With no other option, she trooped back to the kitchen. Naomi stood at the door, nodding.

"See what I told you?" she whispered, closing the door behind them.

"Something's wrong," Gabrielle said, "but maybe he needs a checkup. Has he been to the doctor lately?"

"It got worse when they found that man in the lake. It's the talk of the island. All Hoyt's cronies were at my door at daybreak. Alyssa told me he was a Robert something. Didn't that boy stay at your place?"

"For a while, but he kept to himself except for a couple men he went fishing with sometimes."

"You don't think Hoyt had anything to do with his . . . I can't even say it. Why would he have anything to do with that man?"

"Of course not. Don't even think such a thing. Neither did the other men."

"Check around and see what you can find out."

"Did you mention this to Alyssa?" Even when she asked the question, she knew she hadn't. Alyssa would have mentioned it at breakfast.

"She was leaving town. I didn't want her to worry while she was away. What could she do from Phoenix, anyway?"

"John has lots of contacts in Virginia Beach. Maybe I can pump him for information." John Aldridge had been trying to get Gabrielle to date him.

"Good idea. You talk to him," Naomi said, taking iced tea from the fridge.

"Hmm." Gabrielle turned the option over in her mind. Did she really want to be beholden to John? If she approached him, he'd think she was finally giving in to his advances. Then she looked at Naomi and the worried frown on her brow. For her own peace of mind, Gabrielle needed to know what happened.

"What about talking to Uncle Cleve?"

"Nothing gets done when you bring men into a dispute. Cleve will go straight to Hoyt and ask him. Your grandfather will get angry and stubborn." She shook her salt-and-pepper head, more salt now than pepper. "Some things women have to take care of."

Naomi was right about that. Uncle Cleve would go at it so that nothing useful would get done. Both her grandparents would be in a stew. And nobody would be speaking to each other. They had enough family dramas.

"Yoo hoo!" Wanda Fisher, Naomi's next-door neighbor, pressed her round face against the screen door.

Gabrielle left her seat to unhook the latch.

"I just had to get away from that man. He's driving me crazy," she said as she entered the house, oblivious to the tension circulating in the room. She referred to her husband as "that man." Wanda was cheerful when her husband was out of town. Her navy slacks fit snugly, but most of it was concealed by an oversized white blouse. She was only around five-six, so it made her round figure appear even larger.

"What did he do?" Gabrielle asked.

"This time," Naomi muttered.

"What didn't he do?" Wanda wound up to begin her list of complaints.

Naomi held up a hand. "Before you get started, let me tell you I've got troubles of my own."

Openmouthed, Gabrielle stared at her grandmother. Naomi never turned down an understanding ear. Wanda was a timid woman. Her husband was abusive, emotionally if not physically, and Wanda often vented to Naomi.

"Why don't you just knock him upside the head with a frying pan? Or leave him if he doesn't get in line?" Naomi said.

Wanda reared back as if Naomi had struck her. "Hit him? I can't do that. He'd kill me."

"Leave him. Sometimes you're better off by yourself than putting up with nonsense."

"Where would I go?" Wanda asked, clearly baffled. "I'm not some young chick. I've never worked a job in my life. I married him right out of high school."

"You must have saved something from the grocery money. After all these years, didn't you put something away for a rainy day? You knew what kind of man he was. You're not just finding that out."

"Of course I saved something, but he always needed it when we went through lean times." Wanda clutched at her blouse collar. "I thought you'd be some help."

"I can't deal with your problems now. My nerves are just torn up." Naomi rubbed a hand across her brow.

Gabrielle poured a glass of tea and handed it to Wanda. Wanda's hand trembled so much Gabrielle thought the tea would spill.

The room grew silent; then Wanda set the glass on the table and got up, twisting her hands together as if she were a lost soul.

"I hope everything will be okay with you, Wanda," Gabrielle said quietly. Gabrielle wished she could offer the woman some comfort. "Why don't you come back later?" Gabrielle suggested. "When Grandma's feeling better."

For a moment, Wanda looked around as if she didn't know what to do with herself. As if Naomi had become her right hand and now she'd chopped it off. "Maybe I'll do that," she said, but she soon gave a sad little smile and left the house.

Gabrielle studied her grandmother. "That's not like you."

Naomi squeezed the dishrag in her hand, closed her eyes, and shook her head. "Lord, what's come over me? I've never treated her so shabbily. She's the sweetest neighbor I've ever had. I've got to apologize to her. You see what's happening? Hoyt is driving me crazy. I'm too old for this nonsense."

Then they heard the front door slam. They both moved toward the living room window and peeped out.

Hoyt was hustling down the street. William and Herbert were both heading to Travis's craft store. His daughter and wife ran an art gallery that catered to tourists. The men pulled the four rockers in a circle on the front porch and huddled like a bunch of football players discussing their next move.

"Do you see what I mean?" Naomi repeated.

Resigned to her chore, Gabrielle said, "I'm going to need an extra pie if you want me to ply secrets out of John." This was *not* something she wanted to do. She'd already left Philly because of a botched relationship. She didn't want John to get any ideas about them, because she liked life on the island, and she wasn't leaving her job ever again for a man—or anything else.

"Are the pies for the meet and greet ready yet?" Gabrielle asked.

"In the refrigerator."

"I may as well take them with me."

"Don't forget to tell Cornell about the meeting. It won't be long before the celebration is here."

"I won't. Although you have everything under control."

The meeting was for the Founders Day Celebration in May. Gabrielle was so confused about the family's history that she was going to have to read the documents again. A few years ago, Alyssa had typed up a few conversations on the family history she'd had with Aunt Anna.

At home, Gabrielle showered and changed into black dress slacks and a mauve blouse for the meet and greet. That evening most of the guests attended. She expected Cornell to handle the hors d'oeuvres, but he did all the prep work in the kitchen while one of his employees served.

She saw him in the doorway perusing the crowd, tracking his employee. Gabrielle didn't understand how or why her heart jolted. He wore the white chef's jacket over his shirt, a pair of jeans beneath. There was no reason for her to even notice him. She focused on Mitchell and Graham. They were always together.

Mitchell selected a glass of wine from the waiter.

"How was your trip to Jamestown?" Gabrielle asked.

"Good, good. Lots of wonderful and useful information. Even purchased some books. Think we'll stay here tomorrow. The roads out there were very busy. We considered staying the night in Williamsburg but decided to return. We didn't want to miss the festivities."

"There's nothing like spending evenings on the porch visiting," Graham said.

"I think I'll play a game of shuffleboard tonight. I made a date yesterday," Mitchell said.

Gabrielle knew the exact moment Cornell disappeared into the kitchen. And John hadn't stopped by on his nightly visit for a piece of pie. Nor had he retrieved Robert's things. He was late.

He was definitely going to be Personally Yours's best customer—after her B&B, of course. He wasn't very much of a cook, but he loved good food.

When Cornell conceived of the idea, he must have known exactly what he wanted, because from the very beginning, orders started to come in. Islanders waited for his opening with bated breath.

He employed several residents of the small island, many of whom Gabrielle was related to. Almost weekly articles were written about him in the mainland newspapers.

Gabrielle was among those who would benefit from his personal chef services. Her B&B, at least.

Mitchell nodded his head of stringy hair. "The atmosphere is simply wonderful here. Simply wonderful." He inhaled audibly. "In a few months or so, I'll be finished with my research. I'll be sad indeed then."

Gabrielle wondered how he got his work done. He had a handy laptop on the desk in his room that was never used. A printer was attached, but he hadn't even broken in the cartridge. Maybe he was one of those writers who didn't actually write until he'd finished gathering all his notes.

An hour later, after the guests had been sated and gone for walks or played games on the lawn, Gabrielle spotted John Aldridge parking and getting out of his car. Coming up the flower-bordered walkway, he raked a hand across his short-cropped hair. His uniform looked crisp, and he smelled as if he'd just come from the shower. He was an attractive ebony-complexioned man with brown eyes.

Gabrielle greeted him with a smile.

"I was just on my way to see you," John said. "Did you read the paper today?"

Gabrielle nodded.

"I remember seeing him around town. The sheriff asked me to pick up Moore's belongings."

"Everything is boxed," she said. "Follow me."

"You saved me a piece of pie, didn't you?"

"Grandma made you a whole pie."

"Strawberry?"

Gabrielle nodded. "And I have a tub of whipped cream for you."

"I love that woman."

Gabrielle chuckled.

"You're looking nice today."

She didn't want to go there. "Thank you. The storage room is through here." Gabrielle opened the door and reached for the box.

"Let me get that for you."

"I can do it." She pulled it off the shelf and handed it to John.

"Wouldn't want you to hurt your back."

"There isn't much in there. What did the Virginia Beach PD find in his car? What about the car registration?"

"The car was a rental. Was reported missing. He used a fake ID. We were hoping you'd have something."

"Sorry." They didn't mention finding anything significant in the car. But the police could be holding that information. "Was there anything interesting in the car?"

"I don't think so. Harper has been in contact with them."

How Gabrielle wished she'd known where the bowl was. Or was sure Aunt Anna hadn't told anyone of its location.

Roger's contact could have murdered him after he transferred the bowl.

"Was he murdered?" Gabrielle asked apprehensively. "Do you know what happened?"

"We have to wait for an autopsy," John said. "When was the last time you saw him?"

"Months ago when he stayed here. I left a piece of paper on top of his clothes with the address and number he registered with."

"Any additional information could give us a better range in the time of death."

"Wish I could tell you more. I always wondered what happened to him. He was meticulous, very neat, very precise. And suddenly nothing."

"Hmm," John said as he carried the box to his car. "When was he due to check out?"

"He was only here for the weekend."

"Do you have a list of his phone calls?"

"He used a cell phone."

"We can find out which service he used. Do you know if he was married?"

Gabrielle shook her head. "He never mentioned a wife. Never wore a wedding band."

Someone must be missing him. Gabrielle's family, if you counted aunts, uncles, cousins and the rest, was humongous.

Many of them lived on the island. Come to think of it, that wasn't necessarily a good thing. When trouble came, they called on her. When they were out of money, they came to her as if she were a bank.

John opened the trunk and tossed in the box. He shut the trunk with a snap and leaned against it. "When are you going to let me take you out?" Crossing his arms, he smiled. A dimple winked in his cheek. He nodded in the direction of her house, although it wasn't visible through the dense trees. "Your porch looks mighty cool and inviting in the evenings."

Gabrielle stifled a groan. "Why spoil a good friendship?"

"Maybe some other time." He moved closer to her, cramping her space. "I'll keep you updated on the case."

Gabrielle took two steps back and smiled. "I appreciate that. Wait a minute. You forgot your pie." She ran into the kitchen and brought the pie and whipped cream back to him.

He perused her with unnerving intensity. "I'll have to be satisfied with the pie . . . for now."

"We're friends, John. Let's keep it that way."

"Okay. Okay." After carefully setting his pie on the seat, he got into the car and drove off with a friendly wave.

Gabrielle went back inside and sorted through the next day's checkouts and reservations. It was dusk, and she was headed to her car when Sam Lyon's truck pulled into the yard.

"What are you doing here so late?" she asked.

"I left some tools in the shed. I'm going to need them for another job tomorrow. You're working late yourself."

"What else is new?"

Sam was a quiet soul. Aunt Anna took him in when he was sixteen after his parents died. It struck him really hard. Especially since he was never popular. People thought he was strange because, unless you spoke to him, he wouldn't even think of speaking to you. He'd never strike up a casual conversation, unless it was to talk about his work. Not even with Gabrielle. But

Roger had talked to him often when he stayed there. They went fishing.

Already Sam was striding toward the shed, so she ran to catch up with him. At six-one, his strides were long.

"Sam, do you have a minute?"

Impatience strained every muscle of his caramel face as he turned to face her.

"You heard the news about Roger, haven't you?"

"Sure is a damn shame. Wasn't that good at fishing, but he gave it his best."

"You all became pretty good friends?"

"Nope. He bugged me into taking him fishing with me." Sam was clearly aggravated.

"Am I annoying you with my questions?"

Sam shook his head. "Just thinking about Roger. He talked too much. Always asking questions. Telling stories instead of fishing."

"What kind of stories?"

"About lost treasures. Always asking about Ms. **Anna**'s gold bowl."

Gabrielle's heart skipped a beat. "Did she tell you where it was?"

"Nope. And I didn't ask."

"Did you ever see it?"

"Years back she used to leave it out until someone tried to steal it. Since then, she kept it hidden."

"You wouldn't happen to know her hiding places, would you?"

"Wouldn't be a hiding place if I knew."

Gabrielle tried to remember some of the faces she saw at the bar that night in February before everything went blank.

"Wasn't he friends with Jordan Ellis?"

He shrugged and started walking again as Gabrielle ran to keep up with him. "Can't say they were friends. They fished together, too."

"Aren't you and Ellis friends? Do you know where he is?"

"We fish together. Seems pleasant enough. At least he doesn't ask a lot of questions. I don't get in his business." He threw her an impatient glance. "Why all the questions?"

"The sheriff asked questions about Roger. I was trying to pinpoint who might know useful information so at least they can send the body home."

"I wouldn't know anything. Didn't get into his business."

He wouldn't, Gabrielle thought. He barely spoke to people. You had to draw every sentence out of him.

"Thanks, Sam. I'll see you tomorrow." Gabrielle made her way to her car with no more information than she'd started out with at five that morning.

On the drive home, she let her thoughts float to the night her aunt had died—the night that was completely blanked from her memory. And the fact that Naomi was worried that Hoyt knew something about Roger's death.

Wait a minute. She couldn't have killed Roger. How would she have driven his car into the lake and then gotten home? She couldn't drive two cars at once. So who else had motive to kill him? And why had he been in the lake area in the first place?

CHAPTER 3

It wasn't until Gabrielle made it home that she remembered her last meal had been breakfast—except for one slice of peach pie at the meet and greet.

Eager to rid her cramped toes of the high heels, she moved toward her house. Across the path, Cornell walked briskly toward his front door, swinging a bag on his arm. When he saw her, he stopped and waved.

"Hello," he called out.

Gabrielle greeted him. They should make some effort at becoming cordial neighbors, but who had time for small talk?

"Had dinner?" he asked. Switching directions, he moved closer to the path.

Gabrielle could barely see him with the dim yard light. "No," she said.

"Would you like to share mine?"

Surprise silenced her for a moment. Then she almost laughed. Not at the invitation, but at the thought of her aunt Anna and Cornell's uncle standing at the edge of their properties slinging insults at each other. Gabrielle was close enough now to see Cornell's frown.

"It's not a trick question."

She'd prefer one of his gourmet meals to a sandwich. Why not? "Sure, thanks."

"Come over in half an hour."

"Can I bring anything?"

"Just yourself."

He turned and disappeared into the night.

Gabrielle made her way to the house and headed straight for the bathroom and shower. Quickly undressing, she got under the spray. The warm water flowing over her washed away some of the stress, but not the thought of Roger's death and the bowl.

If only . . . if only she could remember the events of that night.

When Gabrielle got out of the shower, the red light was blinking on the answering machine. Sighing, she pressed the button. Her grandmother's voice came over the line with a hint of annoyance.

"Your grandfather's still marching around here like he's lost his mind. Men. What can I say?" She sighed as if at the end of her rope. "I know you're busy, but with everything going on, I forgot to ask if you've found the bowl. We need it for Founders Day. It's next month, you remember. You need to participate. It's your heritage, too. I can't get your cousins involved. Old folks can't carry on the family traditions forever, you know." A long sigh again. "Almost everything is in place, but there's still work to be done. It's your family obligation. If not for me, do it for your children. Don't forget the bowl!" Her grandmother finished with a snap.

As if she could forget, Gabrielle thought, and she didn't have any children.

There were other things Gabrielle wanted to forget, like the night after they buried Aunt Anna when everyone had gone home and she'd been left with her own thoughts for company. Cornell had come over at her most vulnerable state. Grief had hit her hard. He'd held her in his warm embrace, soothing her.

It was the first and only time he'd kissed her. The erotic memories must have been exaggerated due to her state of mind. She remembered the texture of his skin, his taste, smell, and every contour. The sweet caress of his lips. She would have let their lovemaking go further, but he'd gently pulled back. As gentlemanly as he'd been, she was embarrassed at her own wanton reaction. Still, he hadn't left. They'd sat side by side on the living room couch. And there they'd stayed until she finally fell asleep.

The next morning, she'd awakened snuggled up against him. She had gotten up to go to the bathroom. When she returned, he was gone. Were it not for the note on the table, she would have thought she'd dreamed the events of the night.

He never once mentioned that night. And he never returned to her aunt's house.

Of all the foolish things he could do, inviting Gabrielle to dinner had to be at the top of the list. Before his brain had the chance to fully form the thought, the invitation had poured from his mouth. Too late to cancel now. Besides, he had the extra food.

His brother had planned to spend the evening with him, but called at the last minute to cancel. Probably picked up a date.

He and Gabrielle were neighbors. The least they could do was be friendly, even if he wanted to finish what they started months ago.

Gabrielle, as stunning as she looked, was the last woman he should even consider forming a bond with.

Cornell's family had warned him to stay away from Gabrielle. No telling what bad blood had passed on.

But he didn't believe a word of it. His uncle had loved Anna. They just got along better when they lived in separate residences. When they'd lived together, all hell broke loose.

Besides, he wasn't used to a family breathing down his neck. Or living next door to a woman who expected forever after in the bargain.

He'd taken out steaks for dinner. But was she a vegetarian? Did she at least eat chicken?

He went with his original plan. Steaks. He put the meat in a marinade, then went to shower.

Cornell had finished the pasta salad and just put the steaks on the grill when his doorbell rang.

Gabrielle had changed into a pair of beige jeans and slip-on sneakers with a pretty red sweater. It was too much to hope she'd wear those killer heels with a dress. Give him a look at those legs. She was still a knockout.

Cornell couldn't stop himself from saying, "You look very pretty."

"Thank you." She handed him a bottle of wine.

"You shouldn't have," he said.

But she wasn't looking at him; she was scanning his room, giving him time to take in every inch of her. Thank God for tight jeans.

"I like the remodel," Gabrielle said.

The room was gorgeous. The layout was just like her aunt's, but the recent renovations were astounding. The living room to the right was decorated with a comfortable couch and chairs. The table was the kind you could put your feet on if you wanted to. Even a wooly throw was tossed across it. Unlike hers, he didn't have a TV in his.

To the left was the dining room. It, too, was plain. And the white wainscoting in both rooms added a beautiful touch, reminding her of the wainscoting in the B&B. It made Gabrielle wish she could afford to renovate her house.

"I really like what you've done," she finally said.

"It's small but enough room for me."

To keep her mind off him, she sniffed the air and made small talk—as if that would work. "Something smells delicious."

"Come on back. Steaks are on the grill." Then he stopped. "Do you eat red meat?"

She nodded. "Can I help?"

"Everything's almost ready. How do you like your steak?"

"Medium well."

"I'm glad you aren't one of those people who like their steak well done."

"I don't like it crawling, either."

Stainless-steel appliances predominated the kitchen. But the distressed wood island top and wood cabinets made it seem more homey and comfortable rather then commercial.

"So you did all this?"

"Most of it."

Gabrielle fully perused Cornell for the first time as he passed her. He was strikingly good-looking, with bronze skin, ebony eyes, and thick, dark eyelashes. He smelled fresh, with a subtle tint of woodsy cologne. The T-shirt molded to his chest gave her a glimpse of the muscles he gained from his workouts. She often watched him jogging along the beach. The only thing he was missing was a dog.

He opened the bottle of wine with the ease of a sommelier and filled two glasses. Fighting off a storm of emotions, Gabrielle leaned against the counter and sipped.

She should take her grandmother's advice and leave while she was ahead. Stay far away from Cornell. Holler back and forth across the path where it was safe. He was nothing but trouble and heartache, had already cost her a few nights of sleep. She was no more immune to the bad boy in him than the next woman. But she stayed put, and she watched him move around in the kitchen like the professional he was. So much at ease in his element. There was nothing feminine about him. All masculine grace. He kept the conversation going while she sipped on her wine. By the time he refilled her glass and food was on the table, she was completely relaxed—too relaxed.

"Grandma says your establishment is providing most of the food for the celebration."

"I'm one of the vendors. It took a lot to get them to approve."

"They've got long memories here, especially Grandma."

He pulled out a chair for Gabrielle, and she slid onto the seat, grateful she didn't melt right on the floor. A smile lit his face as bright as the candles around the room. Was he laughing at her?

she wondered as he doused the overhead light to set a romantic mood. She never should have drunk the wine on an empty stomach.

"Your family's really involved in the Founders Day celebration," he said as he sat.

"Although one of my grandmother's ancestors arrived in Jamestown with the first settlers, another landed on this island in 1617. Also, my father's ancestor came over on one of the three ships, too. After his indentured status was up, he worked for a couple of years to earn provisions and crossed the James to move farther out." Gabrielle cut a bite of the steak. "My dad met my mother when he came here for a genealogy search. He stayed at the B and B one month. My mother worked there during the summer. They fell in love and, as they say, the rest is history."

"Which explains why you were the mystery cousin. I spent some summers with my uncle. I met most of your other cousins. Of course, your grandmother always warned them away from me."

"My grandmother disliked your uncle intensely."

"My uncle and your aunt were a strange couple."

"Aunt Anna didn't like to be tied down. But my grandmother blamed your uncle for the relationship's failure, not her sister."

Cornell chuckled. "Every time she sees me, she says, 'There goes that Price boy. Stay away from him.'"

Gabrielle laughed because he mimicked her grandmother exactly. As she ate her steak, she realized this was the first time she'd relaxed the entire day. But she couldn't help thinking about the first generation who came to the new world, and evidently neither could he.

"Your aunt told me stories about your ancestors," he said.

"When?"

"All the time. While you were at work. She liked to talk and I listened."

"She'd talk to anyone who'd sit still long enough," Gabrielle said.

"She was proud of her heritage."

Gabrielle placed her fork on the plate.

Her expression dimmed, and Cornell was sorry he mentioned Anna.

"I didn't mean to upset you. You must miss her."

"I think her favorite tale was of the attack . . ."

It was the year 1617 and during a horrible storm, the ship veered off course. They wandered around aimlessly for weeks. It seemed they came upon storm after storm. They were tossed in the ocean like fish in a basket.

They had no idea where they were, when suddenly in the hovering fog, pirates attacked them. The men fought relentlessly, but the pirates fought fiercely until one by one, the men were dead.

All of them.

There were only seven women. The pirates loaded the meager provisions onto their own ship. As women were scarce in these parts, they took the women, too. They sailed again until they reached choppy waters. The ship rocked and pitched until they finally dropped anchor. They were rowed to shore on smaller boats.

And systematically, the women were raped.

The pirates had attacked a great many ships, Abiola knew, because they had barrels of spices, silks, gold chains, and bars and plates, and other things the captors weren't allowed to touch. They were obviously unaware of the potency of one particular spice. Abiola talked them into letting her use it in a dish from her homeland to add a new taste to the fish and meat. She promised them a feast fit for kings.

Her mother had taught her to be careful using the spice. The proper amount made the dish pleasing to the palate. Too much, her mother had warned, had a poisonous effect.

"I'll need lots of spices," Abiola assured the captain.

"Have your fill. We're celebrating!" Safe in his belief that

*the women couldn't leave, he was already half drunk. They'd
lit torches near the water's edge and built huge fires. There
were great sand dunes and tall sea grass. In the back were
huge trees twisted into strange forms, some so thick it was as
if they'd been standing there from the beginning of time.*

*Under any other circumstances, it would have been a
beautiful setting, with the tide rushing in. The air was warm
on her skin. It seemed they'd traveled forever to get to this un-
familiar land . . . and now this. She wasn't going down without a fight. . . .*

"Gabrielle . . . Gabrielle . . ."

She shook her head. "Yes?"

"You were out of it. You okay?"

She nodded, picked up her fork again, and resumed eating.
"The dinner is delicious."

Gabrielle stayed later than she'd planned. She was actually
enjoying herself. Was actually reluctant to go back to her
thoughts.

After dinner, she helped Cornell clean up, and when he
walked her home, she drew her jacket tighter around her shoulders. He walked so close to her she could feel his body heat.

Spring was in the air. Insects hummed into the night. Cornell's arm brushed against hers. The atmosphere suddenly felt
more intimate. Her stomach dipped, and her nerve endings
shimmered. She inhaled deeply. Gabrielle thought she was in
for a simple dinner, but now her heart beat rapidly as she
heard the flow of the tide in the background. The water
looked black in the moonlight. She couldn't forget the night
he held her in his arms.

"Want to walk along the beach?" Cornell asked.

It was cooler along the water, but she needed exercise after
that meal. "Let me grab a heavier jacket." In the kitchen she
grabbed one from the peg by the door, and the two of them
fell in step together.

* * *

He watched them from the cover of trees. Like lovers in the night, he thought. He had wanted to check Gabrielle's house while she was at dinner, but he couldn't get away quickly enough. Then he remembered Cornell spent a lot of time with the aunt before she died. The valuables could very well be stored in his house.

He silently cursed fate. He wasn't even supposed to be here. This wasn't part of his job. The damn job had gone awry from the very beginning.

He silently continued to watch the couple until they disappeared. Then he emerged from the trees and crossed the path to the cottage. He still needed quiet because sound carried on a country night.

This was his partner's job. But the SOB had disappeared. Hadn't seen him lately. Couldn't trust a freaking soul. First Roger and now this.

He crept up to back door and took out some tools. His partner could be in the place in seconds, while it took him four times as long. Finally, with a click, the door whispered open on well-oiled hinges. Silently he let the door close behind him. Using a tiny penlight, he shone it around the room just in case the guy was fool enough to leave it out in the open as if he wouldn't know what the bowl really was.

The bowl wasn't in the living room or anywhere downstairs. He started up the stairs, started going through closets, boxes. The guy didn't have very much. Most everything was neat and easy to go through. Not like the house across the path that looked like they'd stored stuff from the last four hundred years. Christ, how was anybody supposed to find anything in that crap? It could be right under his nose and he'd miss it.

This was his last job. He damn well better find a way to make enough to last. His nerves were plucked clear through with all the mix-ups.

It was supposed to be an easy job in a one-horse town, with barely a police department to speak of.

Yeah, right.

Cornell had planned to walk her home right after dinner, not prolong the evening, but with one of Gabrielle's sweet smiles, all his plans went awry. Truth be told, he was enjoying himself. He tried to convince himself he invited her to dinner simply because they were neighbors, but he could only fool himself so long before reality set in.

Gabrielle had intrigued him from the moment he moved back to the island. From the moment her aunt regaled him with stories of her youth.

They walked in the direction of the B&B, and soon the outside lights revealed the fabulous gardens. The building seemed quiet and eerie. A light fog had settled in like ghosts swaying in the moonlight. The perfect setting for a gothic novel.

"Do you like it here?" Cornell asked, breaking the comfortable silence they'd settled into.

"Very much. Growing up, it was a fun place to visit. We spent some holidays here and one week each summer, but I never dreamed I'd move here permanently."

Cornell slid his hands into his pockets and gazed out at the ocean. "This was my port in the storm. I loved spending summers with Uncle Lucky."

"How did he get a nickname like that?"

Cornell shrugged. "Better than his real name, Lucius, I guess. They said he was about the unluckiest man in the world, but he didn't feel that way."

They reversed directions and walked toward the house. The light faded into the distance, and their only illumination was the light from the bright moon and stars twinkling overhead—unlike any city view. And then . . .

"Hey, look." He pointed toward the sky. "Quick."

Gabrielle glanced up and briefly saw the burning meteor.

Then it was as if the flame burned out and there was nothing. If they hadn't been looking right then, they would have missed it completely.

"Wow," she said. "This is what I love about this place."

"Yeah, me too."

"You ever regret moving here? The slower pace? The lack of theater?"

"No. All that is a short ferry ride away."

She struck him as the theater and opera kind, especially when she was decked out in designer wear.

Anna had showered him with stories about Gabrielle. He used to tell her he had more sense than to get mixed up with a Claxton. But he began to wonder if his first taste of Gabrielle had been a dream. If her skin was as soft as he remembered.

He should leave her before he did something totally stupid and out of character.

Desire had been clenching his insides all evening, and when they reached her door, he tilted her chin and rubbed his thumb back and forth beneath. In a nervous gesture, she licked her lips. "I hadn't planned to kiss you," he whispered.

"Neither had I." Gabrielle's voice was as soft as a breeze.

He slowly lowered his head. The touch of her lips felt more enticing than he remembered.

Just a little taste, he promised himself. Share something memorable together, like that meteor. His dessert.

He ran his hands down her arms, wishing he could feel bare skin through the jacket. Then he embraced her, pulling her closer. One hand stroked through her hair. The other drew her tightly against him. She moaned softly, and his pulse quickened.

The night and surroundings faded to nothingness, and his world centered on Gabrielle—her fresh smell, the softness of her skin as he slid the back of his hands against her neck. The sweet taste of her. No wonder he couldn't get his mind off of her. His erection strained against them, and he released a low groan.

Her hand pressed against his neck, her tongue brushing across his lips. The kiss was robbing him of control. He shoved her jacket aside. And now that he'd had another taste . . .

Suddenly she jerked back. "I heard something."

"Probably my heart," he said. He pressed against her again and lowered his head once again to kiss her.

"No, really, I heard something. Let's check it out." She moved aside and started around the side of the house.

"Wait, wait, wait, baby. Probably an animal running through the bushes." The only thing on his mind was holding her next to him. He reached out for her, but she was already running around the house.

Damn it. "Hey, wait a minute," he said, trying to cool his ardor. He got in front of her. "Which direction did the noise come from?"

"Near your house."

"All the way from over there?" Cornell sighed. "Go in your place while I check it out."

"We're wasting time."

God save him from obstinate women. Not that he believed anyone was there. He'd go through the motions.

"Stay behind me." Gingerly they crept around the side of the house and across the path. He'd humor her, he thought, knowing very well the mood had been broken. Probably her intention in the first place.

This was usually a safe place. Some people still left their houses unlocked.

He checked the perimeter of the house; then quietly he opened his door, warning Gabrielle to stay outside. As soon as the door cracked open, he heard movement and saw a tiny beam from a penlight. Giving Gabrielle his cell phone, he shoved her out of the door.

Quietly, Gabrielle eased her way outside and dialed 911. When the dispatcher answered, she told him what was happening. Then she heard commotion from inside, dropped the phone, and searched around for a weapon.

Inside she heard the thrashing. *Oh, my God.* Fear streaked through her. She had to help. She found a thick stick and hoped the intruder didn't have a gun. She wasn't naturally a brave person, but she had to do something.

Inside, she pulled a long sharp knife out of the cutting block, then made her way to the living room where the men were tussling in the dark. She popped the light on, startling them enough so that they broke apart. The intruder bolted—straight to her. For a second she stood stunned. He was coming right at her.

Belatedly, she swung the knife with one hand and the stick with the other. With a short yelp, the man cried out and sprinted off as if a lioness was after him. He was quickly out of reach. She wasn't brave enough to run after him.

Dropping the stick, Gabrielle locked the door for all the good it had done in the first place and ran to the living room. "Cornell?"

She heard a moan.

"Oh, my gosh!" She ran over to him. "Where are you hurt?"

Finally she heard sirens. Took long enough. The assailant was probably long gone by now.

After she looked Cornell over, she'd insisted he go to the island's clinic. They roused Dr. Carter from her bed to tend to him.

Cornell had a lump on his head, but that was the worst of it. He insisted that he hadn't lost consciousness and didn't need to stay overnight. Word must have gotten around because her grandparents sent her cousins to spend the night with him to make sure he was awakened every few hours.

Cornell felt stifled. It was bad enough having to deal with the twins. It was just too much having them around at night, too.

Gabrielle and the boys cleaned up the glass and debris in Cornell's house.

"You're going to need a new set of lamps," Chance said.

Lance frowned. "A new coffee table, too."

"I banged my head on the table when I fell," Cornell said.

"Mighty hard head," Chance said.

"I think it's just horrible," Gabrielle bemoaned. "Why would someone want to break into your place, anyway?"

"The police asked the same question."

"You haven't made any money yet. Your business doesn't officially begin until Monday," Lance said.

Gabrielle picked up a pillow and placed it on the couch. This room had looked wonderful earlier that evening. And now . . . "Were you friends with Roger?"

"He, Jordan, and I went out on a couple fishing trips together. But we weren't bosom buddies."

"Did the police question you?" Gabrielle asked.

"No. I can't offer them anything." He had shopping to do. "We've done as much as we can. Boys, walk Gabrielle home. Then you two take off."

They shook their heads in unison. "We're keeping an eye on you," Chance said.

"I can take care of myself."

In the end, Lance stayed at Cornell's, and Chance stayed with Gabrielle, as if her place had been broken into as well. She could not sleep. For years, nothing exciting ever happened on the island, and now they were having a crime wave.

Lance had settled on her couch because there wasn't a television in the spare bedroom. When she went to bed, the TV was blaring, and she heard him talking into the cell phone late into the night.

"Hey, wake up." Gabrielle shook Lance. One arm and one foot were sprawled on the floor along with the blanket. She shook him again. She'd turned the downstairs TV off after he'd fallen asleep during the wee hours of the morning.

Lance moaned and turned toward the back of the couch.

"Lance, wake up." Gabrielle nudged him. When he didn't

respond, she took his pillow from beneath his head and whacked him with it.

"Go away," he groaned, catching the pillow, plopping it over his head.

"Don't you have school?"

With a moan, he continued to sleep.

Gabrielle went to the kitchen and took some ice cubes out of the freezer. After donning her coat and grabbing her purse and keys, she returned to the living room. Lance was still sprawled on his stomach. She slid the ice down his back.

And ran outside. From her car she heard curses rent the air. By the time he made it outside, she was driving off. That'll teach him not to watch TV all night.

Gabrielle started to check on Cornell to see how he fared through the night when she noticed his car was gone. She expected him to go in later. He'd gotten a pretty good lump on his head. She was sure Chance was still sleeping, too.

When she arrived at the B&B a couple of minutes later, the first thing she saw was Cornell's car. And Sam was already replacing the flowers in the foyer. Before she could get inside, he raced over to her.

"You okay?"

"Just fine, thanks."

"I was so worried when I heard. I came over, but it looked like you'd settled in for the night. And I saw the twins' car, so I thought you were okay."

"After all the commotion, I went straight to bed." Sam had been very loyal to her aunt, and he gave Gabrielle the same loyalty.

"Have you eaten yet?" Gabrielle asked.

He shook his head. "Busy day. Had to get started early."

"As soon as you finish with the flowers, come in and eat. Cornell's cooking today."

He scrunched up his face. "He's a terrific cook."

Gabrielle laughed. "I see you won't miss my cooking."

"No, no," Sam said hurriedly. "Your food is excellent."

She touched his arm. "Just teasing. I know he's better."

Inside, the professors were waiting for her. They forced her to sit and tell them what had happened. Since she didn't have to cook, she had a few minutes. Mitchell and Graham gave her a rundown on their research before Mitchell stood.

"Excuse me a minute. Your gardener was going to tell me about the gorgeous plants in the yard. I've tried to get mine to grow with no success."

Gabrielle watched him stride hurriedly across the room before she focused on Graham. "I have to get to work. Enjoy your breakfast, Graham."

In the kitchen, Cornell was working with another cook. Except for the scrapes from the night before, he looked okay. More than okay, if the increased acceleration of her heartbeat was any barometer.

"Don't you get sick days?" she asked.

"You're kidding, right?"

"Everything okay in here? Do you need any help?"

"We've got it under control. Leave my kitchen. This is man's territory."

"I'll just grab a bowl of cereal and fruit."

"Is that all you want?"

"Maybe a glass of cranberry juice."

"We'll bring it out in a minute."

"I can fix it myself."

"Go," he said, skillfully flipping an omelet into a plate. After adding potatoes and a sprig of mint, he handed it to his helper. The young man disappeared into the dining room.

"Do you know why someone would break into your house?" she asked.

"Heck no. There's nothing there to cart away except furniture, a TV, stuff like that. Whoever it was didn't bring a truck."

"Okay." She started to talk to him, but the waiter came back with another order. She was only in the way.

With him at the helm, she guessed it wasn't going to be business as usual.

CHAPTER 4

With a cup of coffee in hand, Regina stood on her front porch regarding her sad flowers. Beyond, the yard was a disaster. There were a few patches of grass that tried to sprout up in spots. She had been given a discount on the house due to the sad state of the yard.

The sellers had at least fixed up the inside by adding fresh white paint, replacing old faucets, gutting the kitchen and adding new appliances and cabinets, refinishing the wood floors. The only thing left was painting the rooms in the colors she wanted. Her father and brother had done that before she moved her furniture in. Gabrielle had given her some of Aunt Anna's beautiful pieces from the storage shed. Regina had waxed them to a bright sheen.

But the yard hadn't been given a thought. Aunt Anna had put the idea in her head in the first place about how pretty the house and lawn had been at one time, when an old lady had owned it in the fifties. How she'd planted a beautiful rose garden and flowers all over the place. White window boxes overflowed with colorful flowers from spring to fall. There were no window boxes now. Even now she could see the place where the boxes had once hung. Her father had promised to build new ones for her but hadn't gotten around to it.

The house had been a showplace, Anna had said. It was where she got the idea for her B&B flower garden. In the eighties, everything had died off when the house was rented out, and no one took time with the garden. Regina liked her sweet three-bedroom house. Small and intimate. She'd turned one of the bedrooms into a study. It suited her.

Aunt Anna had wanted Regina to have the house. Had even left her enough money for the down payment and extra to finish college.

She should plant her flowers—should have done it a week ago. She'd put it off long enough. Since Personally Yours had taken over the kitchen, she went in a little later. She could work on her flowers an hour or so before dressing for work.

Decision made, she set her coffee cup on the table. In the shed in back of the house, she dug out the hoe and gardening gloves. She needed a water bucket, too, so she grabbed the rusted pail the previous owners had left hanging on a nail on the wall.

What did she know about flowers except to dig a hole and plant them?

It was too fine a morning for digging in dirt. She had to start somewhere. She looked around. So many places needed flowers—or something. Finally, she chose a spot. Sam had planted flowers all over the B&B's yard. She wanted her flowers to be like those, in strategic places. She'd make a little grotto in the middle of the yard, maybe to the side. Then she'd plant a few around the house and pray they'd survive.

With the blade of the hoe, she drew a crooked square and stood back to see if it was designed the way she wanted it. She gave it a couple more tries before she deemed it in the proper spot. Then she made little rows of where she'd plant her flowers. Once that was completed to her satisfaction, she began to dig deeper rows. She would put a tree in the middle, so she dug that first. It was hard digging dirt out of hard packed earth, she thought after she'd dug for what seemed like forever. She was just about to put the shovel down again when the dirt moved—on its own. What in the world?

Stepping back as far as she could and still reach the hole in case something jumped out at her, Regina gingerly dug again—and lifted out a baby snake wiggling on the blade.

"Oh, my gosh." Regina jumped back, then inched forward. There were a million little snakes in the hole! Regina dropped the hoe and dashed to the house, locking the doors behind her. With her hand to her chest, she took several deep breaths. She had to do something to protect her space. She found a towel and stuffed it under her door. Then she ran to the phone and called her father.

"Daddy? I've got a yard full of snakes. Baby snakes. All over the place. Please come, hurry!"

Hanging the phone up, Regina glanced around. How on earth was she going to get to her car without getting eaten alive? Were they in her house?

"I need a man," Regina said later that afternoon when she marched into the laundry room.

With a chuckle, Gabrielle glanced up from the towel she was folding. "Been that long, huh?"

Regina rolled her eyes.

"May I ask why?" Gabrielle asked.

"Other than the obvious, I went to Sam's place the other day and asked him to suggest some flowers for my yard. Well, I brought all these containers that've just been sitting on my porch until I have time to plant them. I mean, I've been studying for exams." Regina reached for a towel and began to fold. "Anyway, this morning I finally started digging a hole in my front yard. And what do I see? A million little snakes crawling around. Scared the shit out of me."

"What did you do?"

"I called Daddy. He took care of them. I don't know how

and I didn't ask. But I'll tell you one thing, my yard needs fixing, and I'm not going to be the one to do it."

"Did you talk to your dad and brother about helping you?"

"They'll take their own sweet time. I need someone a little more reliable. Besides, Mama's yard doesn't look that great. I want my yard to look like yours."

Gabrielle started a load of laundry and took a load out of the dryer while Regina continued to fold. She was right about her father. He'd rather go out on a boat and fish than do yard work.

"I wonder what I could do for a man who can already cook better than I do?" Regina pondered. She sighed, placing the towel on a pile of folded ones. "He probably doesn't know a thing about plants."

"Sam knows," Gabrielle said. "He'll probably give you a discount." Regina setting her sights on Cornell was unappealing.

"Hmm. I would talk to him, but he's too weird."

"He's not weird. Why would you say something like that?"

"Who can get a decent conversation out of him? What would we talk about? I'd ask a question, he'd mumble an answer, then silence. In moments I'd be bored to tears. I wonder if he's a virgin?"

"What a question."

"I've never seen him on a date. Have you?"

Come to think of it, Gabrielle hadn't, but she hadn't given it much thought, either. "He talks to me."

"You mean after you go tripping after him. He's never still long enough. He was a couple years older than me in school, and he was strange even back then. Even when Aunt Anna took him in, he never mixed with the family. Always stood by himself."

"His parents died around that time. He took it pretty hard. Anyone would."

"I know. And I felt sorry for him. But it's been years and he's still the same."

"You ever consider that he's responding to the way people react to him? Not everyone has a huge family to lean on the way we do."

Regina sighed again. "I know, I know. But I was trying to find someone I could afford, like a boyfriend or something. I can't afford to pay him."

"Maybe he'll do it on a payment plan."

"Maybe. You always had a soft spot for Sam, just like Aunt Anna."

"I just don't think he deserves the rap he's getting."

"Always for the underdog."

"Somebody's got to cheer for them." She should know. She was always an underdog herself. Maybe she and Sam understood each other because they were kindred spirits.

Lisa joined them in the laundry room with a load of dirty laundry. It seemed all the guests were either out for the day or sitting outside on the porch facing the ocean and enjoying the warm spring day.

"What are you talking about?" she asked.

"My disaster of a yard," Regina said.

"At least you have one."

Here we go again, Gabrielle thought, waiting for Lisa to start on her woe-is-me story. Lisa was jealous of everybody. Aunt Anna had left her something in her will, too.

"Well, the whole town is talking about Roger," Lisa murmured.

"He's the latest hot topic," Regina said. "Strange he used a fake identity. He could have been a hit man for all we know."

Gabrielle had told Regina the bare basics about Roger. Not what had happened on Valentine's night, though.

"He used to date Melinda," Lisa muttered.

"Alyssa's friend? I thought she was dating Skeeter," Regina said.

"She was. And Skeeter didn't like it one bit when they broke up. He's the real jealous type."

"Why didn't I hear anything about this?" Gabrielle asked.

Annoyance flickered across Lisa's face. "You were trying to get this place fixed up. And Aunt Anna had you dancing to her tune. Didn't have time for island gossip."

"How long ago did they break up?"

"Just after Christmas," Lisa said. "He gave her a diamond necklace and earrings."

"I wonder if he stole them?" Regina asked. "Must be nice to have a boyfriend, somebody to give me something."

"I wouldn't know about that, but I know he was surprised when she dumped him." Lisa put sheets in the washer. "And then he just disappeared."

"You don't think Skeeter killed Roger out of jealousy, do you?" Gabrielle asked.

"Why would he? Melinda had already dumped Roger by then."

"Still . . ."

"Girl, please. Skeeter's all talk. He doesn't have a violent bone in his body," said Regina.

"I don't know. Roger's dead, isn't he? But it doesn't mean he was murdered," Lisa said.

"Roger was always talking about ships and stuff. I wonder if he lived in the Norfolk area?"

"Who knows?" Gabrielle mused. Most of the people around there had either been in the navy at some time or worked at the navy yard. Norfolk Naval Base was also the largest naval facility in the world.

"I don't know. Skeeter was soft. He may have belted Melinda a time or two, but she kicked his butt afterward."

"Good for her," Regina said. "And she could shoot, too. Skeeter was always scared of the noise. You know how he was as a boy. Never liked guns. Melinda used to go hunting with her grandpapa when she was a girl on account of he didn't have any grandsons to take with him. She wasn't scared of nothing. Heard tell she chased Skeeter away just before they broke up. He'd tied one on, and he was a mean drunk."

"He'll think about that the next time he hits a woman," Gabrielle said, and filed that information away. Seemed like Roger had any number of enemies. "Where's Skeeter now?"

Lisa placed a sheet on the pile. "Come to think of it, he disappeared a while ago."

"Maybe he did kill that fellow and took off. His grandparents should know. They were always close," Regina said before a teasing glint appeared in her eyes. "You better be careful, Gabrielle. Melinda has an eye on Cornell. But don't worry. He hasn't given her the time of day. His eyes are glued to you."

"Get out of here."

"Play dumb if you want to," Lisa said.

"You know those little dinner packages. Well, Melinda drops by Personally Yours to pick up her own," Regina said. "She'll be there today."

"We got her timed like clockwork."

Gabrielle shook her head at her cousins' teasing. "I hadn't noticed."

"Like that's news. You don't notice anything outside this place," Lisa said. "And running after old folks. You need a life."

Gabrielle tried to ignore that remark. The B&B required a lot of time. Especially when she had guests like Roger who left a ton of trouble behind. They'd revealed a couple of Roger's enemies. It was a matter of which one he'd ticked off enough to kill him. Gabrielle didn't believe he just happened to get lost in the lake.

"Did they take anything last night?" Naomi asked Gabrielle later that day.

"We caught him in time," Gabrielle said. The kitchen was filled with the scent of cooked fruit.

"We? What's this *we* business? What were you doing over there?"

"We had dinner together."

Naomi shook her index finger for emphasis. "I told you to stay away from that boy."

"That's going to be difficult with him living right across the path, Grandma. Especially since he's the only neighbor I have," Gabrielle said. "These pies for me?"

"Some are."

"Is Grandpa acting any better?"

"Don't think I'm too old to know you're changing the subject. There's nothing wrong with my memory. We'll discuss this later. Oh, by the way, your grandfather has spent his little stash."

"What stash?"

"He's always kept some money hidden. I checked his hiding place yesterday after you left. Nothing's there but an empty envelope."

"How much was it?"

"I don't quite know. I haven't counted it in a year. The last time I counted, there was five grand."

"If it was a secret, why do you know about it?"

Naomi looked at Gabrielle as if she were missing a few marbles. "I know what's going on in my own house. And come to think of it, William's grandson, Skeeter, disappeared the same time that man disappeared."

"Probably moved back with his parents?"

"He was working in Norfolk but living on the island. I know they gave him a leave of absence from his job. Heard Hoyt and William discussing it, but they'd moved off before I could find out why. The next thing I know, he's gone."

"I'll casually bring the subject up with Grandpa, see if he's ready to loosen up."

"They're over there hovering on Travis's porch now." Naomi shook her head and rose from her chair. "Come on. Help me take these pies to Wanda's. I'm not going to worry myself into an early grave."

"I think I'll give Cornell one as a thank-you for dinner."

"Stay away from that boy, you hear me? He's nothing but trouble."

"It was a neighborly dinner, not a marriage proposal, Grandma. You're making too much of it." Gabrielle took three of the pies and headed for the door.

"You better not hold your breath for a proposal. That boy isn't going to marry anymore than his uncle did. The time he and Anna were married was a nightmare." Naomi shook her head. "I hope to God your grandfather and those crazy men didn't do something foolish," she said, despite her promise to stop worrying. They made their way across a vivid green lawn.

"They didn't do anything, Grandma. That's the last thing you have to worry about. They may be eccentric, but that's as far as it goes."

"William fought in the Korean War. Sometimes they get it into their heads they have to protect the town. Like they could really do something."

"Protect the town from what?"

"Who knows what those foolish men think? They've done crazy stuff before, and when they don't have enough to do, they make up stuff. I'll tell you this, if they hadn't done anything, they wouldn't act guilty."

Wanda opened the door only seconds after they knocked, as if she was watching them as they approached. Wanda spent a lot of time at the window looking out—that was, if she wasn't at Naomi's.

"Wanda, forgive me for treating you so shabbily yesterday," Naomi said. "I feel so awful."

Wanda gave them a stunning grin, then hugged Naomi. "Don't give it another thought. You're my best friend in the world. Settled your troubles yet?"

"Don't even mention it." Naomi moved past Wanda and headed straight for the kitchen. They set the pies on the countertop.

"What have you got there?" Wanda asked.

"Strawberry, blueberry, apple, and peach. I baked them this morning for you." Naomi sniffed. She had the most sensitive nose when it came to odors. "Smells like you've been cutting fresh meat."

"After I dropped Harvey off at the airport this morning, I drove to Smithfield. Pork was on sale. My freezer is packed with enough to last a while. I got some for you, too, in the fridge. You saved me a trip. Don't forget to take it with you when you leave."

"That was kind of you, especially after the way I treated you. What do I owe you?"

"You don't owe me one penny. That's enough of that. We all have bad days." Wanda covered her cheeks with her hands. "Oh, my goodness. I'm going to freeze some of my pies. I just love your pies. You've got the magic touch." She waved her hand toward the table and started moving about like a wound-up jack-in-the-box. "You and Gabrielle have a seat. I'll freeze them later, after they cool. I just made a cake. Have some with ice cream."

"Wanda, what did I tell you about saving a little on the side?" Naomi said. "If you needed to move into a hotel for a few days, you don't have to go begging to your husband for the money. Now, I'm coming back here later to pay you for the meat. Meat's expensive. Gas alone cost a fortune."

"I had to go, anyway."

They really didn't have time to stay, but they sat anyway and waited for Wanda to serve them. She tried so hard to please everybody. It was sad to see her work so hard at pleasing. Nobody ever told her it was an impossible task, or her self-esteem had been whipped until she still spent her life trying.

Gabrielle stood. "Let me help you, Wanda," she said.

"No, no. I have it. Just sit."

Gabrielle sat and waited while Wanda and Naomi carried on a conversation. Gabrielle tuned them out.

The kitchen was very neat and homey with little knick-knacks. Wanda loved birds of all kinds, and little porcelain birds of a variety of breeds were displayed on shelves. Even her decorative cup towels were embroidered with birds.

Wanda fixed herself a big helping and sat at the kitchen table with them, as happy as a lamb. Wanda was always happy when her husband left on an assignment. But when her husband was home, she was nervous and jittery, always looking for an excuse to leave the house. It just wasn't healthy living life like that. Having a man just wasn't worth it.

"Your flowers are so pretty," Naomi said. "My yard is in a real mess. Moles are just tearing up my grass, leaving rows of brown streaks."

"Caster beans work for me."

"Maybe I'll try it. Your yard is the best-looking on the street. Such gorgeous flowers."

Wanda beamed. "Pretty flowers just brighten the day, don't you think?"

Gabrielle glanced at the pretty flowers in vases on the countertop and table and had to agree they brightened the room considerably.

"They certainly do," Naomi said.

"I know I'm weak," Wanda said. "I'm not strong like you, Naomi."

Naomi patted her hand. "Everybody's weak sometimes. Even me. We all need somebody to lean on."

Gabrielle knew Naomi was thinking of Hoyt and what she was going through with him holding secrets.

"It was just one of those days. But Harvey got a new assignment, and I took him to the airport this morning, thank heavens." She looked up toward the ceiling and closed her eyes briefly.

"He's not always going to have an out-of-town job to go to. What happens when he retires? He's going to be underfoot all the time. What are you going to do then?" Naomi wanted to know.

"I'll worry about that when the time comes. Right now, his contract is for two years," Wanda said around a bite of cake. "For two years I'll get some peace."

"Oh, Wanda. I hate for you to go through life like this. Marriage should be with two people who love and communicate with each other. Not for people who want to get away from each other."

"Naomi, most marriages aren't like yours. You watch too many of those TV pictures. Most men aren't that nice. But I'll survive. I'll be fine." She patted Naomi's hand. "Don't you worry now. I've loved it here better than any other place I've lived."

"You've been the best of neighbors," Naomi assured her, squeezing Wanda's hand in turn.

And she looked fine, too. As happy as could be as she dug into the devil's food cake and ice cream. "Everybody's been talking about that man who was murdered. Did you know him?" she asked Gabrielle.

"He stayed at my place on and off for a year," Gabrielle said.

"Was he nice?"

"He was kind enough, I guess. Grandma, he was one of the people who wanted to buy Aunt Anna's bowl."

"Have you found it yet?"

"No."

"She was always good at hiding things, always paranoid. You'll find it one day. I wouldn't be surprised if she'd dug a hole in that backyard and buried it there. In a flowerbed or something."

"She wasn't that bad."

"You didn't know her like I did. She could squeeze a penny tighter than anyone I know. Which was why you had to make all those repairs when you came. Anyway, I can't get my mind off that man. His family must have been mad with worry about him."

"Have they located them yet?" Wanda asked.

"He registered with false information. I hate to eat and run, but I have to get back to the B and B," Gabrielle said, taking her dishes to the sink. "I'll take the meat back for Grandma."

Wanda hopped up and filled a paper bag full of meat. "Business good?" she asked.

"Wonderful. Anytime I'm full, it's wonderful," Gabrielle said, and left the two women sitting at the table.

She packed the freezer and collected her pies. It took only a few minutes to make it back to the B&B.

Cornell had a giant headache and the last person he wanted to see walk through his door was Melinda. He was trying to get out before she arrived, but somebody spilled a tray of mini-casseroles. He had to order more ingredients for the next morning. Melinda reminded him of Alyssa. A man-eater-hater.

He studied Melinda as she exited her red Camaro and strolled toward the door with purposeful strides.

Melinda was about Gabrielle's age. She wore a hot-red short-sleeved suit, the skirt several inches above her knees. Melinda was very fit and had long legs—legs boys ogled over. Her rich brown creamy complexion was so smooth she didn't need hosiery.

He heard Melinda asking one of his employees if he was there. And of course the employee said yes.

He sighed and geared himself up for an uncomfortable conversation with her as Gabrielle drove into the yard as if she were running from a fire. Always in a rush. He waited until she entered the building before he joined them.

It was as if the women were squared off against each other. Two combatants with him dead center. And while it might have done his ego a bit of good to have two women vying for him, he didn't think Gabrielle cared enough to put up a fight.

"I'm sorry about your loss, Melinda," Gabrielle was saying.

"What loss?"

"Roger. I mean, the two of you were dating."

"We weren't dating. We went to dinner once, but that was it. It sure is a shame, though, about his death."

"Didn't Skeeter go missing around the same time? People have started to ask about Skeeter," Gabrielle said, and Cornell wondered why she was broaching that topic.

"I wouldn't know."

"Skeeter was possessive, though. I heard he gave you a hard time about leaving him."

"He eventually got the message," Melinda said, checking her manicured nails.

"He also disappeared. Leaves one wondering, doesn't it?"

Clearly amused, Melinda laughed. "Gabrielle, are you asking me if I murdered Skeeter and Roger?"

Gabrielle shrugged.

"If I had killed Roger, I wouldn't have been stupid enough to leave his body in his car in some dingy little pond that eventually shrivels up when the weather gets too dry. There are too many places in these parts to lose a body—if I were so inclined. Obviously, the person didn't know the area that well."

"Hmm. There's still Skeeter."

"Now you think I murdered stupid Skeeter. I wouldn't waste my time on that worm. And, Gabrielle, give the sheriff something to do. That's what we pay him for. As for Skeeter, he probably went home to his folks."

Dismissing Gabrielle, Melinda straightened from the railing and focused on Cornell. "So what's cooking today?"

"Good evening, ladies," Cornell said, looking directly at Gabrielle. "I tried to call you earlier. You didn't tell me what you wanted for dinner. Your timing's good, though. I was just getting ready to leave." He turned to Melinda before Gabrielle could speak. "What can I get for you?"

She looked at Gabrielle, then at him. "I stopped to pick up dinner."

Okay, what game was he playing? Gabrielle wondered. He knew as well as she did that they had no dinner plans. She actually stopped by when she saw his car, surprised he was still at work. He looked like he could fall down where he stood.

"I also came to see how you are," Melinda said, lifting a hand to brush across his temple. Gabrielle wanted to break it. "I heard you were under the weather."

"You do look under the weather," Gabrielle murmured. "I wonder if God missed the sense gene when he was dispensing it to you. You had no business working in here all day."

"Leave these crazies alone? I don't think so."

"Should you even be driving?" Gabrielle asked.

"I'll take you home if you need a ride," Melinda offered too eagerly.

"His car is outside," Gabrielle said.

"But if he shouldn't be driv—"

"If he can work here all day, he can drive himself home," Gabrielle said.

"Witch," Cornell mumbled under his breath. What could a man expect from a Claxton? Certainly not tender loving care.

Gabrielle's narrowed eyes searched his. "What was that?"

"I'm fine, really." He focused on Melinda. Regardless of what he'd first felt, it was safer. "What can I get for you?"

"If you're sure. I'll take the chicken and sweet potato special you advertised."

Cornell called for one of his workers to get the dinner for Melinda. As soon as it arrived, Melinda said, "Well it's a bit chilly in here. I'll leave. But if you need any help, sugar, remember we're neighborly on the island."

"Thanks."

Could Melinda really have shot that poor man? Gabrielle began to wonder. Of course not. If she'd shot him, the entire island would know about it and exactly why. Melinda wasn't subtle by any means.

"What the hell was that all about?" Cornell asked.

Gabrielle shrugged. "Just island stuff."

He glanced toward the kitchen where Melinda had disappeared. "Watch yourself around that woman." But he was looking at her too closely, as if he was searching for something.

She wasn't really worried about Melinda. Roger was the one with secrets.

"You want to tell me what's going on?" Cornell asked.

Gabrielle picked a piece of imaginary lint off her blouse. "Nothing's going on." Except she'd probably made a total ass of herself.

He assessed her with disbelieving eyes.

CHAPTER 5

After Melinda left, Cornell moved closer to Gabrielle with a relaxed smile. "So, are you going to make sure I get home safely? I'm a sick man."

"You want me to tuck you in, too?" Gabrielle said with a saccharine smile. His sexy voice was at odds to the man who looked as if he'd keel over any second.

"I'm all for it."

"I bet you are." Sometimes, Gabrielle just didn't understand the masculine mind. "Can you leave now?"

"Yeah. I'm done for the day. Let me lock up."

"Can't one of your employees do that?" Gabrielle inquired crisply.

"Yeah. But I usually check to make sure everything's turned off and put away."

"I'll help you." Since she was a control freak herself, she understood his need to see things done to his satisfaction. Teenagers weren't careful. Their minds were on graduation or getting the next hot babe underneath them. Heat seeped into Gabrielle's cheeks, and she cursed her fair skin that revealed everything. She ducked her head for a second and glanced at Cornell, hoping he missed her heightened color, but he appeared to be using all his concentration on placing one foot in front of the other.

He pushed open the double swinging doors that separated the kitchen from the dining area. Suddenly Cornell swayed as if fatigue had finally gotten the best of him. Gabrielle guided him to a chair and stood in front of him while he got his bearings. He was a proud man. Although her education was lacking in the complexities of the male sex, she knew enough to know Cornell hated any kind of weakness, especially his own.

In the background, rap poured from strategically placed speakers. One of the teens was scrubbing the floor, another taking dishes from the dishwasher and storing them. One had taken the cup towel and slapped it at a coworker. Laughing, his partner danced back a couple of evasive steps. They both stopped when they spotted Gabrielle frowning at them.

"You need a couple of older women working here," Gabrielle offered to Cornell. "They're more reliable." She spoke soft enough so the teens couldn't hear her.

"My older workers are here during the day. Most of them prefer part-time so they can spend more time with their families. The younger ones like to work after school." He sighed as if he couldn't say another word even if he wanted to.

"I'll be right back."

Cornell couldn't understand what had suddenly come over him. He hadn't felt fatigue like this since the accident three years ago that had brought him to the island to recuperate. Although he'd had a headache all day, he'd been able to work his regular schedule. Suddenly, putting one foot in front of the other seemed a Herculean feat. What he needed was a good night's rest. He was sure he'd be okay by the morning.

Gabrielle was back. The kitchen was quiet. He realized the lights had been lowered. Gabrielle had instructed one of the teens to help her lock up.

Cornell stood and swayed as he fished his keys out of his pocket, but she took them and urged him back into his seat.

What the heck had come over him? he thought as she walked away. It seemed only seconds had passed before she was back. With her arm firmly around his waist, she walked with him outside. Once he was settled in her passenger seat, the next thing he remembered was waking up in her car—in his yard. She led him into his house and to his bedroom. He remembered her pushing him onto the bed, thinking she was going to join him there. Okay, maybe having a feisty woman in his bed wasn't so bad, after all.

Finally he was really going to have her in his arms. How many times had he dreamed of this day and forced it from his mind?

He felt her remove his shoes and socks; he helped her as she pulled his jeans down his hips and shrugged off his jacket and shirt. Feeling himself hardening, he cursed the malady that kept him from enjoying Gabrielle's lush body.

When she finished undressing him with soft, silky hands, he was left in his briefs and T-shirt. Then she urged him under the covers. His brain felt fuzzy as he shifted toward the center of his bed. He lifted the covers for her to slide in beside him but thought he heard a testy "In your dreams." He couldn't be sure, 'cause he was certainly having a fascinating fantasy right now. He smiled, anticipating her warm, soft body in his arms. She patted his arm down, and since his arm had started to feel like a dead weight, he lowered it. She'd probably go to the bathroom to take off her makeup before she came to bed. He wanted to tell her where the washcloth and towels were, but she could probably find them on her own.

Cornell closed his eyes and waited for Gabrielle to return.

And that was the last thing he remembered before the alarm went off at quarter to five the next morning. Smiling, he rolled over, seeking Gabrielle's warm body beside him. He was already hard—was bursting with energy.

He reached out, felt for her, and came up empty. He opened his eyes. He was in bed alone. Lifting his head, he looked for an indentation in the other pillow, but it was as smooth as the morning before. Cornell closed his eyes with the alarm clock blaring in his ear. Totally disgusted, he fumbled, searching for the clock on the bedside table.

For the first time in many years, he pushed the SNOOZE button.

He felt like hell. His back still throbbed as if someone had taken a stick and beaten the heck out of him. His partner still hadn't contacted him. And the cut on his arm hurt like hell.

The bitch had swung the knife like a machete and brandished the stick like a demented wild woman.

He wanted to punch her lights out.

Flipping open his cell phone, he dialed his partner's number. It immediately threw him into voice mail, which meant he hadn't retrieved any of his messages in days. He closed the phone, wondering where the heck he'd gotten to.

Everything about this project had gone to hell. Roger was dead. His other partner was missing. There was some conspiracy against them.

In the bathroom, he filled a glass with tap water. To keep himself from walking around like a decrepit old man, he returned to his bedroom and dug in his secret stash for a painkiller. Retrieving ointment from the medicine cabinet, he had to twist his arm into an awkward position to apply a small amount to his cut and got pissed off again.

Damn it. It wasn't his job to search the houses. It was his job to find the mark and gather information, not crawl through some sicko's house getting attacked. And certainly not keep up with the players. Why the heck hadn't his partner called him?

When the clock buzzed at five, Gabrielle hit the SNOOZE button instead of bouncing out of bed as she usually did. She wouldn't even let her mind wander to Cornell and how much she wanted to spend the night in his arms. Men were like little cuddly kittens when they were sick, but once they were on their feet . . .

Ready to turn over and sleep another ten minutes, she suddenly realized he might not be able to work. She turned the alarm off and dragged herself out of bed and into the shower.

As she dressed, she realized she needed more information to work intelligently with the Roger dilemma. It was true the sheriff should be working on it, but she wasn't about to reveal what had occurred on Valentine's night. She wasn't about to get herself locked up, especially when she didn't have all the cards in the deck.

It was cooler outside than she expected. She went back in and retrieved a heavier jacket.

Cornell's car was at the B&B when she drove into the parking area. Making her way inside, she shook her head at the stubbornness of men.

"Why didn't you sleep in?" she asked him. He looked better but not quite himself yet.

"I had work to do. What are you doing in here so early?" he asked.

Gabrielle reached for a cup. "I was going to cook."

"Not when you're paying me."

"I don't expect you to come in to work when you're sick, Cornell."

"When I can't make it, I'll send one of my employees. Anyway, Silas is almost ready to take over." He finished off an omelet, slid it neatly onto a plate.

Gabrielle had spotted Mitchell at the table waiting when she walked through.

"Have dinner with me tonight," Cornell asked.

"Okay," Gabrielle said before she gave herself a chance to reconsider, acutely aware of how masculine he appeared wielding a frying pan. "My treat this time." What Cornell needed was a good night's rest, not preparing dinner for her.

He regarded her as if he wondered if she even knew kitchen basics.

"I can cook one or two items, you know."

"I didn't say a word."

She cleared her throat just as the bell tinkled at the registration desk. "A few guests are checking out today. I have to go take care of that."

"Would you like breakfast?"

"Sure," she said absently as she left.

An hour later, Regina arrived and started cleaning the lobby area. She had afternoon classes, and with only fourteen rooms booked the night before, Lisa could take care of the rooms. Regina was cleaning the front door glass when suddenly she dashed for the kitchen. Gabrielle wondered if her cousin had taken leave of her senses when she came out with a cup of coffee and charged outside.

Regina had been acting strange lately. Then Gabrielle noticed Sam getting out of his truck with a couple of his workers. The men were unloading two lawn mowers when Regina caught up with Sam and handed him the coffee. With a puzzled frown, Sam pulled off his gloves, said something to his workers, then took the coffee.

Regina was yakking a mile a minute while Sam nodded.

This man is so lame, Regina thought, disgusted with herself for running outside with coffee like a lovesick fool. She usually had men eating out of her hand. This one acted like she had leprosy or something.

She was beginning to notice things about him that she never had before. Like the hint of some earthy cologne. The pleasing aroma was so subtle it was easy to miss. Or arms so solid, she wanted to wrap her fingers around them and stroke.

Regina cleared her throat. "So, what do you think about Snake Away?"

"You can try putting sulfur around your house. Moth balls will be cheaper than Snake Away."

"Excuse me?"

"The best plan is moth balls. You can scatter them around your house."

"What do I do about the snakes buried in my yard?"

"Nothing."

Horrified, Regina shuddered at the thought. "I can't have snakes in my yard."

He shrugged his wide shoulders. "They hibernate. You live in the country. You've got to expect a few snakes around the place." He handed her the cup. "Thanks for the coffee. I've got to get to work." His crew was already on mowers cutting the grass.

Leaving her where she stood with the cup dangling from her fingers, he tugged on his gloves and got something—she didn't know what—out of the truck bed and went to a plant farther over in the yard.

If this wasn't nothing. She went back inside where Gabrielle was watching her like a darn hawk.

"He agreed to service your lawn?"

Incensed, Regina said, "We didn't get around to that." Men were not immune to her.

"So what are you going to do? Those flowers can't hang out in those pots forever."

Regina sighed. "I don't know. You think maybe he likes smaller women? All the men seem to go after tiny women now. The anorexic size zeros."

"I wouldn't bet on it," Silas said, looking Regina up and down. "I like a hippy woman. Somebody with meat on her bones."

"Guests are waiting for breakfast in the dining room." Gabrielle said to him. What the heck was he doing out in the hallway listening to their conversation?

Grinning, Silas sauntered back into the kitchen.

Gabrielle shook her head. "It's not your size that's the problem, but the fact that you want to use him."

"I'm doing him a favor. He needs a woman to stir up his life, even if it's only temporary."

"Don't, Regina. Don't hurt him that way. He wouldn't get involved with you unless he was serious."

"Oh, for crissakes, I'm not going to hurt him. He's a grown man, not a baby. You and Aunt Anna were too overprotective." She blew out a frustrated breath. "So far he won't give me the time of day. So there." Regina flounced off with the rag and spray to finish washing the glass door.

Gabrielle shook her head and went to her office. She had a ton of work to do. She didn't have time to indulge Regina's misdirected love life.

It seemed Gabrielle spent half her time hopping from the B&B to her grandmother's. She'd called for an update on the body in the lake—Robert.

"Grandma, I know you don't want me to talk to Grandpa, but I need to. There are too many variables if I don't. It could have had something to do with Skeeter. Who knows?"

"That old man is not going to tell you anything."

"So what do I have to work with? I'm not a trained investigator or a police officer."

Naomi threw up her hands. "So talk to him. Don't forget I told you you're wasting your time."

If she spent a great portion of her time between the grands and the B&B, her grandfather spent most of his between his house and Travis's front porch with his cronies. At least it was a good form of exercise, Gabrielle thought as she met him on the front porch.

The screen door slammed behind her. "Grandpa, I need to talk to you."

"What about, doll baby?"

"I've noticed you've seemed worried lately." She sat in the glider, hoping he'd do the same.

"That's life. Always something cropping up. What, you've got a problem Grandpa can help you with?"

"Actually, no. I thought you might have a problem I could help you with."

"I'm just fine, baby girl."

"Do you remember the guy who stayed at my B and B?"

"There's always outsiders coming around."

"He's not quite an outsider."

"If he's not an islander, he's an outsider."

Gabrielle was silent for several seconds. "I didn't grow up here. I'm one of those outsiders. No one lets me forget that."

"Your mama was raised here. You've got family here. This is your home. This is where you belong."

"What is it about the guy they found in Heron Lake that bothers you?"

He shook his head. Worry creases aged him. "Don't you worry yourself about this old man. I can take care of myself."

"You've got family to help you."

He squeezed her hand. "I know that. When I need help, I'll ask for it."

"I'm worried because Skeeter disappeared, too. Do you know where he is?"

"The boy's fine. William was just talking about him the other day. You never hung out with his crowd. Why are you worried?" Hoyt asked.

"Because the two disappeared around the same time. I wonder if it's connected."

"Solving the murder isn't your concern. Let the police do their job. We pay that new city sheriff a fortune to keep this island clear of crime, not that he's doing that good a job."

"Why do you say that?"

He shrugged.

"If you're mixed up—"

"You worry more than your grandma. Woman 'bout to drive me crazy."

"But, Grandpa—"

"You go on now and give an old man some peace. I think I'll take a nap."

Gabrielle kissed him on his weathered cheek and entered the house with him.

"Told you so," Grandma said. "He's got that stubborn streak. Won't talk to anybody," she said tersely. "I've got to go to a meeting later on. Wanda's taking me. There's so much work involved in the celebration. And since that old fool continues to be so stubborn, I've washed my hands of the entire affair."

She'd said that before, but Gabrielle didn't remind her.

"I'll help you any way I can."

Back at the B&B, Mitchell sat in the rocker, taking in the crisp breeze while he read his newspaper.

"How did the writing go today?" Gabrielle asked, balancing the pies as she climbed the stairs.

He folded the paper, put it on a side table, and hopped out of his seat. "Need a break and take in the atmosphere. I'm thinking about going to Virginia Beach. It's early yet."

"Very crowded."

"Lots of people, lots of ideas," he said.

"I guess that's what a writer needs."

"Indeed. I'm getting so many ideas, I'll be able to write books forever."

"Let me put these pies inside," Gabrielle said.

Mitchell followed her, held the door. "I've been reading about the young man who was killed."

Gabrielle tried to steer away from that topic. She didn't want her guests worried about dying while they were at her

B&B. "It's a sad thing. Safety is the one thing we take pride in on Paradise Island."

"I've heard it whispered that he stayed here."

"Yes, he did," Gabrielle said, setting the pies on the buffet and steering Mitchell outside. "But you don't have to be concerned about your safety. Our island is one of the safest locations in the country. It's not that easy for a criminal to get away once he commits a crime."

"I wasn't worried about safety. The peace and solitude are unlike any place I've been. I wonder why my ancestors ever left. I could have a summerhouse here."

Gabrielle smiled. "I'm glad you think so, but your ancestors never stayed on the island. They lived on the mainland."

He nodded. "Virginia Beach isn't bad. Well, I'm going to try to catch the next ferry out. Did I tell you we visited the area where my family once lived?"

"No, you didn't."

He shook his head, some strands of his hair falling to the side. "All that land. It's a shame it got out of the family. You know, your family did a wonderful job of holding your land intact for future generations. Who could ask for a better place to live? Like having a year-round vacation."

Gabrielle agreed. "This has always been my refuge."

She wondered if people were indeed worried about the murder. The body was found in Virginia Beach, not on Paradise Island. Still, that kind of worry was bad for business. She was hopeful. So far, people weren't calling in with cancellations.

That evening, Gabrielle was so tired she didn't even want to eat supper, much less cook it. She just wanted to go to bed and sleep for ten hours. But just as she was about to take her chicken out of the marinade, her doorbell rang. She put the plastic bag on the counter.

Her cousins Lisa and Jackie—the two biggest troublemakers in the family—were impatiently standing on the porch.

"Come on in, ladies." She stepped aside to let them pass, gearing herself up for a confrontation. Lisa never showed up unless she had a complaint.

They sailed in ahead of her. "We won't be long," Jackie said.

"Have a seat. I was preparing dinner," she said, hoping to cut whatever they wanted short. "Can I get you a drink?"

Jackie turned up her nose. "No."

It was all Gabrielle could do to stop an eye roll.

"We came here to talk to you about the bowl."

"We know Aunt Anna gave you control over the bowl, but it doesn't just belong to you," Lisa said. "It belongs to the family. We think it should be sold and the money split between all of us. We should hold a family meeting to decide. It shouldn't be your decision alone."

"This family is huge. After the proceeds are split between everyone, how much do you think you'll get?"

"Enough."

"This bowl has been in the family for centuries. I'm not about to sell it. We've discussed this before. I don't know why we have to keep rehashing it."

"I need money," Lisa said.

"You always need money."

"I bet you've already sold it," Lisa said. "And kept the money for yourself."

"Listen, we've been over this a thousand times. I can't sell something I don't have possession of. Besides, I can't sell it alone. Aunt Anna left three of us in charge of the bowl. It would take the okay of all three to sell it. You know the conditions of her will as well as I do."

"You mean the three of y'all. You, Alyssa, and some cousin we haven't seen in years."

"And that bowl has conveniently disappeared," said Jackie.

"It's around here somewhere, I'm sure," Gabrielle said tiredly, wishing she had nothing to do with the darn thing.

"Only you don't know where," Lisa said skeptically.

"Like we believe that," said Jackie.

Gabrielle stood and headed to the door with the two women following her. "This meeting is over. I don't care what you believe."

But Lisa wouldn't budge. "You were in here with that batty old woman for a year. I know she told you something. I would have known if I'd a been here."

"Both of you were on the island. You could have taken care of Aunt Anna and the B and B, and maybe she would have told you where it was."

"I had a family to take care of," Jackie said.

"So don't complain about me. You weren't willing to lend a helping hand, but you come sniffing around here for anything you can get."

"You're the sneaky one," Lisa snapped. "You ended up with her house and her business."

"And your family ended up with her money. She saved like a miser."

"None of it came to me."

"Yes, it did. She left both of you twenty-five grand. And she left plenty to your father. So why are you always so broke?"

"That's none of your business," Jackie said.

"She should have left the bowl to family and this place to family, too. Not you. You didn't even grow up on the island, with your white self," Lisa said nastily.

"I tell you what. The next time you need a loan until payday, don't come here. You go to family. A loan, by the way, that you never pay back."

Lisa turned around and glared at Sam who was standing at the door getting ready to knock. "Who you looking at, you freak?"

"Don't talk to him that way," Gabrielle said. "Come on in, Sam. They're just leaving."

Sam ignored Lisa and Jackie as if they were nasty insects. "Are you okay, Gabrielle?" he asked.

"And you need to fire him," Lisa said just before she and Jackie walked away.

"Mind your own damn business." Gabrielle shut the door in her face. She was sick of them telling her she wasn't family because her father was white. Her mother and their father were brother and sister. What right did they have to ostracize her?

"I'm sorry my cousin is an evil witch."

"She's got issues. No wonder Mrs. Anna never trusted her. I saw them driving up here. Thought you might need some help," Sam said.

Gabrielle was weary to the bone. "Don't worry about her. I don't." She sighed. Sometimes she felt she didn't fit anywhere. Either she was too black or too white. Her complexion shouldn't even matter. It never mattered when someone needed money.

"How do you like it?" Sam asked.

"Like what?"

Sam nodded toward the ocean. "Look out back."

Gabrielle took a deep breath. She couldn't take her frustration out on him.

"Okay, come on."

She led the way out back onto the porch and down the steps. Then she saw it. A hammock. And he'd replaced the screen door.

"It's lovely. And thank you for the new door."

He rocked back on his heels. "Thought you'd like it."

"I do. I do."

"I'm going to plant more flowers out here. Make it prettier. I tell you, I've been busy as heck lately. I usually have a nice garden going for Mrs. Anna by now."

"Whatever you do is always pretty. Can I get you a soda or something, Sam?"

"No. I already had dinner." He started walking away. "Just wanted to make sure you were okay."

Gabrielle watched him walk down the path to his car. She wanted to warn him about Regina but decided he could take care of himself. It would be nice if he could find someone kind to date. He'd had such a hard life. Regina would be a good fit if she loved him.

But so far he ignored Regina. As long as he knew the score, she'd keep her nose out of it.

Gabrielle closed the door and was headed to the kitchen when the phone rang.

It was Cornell, saying something had come up. Regrettably he'd have to beg off dinner, but he'd make it up to her. Gabrielle dug into the bag of marinating chicken. She grilled it, anyway, then fixed a sandwich with one of the pieces.

Afterward, she cleaned up and roamed around the old house. She must have gone through it a thousand times, trying to find places large enough to hide the bowl. She'd even checked the attic and the shed out back. But so far she'd been unsuccessful. She just didn't know where else to look. Founders Day was quickly approaching. This year for the first time, they probably wouldn't have a bowl to display.

Gabrielle headed to her aunt's room.

It had been months since she'd entered it. Alyssa and her grandmother had helped her sort through Aunt Anna's clothing. She'd kept the furniture, except for the pieces she gave Regina. Alyssa wanted a bedroom set, too, and Gabrielle would give it to her when she returned from her trip.

Naomi had told Gabrielle she should move into Anna's room since it was larger than her own bedroom, but it didn't feel right somehow. It belonged to Anna. It was a beautiful grouping, really—a four-poster bed, huge armoire, bureau, and dresser with the large mirror.

The furniture, painted a deep, dark brown, almost appeared black. Gabrielle knew if the old paint was sanded off, a rich beautiful wood would be revealed. After sanding, some people applied a clear varnish to let the rich wood grain show through. But the paint of the antique furniture had never been changed.

Furniture was the furthest thing from her mind right now, though. The room still smelled like Anna. Gabrielle knew it was fruitless, but she went to the closet. Most of Anna's clothes were gone. Anna had been a pack rat. Gabrielle had saved some old period pieces just in case a family member wanted it for a Founders Day function or the children needed it for school for period dressing.

Gabrielle gathered boxes from the top closet shelf and set them on the dresser. Having only given them a cursory glance before, she knew pictures were there, but maybe Anna had hid the bowl under them.

When she was putting a box back, she found a rolled-up portrait in the back of the closet. It was a painting of a white woman Aunt Anna had talked about—the woman who'd run away in the mid-1800s.

Gabrielle gingerly took out the portrait and carefully unrolled it. She should have it framed.

Mary was paper-white. Unhappiness was clear in her vivid blue eyes. Gabrielle thought of the story Aunt Anna had told her numerous times from the time she was a tiny girl. . . .

Mary's husband hated her. Had never loved her, really. They hadn't married for love, but she'd at least expected their relationship to settle into comfortable respect and fondness.

Her father wanted her to marry a man who would take proper care of the land and of her. Her husband, a man of European aristocracy but broke, wanted a wife wealthy enough to lift him from penury. His father came to America ten years ago, and they'd struggled to raise their station. It didn't happen until he married Mary.

Mary had lost her baby the winter before from fever. She'd sunken into a state of melancholy that refused to abate. Her husband became more abusive by the day. She had to get away from him.

Her father had indulged her, and she wasn't accustomed to being treated so shabbily.

So on the day her husband left for the governor's estate in Williamsburg, she'd told the servants she would spend a week with her best friend in Suffolk. She'd packed bags for two of her slaves and herself, meticulously storing the beloved painting her father had commissioned before his death—and the gold bowl and bullion that had been in her family since 1617. They were a point of pride for her husband, but she'd be damned if she was leaving them behind for him.

She'd sent a message to have someone waiting for them with a boat to whisk them away to the island in the dead of night. Every move was meticulously planned. They climbed aboard the boat, and someone drove her carriage in the opposite direction to Suffolk, for she knew her husband would search for her there first.

All three of them were going to freedom, she thought as they left. She watched the shore disappear until it was a speck on the horizon. She felt like Elizabeth, who had made her journey across the ocean in 1617. Elizabeth's courage augmented her own. Elizabeth had survived and so would Mary.

A month later, they arrived in Philadelphia. She'd sold the bowl and bullion to pay for their transport and living expenses. With new names and a new beginning, they disappeared into the flow of the city.

CHAPTER 6

As expected, Lisa didn't show up for work the next morning. Regina could only work for three hours and sixteen rooms were occupied. Regina cleaned six rooms before she left, leaving Gabrielle with ten. Good thing Cornell was working in the kitchen, because as guests went down to breakfast, Gabrielle cleaned. She especially tried to get the professors' rooms done quickly since they loved to talk, and she didn't have time for lengthy conversations.

Looking at Mitchell's room, she couldn't see one sign of the care she had put into selecting the floral sheets, bedspread, and knickknacks. She'd chosen Victorian rose and white patterned wallpaper. Rose towels and washcloths were thrown haphazardly on the floor. Early twenties-era pictures hung on the walls. There was even a writing desk and a chair. The reupholstered love seat was topped with papers, books, and clothes.

Gabrielle itched to clean it up, but she didn't touch customers' personal belongings. It was a good thing she didn't clean these rooms on a daily basis. It just hurt her to see the room in this shape. Mitchell wasn't a neat man by any stretch of the imagination.

On the desk, papers were scattered about—Post-it notes,

small and large notebooks, sheets of stationery, and little pieces torn from tablets. Gabrielle dusted the top of his computer. Obviously it still got very little use. His room was the polar opposite of Graham's. Graham's computer got plenty of use.

"Damn it." She'd just noticed a thumbtack stuck in what had been flawless wallpaper. She took it down and placed the paper on the table, tossing the thumbtack in the trash.

Gabrielle found a pair of eyeglasses under the bed. She placed them neatly on the bedside table.

As luck would have it, she was still in Mitchell's room when he roamed back upstairs from breakfast with Graham.

"Gabrielle. I missed you downstairs. Is Lisa sick?" Graham asked.

"No. Your room's already clean," Gabrielle said, gathering towels from the cart to place in Mitchell's bathroom.

Graham's room was on the third floor at one end, where he was afforded more privacy. There were only six rooms on the third floor. He liked being up high where he could look out at the ocean.

"I always wanted to ask about the pictures on the wall," Mitchell said. "Are they relatives?"

"Yes, they are. I had them photocopied from Aunt Anna's collection when I redecorated."

"What a lovely selection," Mitchell said in awe. "I would love to see your pictures. How far back do you have them?"

"I believe to the late eighteen hundreds. There are a couple of primitive paintings. How close they are to the actual people is anybody's guess."

"When you have time, please bring in your pictures, or I'll be happy to go out to your place to view them."

"I'll let you know." Hopefully after Lisa returned. If the temperamental woman came back at all.

She always returned when she ran out of money. She'd be back next week for her check at least. If Lisa wasn't so good at her job, Gabrielle would just fire her and be done with it. Still, she wondered if keeping Lisa was worth the aggravation.

It was early afternoon when Gabrielle completed the rooms. She still had laundry to do, but she was surprised when she found her grandmother and Wanda in the laundry room, folding.

"Regina told me Lisa quit again. I'm not about to climb those stairs, but we did your laundry," Naomi said.

"Can I kiss you?"

"Not until you shower."

"We cleaned the downstairs public area," Wanda said.

"Thank you, thank you."

"Cornell called," Naomi said, pursing her lips as if she'd sucked on a lemon.

"What did he want?"

"Said he'll bring dinner. Thought I told you to stay away from him."

"We're not going through that again."

"Never could tell you hardheaded girls anything."

The best way to get on Naomi's good side was to change the topic. "I was going through Aunt Anna's things last night. I found Mary's portrait in the back of her closet. I'm going to frame it before it's damaged."

"Mary was afraid her portrait would get damaged on the trip. And she had to leave quickly. She knew the island would be the first place her husband looked, and she couldn't take much with her. She and the slaves traveled through the Underground Railroad to Philadelphia. But as the story goes, she never returned. The islanders never heard from her again. She was probably afraid any letter she sent would be intercepted."

"Interesting," Wanda said. "The more I listen to you, the more intrigued I become. I know very little about my ancestors."

"I keep trying to get my grandchildren interested. Someone has to carry on the torch."

"Alyssa keeps tabs on the family history, Grandma. She's typed it up."

"Not all of it. She shouldn't have to do it alone when I have so many grandchildren to participate. You're going to want to know your roots when you get old so you can tell your children. Then it'll be too late," Naomi said, her face pinched in disapproval. "Because the people who know will all be gone."

"You're right, of course." Gabrielle wasn't up to a long lecture. Agreement was the easiest way to get her grandmother to come down off her soapbox.

"Aren't I always?" Naomi sighed. "I know Cornell's serving brownies for the meet and greet this evening, but I brought the pies over with me, anyway. Baked a few extra you can stick in the freezer. I left the instructions for thawing."

"Thanks, Grandma."

"The strawberries will be ripe for picking soon. Wanda is going to help me freeze them for my pies."

"And I get to learn her recipe," Wanda said.

"It's time you learned, too, Gabrielle."

Gabrielle had enough on her plate. "Maybe next year."

Cornell caught himself staring into space when the twins erupted into his office.

"We have a proposition," Chance said.

"Whatever it is, I don't want to know," Cornell said.

"We want to have a party here."

"Hell, no. You're out of your mind." Cornell shook his head. A party with a bunch of teens in his freshly renovated building?

"But you haven't heard our proposition yet," Lance said.

"What part of no don't you understand?" Cornell asked.

"But we don't have anywhere decent to go on the island."

"Don't you have work to do?"

"But—"

"You're on my time."

As the boys filed out, Cornell shook his head at their foolishness but quickly cast them from his mind to focus on the previous day's event. By the time his head had cleared, he knew he'd made a colossal mistake in inviting Gabrielle to dinner. By the time he'd reached his shop, he'd reasserted his position to get himself a sweet, gentle woman. The lump on his head had his thinking all screwed up.

His brothers had called the night before, inviting him to go partying with them. That was when he'd decided to break his date with Gabrielle.

They'd hit a sports bar. A few women his brothers worked with were there along with some of their friends. He'd found himself singling one out. She was exactly the kind of woman he was looking for.

Except throughout the entire conversation, he was thinking of the sassy Gabrielle. Thought of her barking orders at him when his brain was just too fuzzy. Thought of her taking his shoes off, tucking him into bed—sliding his pants down his legs.

Worse, he thought of the sweet kiss the night he'd gotten knocked upside the head and how she'd stayed to help him out, brandishing a stick and knife like she was fighting alongside her pirate.

Damn it. He liked strong, sassy women, and he liked one in particular.

So he'd left that night without asking the woman for a phone number or if he could see her again. She'd slipped him a piece of paper with her number on it, anyway. And when he went outside, he'd found himself tossing it into the trash.

After Gabrielle's altercation with Lisa, he felt like easing her evening by making sure she had dinner. So now he had a date with the woman he wanted to completely banish from his memory. He needed to admit it to himself if to no one else.

Hell, he was one sick fool. Why didn't they just slap a sign right across his forehead?

By the time Gabrielle made it home, she didn't want to talk about family. She didn't even want dinner. She only wanted to take a shower and quickly fall asleep on her soft mattress. The problem was she didn't work out anymore, and she could feel the difference. She'd stopped her daily walks a couple of months ago. She wasn't going to start again today, though. Cleaning ten rooms was enough exercise.

She headed to the shower. She had just finished dressing when Cornell arrived.

"How's the head?"

"I'm back to my old self."

He went to her kitchen, and Gabrielle couldn't help but compare the two. Hers was old and clearly needed updating. The cabinets were scarred and rubbed raw from repeated cleanings. Her kitchen was without a center island. But just like his, it had good bones, it was clean, and it aged gracefully. Still he kept a running conversation while he finished preparations as if he was working in a gourmet kitchen.

"We can use paper plates," he said.

"If this is anything like the other night, we need crystal, china, and silver."

He was out of his mind. He did not need this distraction right now. But something about Gabrielle intrigued him. "Whatever suits you," he said, putting on the finishing touches. "You know, if we ate in front of the TV, we could watch the game," Cornell said.

"Okay. So what do you want to watch?"

"The basketball game."

In the end, they ate at the cocktail table watching the

Lakers. He kept only half his mind on the game, though. The other half was on Gabrielle. What was it about that woman that kept getting to him? That had him preparing dinner for her? But her focus was someplace else.

"Something's bothering you," Cornell said.

Gabrielle sighed and placed her fork on the table.

"Talk to me. Is it the bowl your cousin's always pestering you about?"

She shook her head. "I haven't discussed this with anyone."

"Maybe it's time you got it off your chest. I never heard the entire story of the golden bowl. Just snippets your aunt told me while she was sick."

Her gaze flickered to his.

"Used to visit her all the time. Usually during the day. I'd bring over a meal or two."

"And she allowed it?"

"Of course. That's how I know how much she loved Uncle Lucky. If it's any consolation, he loved her, too. It's tragic in a way for two people to love each other and yet can't live together."

Gabrielle nodded. "Some people are meant to be alone. They didn't know how to compromise."

"I think they preferred their own company." He brushed silky strands of hair from her face.

"Do you really believe that? I mean, I know my aunt missed Uncle Lucky."

"What can I say? I'm not a good gauge. My parents certainly aren't the model couple of the year. Sometimes I wonder what they ever saw in each other. Was it all sex or what?"

"Yet, they're still together," Gabrielle said quietly.

"Probably been together so long, they wouldn't know what to do on their own."

"Something brought them together in the first place," she said.

"Marriage was different back then. It was expected to last even if you grew apart. Anna and Lucky were the oddballs of their time."

"Expectations make the difference. If you go into it thinking you can leave if it doesn't work out, do you really work at it to make it last? The divorce rate proves you don't. Second marriages are even worse, so that isn't the answer, either."

Clearly uncomfortable, Cornell said, "How did we get from the bowl to marriage?"

Gabrielle sighed. "The truth is, I don't know what happened to the bowl. But in the early eighteen hundreds, one of the descendents of the women who came over with our ancestor ended up with . . . I guess I have to go back to the beginning. The pirates who captured my ancestor had captured another ship that was filled with spices and other valuables. The women poisoned the pirates with one of their spices. . . .

The women quickly got into a small boat and rowed to the ship docked offshore. Nervous energy buoyed them. They climbed aboard and began checking the ship for whatever they could use.

"How are we going to leave here?" one of the captives asked. "We don't know anything about ships."

"We've been aboard one for months," Abiola said. Some of the men had gotten sick, and the women had been recruited to help out.

"We can do it," Elizabeth offered in encouragement. "We have to."

"Now let's check the ship for valuables. See what we can take with us."

"These waters are so treacherous. We barely made it here, and then only because the pirates knew the area."

"We'll make it. Think of the alternative. But first we have to check the ship and see what we have. We need enough

*provisions to last us until help arrives." Abiola didn't voice
her fear that they might be on their own for the duration.
Just the thought of it sent chills up and down her spine.*

*The women split up. As Elizabeth and Abiola made their
way to the captain's quarters, Abiola realized she was shaking
all over. She pressed a hand to her heart. The fear in Elizabeth's eyes was reflected in her own.*

*"Well," Abiola said, trying to boost their courage, "it has
to get better from here."*

*"We have so much work to do," Elizabeth said. They both
knew their situation had worsened on this journey as time
elapsed.*

*They entered the captain's quarters and began to search
through his trunks.*

"Oh, my. Look at what we have," Abiola said.

*"What?" Elizabeth looked up from the trunk she was
checking, which was filled with fine silks and cloth.*

*"We will do very well in the New World," Abiola said. When
Elizabeth moved close to her, she revealed a treasure trove of
Spanish golden bowls, some jewels and gold bullion, and
doubloons.*

*Elizabeth raked her hands through the doubloons. "Oh, we
will do very well indeed."*

*"But first we have to get out of here. Other pirates may
come."*

"May the good Lord guide us."

*They both prayed, for although they had worked with the
men, this was the first time they would steer alone. And none
of them knew where they were going or how to navigate. They
could not sail back to England.*

*Elizabeth grabbed Abiola's hand and squeezed hard. "I
don't like to show it, but I'm afraid. We might never see dear
England again."*

*Abiola squeezed back. She had been born in Africa. Her
family had traveled to England to be near her father, who*

sailed the world on one of England's ships. She was familiar with being in a new land but feared what they would find once they reached this new land. Would other people be there? Would they be friendly? Where would they be and how would they survive after their provisions ran out?

Abiola hugged Elizabeth tightly, then let her go. "We can't show the others our fear. We must go on this new voyage with courage and determination. We will survive. We will conquer whatever problems we encounter.

Luckily, one of the women knew how to sail as well as any man. They had no idea if other pirates would soon be in the vicinity. They made haste in leaving the island, flowing with the current. On their journey, they searched through the pirates' things and found amazing riches. In addition to the gold and jewels, they found silk fabrics, spices, seeds, and enough supplies for them to begin their lives as women of means wherever they sailed instead of as indentured servants. After all, the boat they arrived on had sunk to the ocean's floor. They decided to change their names.

The boat hit an obstruction near an island a few days later, and they knew they'd traveled as far as they could go. They expected to find people there, but none were in sight. They unloaded as many goods as they could before going inland.

The island looked as if a strong wind had come through and left it desolate. Trees had been blown over. Huge trees— big enough for several buildings—stood as if grounded in stone.

"So what happened to the bowls?"

"Two of the women—Abiola, my grandmother's ancestor and, believe it or not, Elizabeth, my father's ancestor—each took two bowls. The riches were distributed equally among the women. My father's white. I guess the islanders have talked enough about that."

Cornell chuckled. "You better believe it." He regarded her for several seconds. "Something's bothering you. Do you feel comfortable enough with me to talk about the bowl?"

Gabrielle glanced at her hands, then up at Cornell. "To tell you the truth, I don't know what happened to it. At one time I knew where it was stored." She inhaled sharply. She needed to tell someone, to get the boulder-size burden off her chest or she'd explode.

"Cornell, I need to talk to someone. I usually confide in Alyssa, but she's away and I don't want to burden her."

"I'm here, Gabrielle." He took her hand, held it securely in his grasp. "Talk to me."

Gabrielle inhaled deeply, some of the tension already easing just knowing she could share, that she wasn't alone. Since February, she'd felt as alone as she could be. And a heavy weight had settled on her chest.

"The night my aunt died, I stopped by the bar for a few minutes. My aunt had encouraged me to go out. It was Valentine's, after all, and I was just sitting around at home. She wasn't well, but usually she took a sleeping pill at night, so I didn't have to worry about her wandering. After she fell asleep, I took her advice and went to Pete's. I had only planned to stay a half hour or less. But, anyway, when I got there, Roger was nursing a drink and selecting songs on the jukebox. He was in a jovial mood. Asked me to dance. I didn't really want to, but it was Valentine's Day and I thought what the heck. One dance to celebrate.

"After the dance, he wanted to talk. Before he could broach the subject, I told him that I wasn't going to sell the bowl to him, didn't even know where it was. I'm not as nostalgic as my aunt, but it meant a lot to her, and I'd never sell it. He said he wouldn't bring up the subject. He was staying at the B and B and he was a great customer. So when he offered to buy me a drink, I complied." Gabrielle fell silent.

"What happened?" Cornell asked softly.

"I started thinking about Aunt Anna, and after I finished the drink, I told Roger I had to leave. He walked with me outside. I started to feel dizzy, but Roger kept talking to me like nothing was going on. Then he was asking me what was wrong. I must have passed out, because I don't remember anything until the next morning when I woke up on the living room couch.

"When I went to my aunt's room . . . she was dead." Gabrielle closed her eyes briefly. "It wasn't until her body was taken away that I thought to look for the bowl. It wasn't where I'd last seen it months before. I always wondered if Roger brought me home, killed my aunt, and took the bowl. You know the rest, because you came over when you saw the police car."

Cornell captured her cold hand in his and rubbed some warmth into her fingers. He didn't want to depress her, so he steered the conversation from her aunt.

"So you've looked all over for the bowl and can't find it."

She nodded. "I've looked in every hiding place I can think of. I even searched her room again last night. The celebration is coming up next month, and I'm at a loss." She needed to say the rest. "There's more."

"What is it?"

"I believe Roger was killed that night. I haven't seen him since the bar. At first I thought he'd stolen the bowl. But after they found his body, for a while I thought I might have killed him, but I realized I couldn't have driven his truck to Heron Lake and then driven my car back here. I don't know what happened that night," she said finally. "And I need to know for my peace of mind."

"Let the police investigate. It's their job to find out."

She was willing to compromise herself but not her grandfather. "What if I was involved in some way?"

"You can't believe that. Obviously he slipped something

into your drink. More than likely you were out the whole night. You didn't see anything."

"But what happened after that? I need to know. I need to know how I got home and what happened afterward. I need to know"—she swallowed the lump in her throat—"I need to make sure Aunt Anna wasn't murdered, that I didn't cause her death."

Gabrielle couldn't prevent the tears that stole down her cheeks. Even more than the artifacts, she couldn't live with the idea of being responsible for Aunt Anna's death.

And then Cornell was wrapping his arms around her, holding her close.

"You didn't kill Roger."

She pushed him aside. Wiped her hands across her eyes. "Tears aren't going to help."

"You can't keep that kind of tension bottled up inside," he said, tugging her against his chest. "Something's got to give somewhere."

Gabrielle hated leaning on anyone. But she couldn't deny the pleasure of his gentle stroking. She was astonished and a bit dismayed when she felt goose bumps rising on her arms. She finally relaxed enough to lean fully against him. She felt as if a thousand-pound weight had lifted from her chest, but she also felt the muscled hardness of *his* chest, the staccato beat of his heart against hers.

When had his stroke changed from gentle to erotic? Or maybe it was just her reaction to his touch.

She tilted her head, shifted her gaze to Cornell's. He hesitated only a moment. It seemed time stood still until his lips claimed hers. Her hands stroked his chest. Desire shot through him like a jolt of electricity. He kissed her chin, her throat. And her hands on his body shook his control, and he felt himself pressing her flat on the sofa. It was her sweet moan that brought him to his senses.

He had to leave. He couldn't stay another second. It took every fiber of his being to tear himself away from her.

He shook his head and looked toward Gabrielle's house. The light came on upstairs. He'd had to get out of there. He wanted to make love with her so badly he ached with need. But he couldn't take advantage of her in her emotional state. He swiped a shaky hand across his face.

Against the curtains, he saw her silhouette undress. Feeling a bit overheated, he drove to the local bar—the only bar on the island.

"Hey, Mike, how's it going?"

"Everything's everything. What can I do for you?"

"The usual." Cornell always ordered dark beer. A minute later, Mike put a Sam Adams on a cocktail napkin in front of him.

The tube was on, and the game was still playing. Shaq and Kobe were still hustling for the ball.

"Seen many strangers around lately?"

"Always see strangers."

"This one is about five-ten, on the slight side but pretty strong."

"Nobody unusual. Heard about your break-in. Sorry I can't help you, man."

"Did you see anyone with cuts? Like he got into a fight with a cat and lost?"

Mike shook his head and went to wait on another customer who sat farther down the bar.

Cornell finished his drink and left. The game was still playing, but he'd lost interest.

Upstairs in his own house, he showered. People always said he never had to go looking for trouble. It always came to him.

But he didn't forget Gabrielle. She even invaded his dreams.

* * *

The bushes swayed as he watched the lights go out in Gabrielle's house. Cornell had left, but he'd already checked his house. Too bad he didn't get out early enough the other night. Now he was suspicious, and Gabrielle would take extra precautions.

His vigilance had paid off. Gabrielle had been in the aunt's room a very long time the night before. He wondered if she'd found anything. On his next visit, he'd be sure to concentrate on the aunt's room again. He'd checked it once already. Gone through the boxes of pictures. Dug under the bed where dust bunnies had formed since the aunt's death, but he found no coins or gold bowls. He'd found no emeralds or sapphires. They were in that little cottage somewhere.

But even more puzzling was where the hell was his partner? He was supposed to meet him already. He'd thought he'd left to scout out another job. If he'd just help find the jewels on this job, they both could retire for life.

He was getting royally pissed at the way things were turning out. No wonder they had to work job after job. They were so inept, it was a wonder they could stay in the business.

And why wasn't his partner getting any info?

With one last cursory look, he turned and left. He'd return the next night, and the next, and the next, until he had what he'd come for.

CHAPTER 7

Ever since Lisa graduated from high school, she'd worked off and on at the B&B. When she decided to show up, things went well. The B&B was a daily operation, and Gabrielle couldn't afford to hold Lisa's job for her if she was going to run off in a huff whenever it suited her, leaving Gabrielle to do her own job as well as Lisa's.

If Aunt Anna were alive, she'd tell Gabrielle to be patient yet again. If Gabrielle kept giving in to Lisa's impulses, she'd never have a comfortable work schedule. The world didn't revolve around Lisa, and she was doing her a disservice by letting her believe she could continue to disrupt everyone else on a whim.

As much as Lisa complained that Aunt Anna left her nothing, the older woman had left Lisa twenty-five grand to buy a cute little two-bedroom fixer-upper on the other side of the island. It needed less work than Gabrielle's house. Her father would have gladly done the renovations to get her out of his garage apartment. And the cost of housing hadn't skyrocketed here the way it had in other places. She could buy the place for well under a hundred grand, which was affordable.

Lisa had already blown the money. She'd run away to New York with some man, like she usually did, soon after Aunt

Anna had died. And as soon as the man had spent all her money, he left her for greener pastures. Lisa had no option but to come back home broke.

She never learned from her mistakes—kept finding and trusting the same kind of man.

Gabrielle was sick of it. She couldn't have an unreliable worker during the summers when all the rooms sold out. And Regina wouldn't be there very long. She was working part-time in the clinic during the summer.

Still, Gabrielle hated to lose Lisa because she was good with the guests and they loved her. If Lisa had her head on straight, Gabrielle could have involved her with other segments of the B&B, had the two of them split more duties.

She needed someone more reliable, and now Aunt Anna wasn't there to intervene. Guilt stabbed at her conscience, but she wasn't going to keep putting up with Lisa's bull. She wasn't Lisa's whipping girl.

Gabrielle drove through the small downtown area. There was a hardware store, an ice cream and burger place, a pizza parlor, an art shop that catered to tourists, a bank, and a combination real estate/insurance office. Farther down the street were the marina and ferry dock. On the outskirts of town was a small grocer. Five miles out of town was an artists community. A few poets and artists lived on the island.

Inside the grocery store, the bulletin board was peppered with flyers, posters, and notes. One poster advertised the Founders Day celebration, and one announced the grand opening for Personally Yours.

After making small talk with no less than six locals, Gabrielle tacked her note dead center on the message board—an ad for a full-time housekeeper. Then she rushed out before she was waylaid once again. Everyone was curious about her encounter with the burglar.

It was warm outside, and the picture of a milkshake made her mouth water as she passed the ice cream place. Between her grandmother's pies and Wanda's cakes, she was gaining weight, but she reached for the door and found herself at the counter ordering a peach milkshake. She was going through the door, closing her eyes on the first heavenly sip, when she heard a familiar voice.

"Got enough for me?"

Gabrielle's eyes flew open, her heart pounding. "I . . ." She was stammering like an idiot. Yeah, the lovemaking was slightly this side of heaven. She wanted to complete what they'd started. She still didn't understand why he'd stopped. For some vague reason, he was determined to keep their relationship platonic, but his kisses let her know he desired her.

He took the drink from her hand, and with one sip, half the milkshake was gone.

"That hit the spot."

"I guess it did," she said, but her words didn't have the intended sting because she was remembering how those lips had done amazing things to her body the day before and how her body sang and squirmed under them.

"What are you doing here? Thought you'd be too busy preparing for the grand opening."

"Don't remind me. Had to get a part from the hardware store. Since you're here, I wanted to make sure you were going to be there tonight. Forgot to remind you last night." He chuckled. "My mind was captured by other things." He leaned down and kissed her. "Umm, sweet."

"You keep running hot and cold on me. I want to know why you stopped last night and not a mumbled vague excuse, either."

He moved close to her and brushed a thumb across her chin. "I stopped because when we make love, it's going to be because we both want it, not because you're dealing with an emotional issue."

"When?"

"It's just a matter of time, baby."

Gabrielle grabbed hold of him and kissed him again. "Don't keep me waiting too long."

"I like a woman who knows what she wants."

Gabrielle laughed. "You're too full of yourself."

Chuckling, he started down the street. "See you at six."

Gabrielle tried not to think about their lovemaking. Had never intended to get involved with him. He was taking things much too slowly for her.

Gabrielle might not bake pies and cakes, but she pampered her guests just the same. When she returned to the hotel, she gave tour suggestions to a couple from Detroit with two toddlers. And she gave them directions to the Virginia Marine Science Museum in Virginia Beach and the Children's Museum in Portsmouth.

"I think we'll do one each day to keep the children from tiring out," the mother said.

"That's a great idea."

"The weather should be warm tomorrow. No rain expected. I'm thinking we can spend the afternoon on the beach. Maybe take in the Children's Museum in the morning. Do you offer picnic baskets?"

"Yes," Gabrielle said. She grabbed a menu from behind the desk and handed it to them. "If you give a staff member your selection by tonight, we'll have it ready by tomorrow morning."

"Wonderful. Okay, kids. Let's go."

"Enjoy your day," Gabrielle said. Next, she spent a few minutes with guests who were breakfasting, and she worked on paperwork for an hour before she joined Regina in cleaning rooms. After that, she checked on supplies and made orders.

"I was just telling Grandma the other day," Regina said, "that Aunt Anna had put a lot of things in the storage shed out back. Did you go through that stuff yet, Gabrielle?"

"What kind of things?"

"I don't know. Papers and stuff, I guess. Anything she didn't know what to do with. Just about anything could be in there."

Just one more bunch of stuff to go through. Was the bowl there? "I'll check it when I get the time. I thought Sam stored his equipment there. Although, I don't think she would have put the bowl near the B and B."

Regina shrugged. "She was paranoid about that thing. Probably wouldn't think it was safe here."

"Think she put it in a safety deposit box?"

"She wouldn't trust a bank to that extent. Remember, she was around in the thirties."

"She had accounts there?"

"The bowl was different. . . . Oh, there's Sam. I need to tell him something. Check you later." Regina dashed to the kitchen as if a fire were chasing her.

"Poor Sam."

Regina's heart was beating so hard and her hand was shaking so much she nearly dropped the container of juice. Steadying her hand, she poured a glass of cranberry juice. Using the time it took to return the jar to the fridge, she willed her heartbeat to slow. Calmly she made her way outside, hoping no one noticed her acting like a fool. She was on a mission here. And she could be as stubborn as Sam. It was more than the garden. He'd become a challenge. She unbuttoned the top two buttons on her blouse. *Let's see the effect of a little cleavage.*

"Hi, Sam." The smile she gave him would melt sugar.

Sam barely spared her a glance as he mumbled a greeting and kept taking whatever out of the truck bed. *I know he didn't ignore me that way.* And after she'd worn the lavender blouse that accented her brown complexion. With a little cleavage as a bonus, he should be tripping all over her. This was the second time in as many days she'd tried to get his attention, and she wasn't going to let him ignore her. As antisocial as he was, he should be grateful she was giving him the time of day.

"It's getting hot already. I brought you a glass of cranberry juice."

"Still early. Pretty cool still."

Like she didn't know that, nitwit. Maybe she needed a college course on dealing with assholes.

"I'm sure after you finish doing whatever you're doing, it'll be pretty steamy." She did her best to keep her smile in place, but he was making it hard.

For a moment she thought he was going to continue ignoring her. She wished she had the largest hypodermic needle in existence so she could jab his lame behind. But suddenly he glanced up from his work and paused. Then he pulled off his gloves and laid them on the truck bed. She handed him the glass. Careful not to touch her, he took it from her as if he'd catch something if he got too close.

His gaze was so intent, she thought he peered past her eyes, past any false pretenses and stared right into her core. For the first time, Regina felt uncertainty, and she didn't like it one bit. Of course, he saw only what *she* wanted him to see. He wasn't that deep.

She watched the play of his throat muscles as he drank half the glass. He swiped his tongue over his lips. Funny, she never noticed how nice his lips looked.

"Thanks," he finally said, but held on to his glass.

"It's Friday and Personally Yours is serving dinner tonight for their grand opening. I was thinking about stopping by there later on after I finish working," Regina said. "I'm doing overtime to make a little extra money."

"Don't you have classes this afternoon?"

Regina's heart lifted. "No Friday classes." So he did notice things about her. The sneaky devil. But for some reason her crazy heart gladdened. She knew Sam wasn't the man for her by any stretch of the imagination. She preferred them more outgoing, more polished, more like Cornell, although he didn't turn her on. But it had been a long time between men, and she was feeling lonely lately. She gazed the length of Sam.

He looked all nervous, as if he'd noticed her ogling him. Regina stifled a smile as he nodded and tugged at his hat and looked anywhere but at her. He needed somebody to shake up his world.

And she was just the one to do it.

"I was thinking about stopping there, too. Maybe later on," Sam said.

Regina was pissed off again. What the heck did she have to do? Wear a damn sign stamped on her forehead saying "Invite me out to dinner, you dunce?" She smothered her aggravation, or else she'd turn him off completely.

"So, what time are you going?" she asked.

He shrugged. "I'm working late, too. Just got a new customer. Have to make up an estimate before I call it a day."

She glanced around. "Suddenly everybody wants a showcase front yard."

"I'm not complaining. More business for me," he said.

"You have a gift with flowers. Everything I plant dies. My yard looks like a disaster area."

He chuckled. "You ever do anything about those snakes?"

"I threw some moth balls around the place, but the flowers are still in the pots on my front porch."

"They're not going to last long there." He glanced away. "I could help you."

She was so shocked she almost swallowed her tongue. Took him damn near forever to make the suggestion.

"Really?"

"Sure." He drank the rest of the cranberry juice and handed her the glass. "I'll stop by sometime this weekend and look your place over."

It sounded like the answer to a prayer, but she was in school and . . . "I really can't afford your services."

"Just buy your flowers from my shop."

She smiled. "You've got a deal."

He started working, and she watched him for a couple of minutes, holding the glass against her chest before she sedately walked back into the B&B . . . and danced a step in the foyer. A toddler she'd met the day before ran to her and begged to be picked up. Regina picked him up and danced around in a circle to his hilarious giggles. The parents were talking to Gabrielle.

What was she getting all excited about? She and Sam weren't dating or anything. Sam was definitely not her type. She just wanted her flowers planted. So why was her heart tripping like she'd just gotten a date with Blair Underwood?

The parents beckoned for the child, and Regina put him on the floor. They waved good-bye.

"What's with you?" Gabrielle asked after they left. "Carrying on like that."

"Oh, nothing." But she couldn't stop herself from grinning like a simpleton.

Gabrielle shook her head and went back to work.

Regina peeped out the window at Sam and watched his muscles bulge as he lifted bags off the truck. She never realized how well built he was. But she guessed anybody who hefted heavy fertilizer and soil bags couldn't be a wimp. When she caught herself staring at him another minute, she forced herself to go upstairs to continue her own work. She could not stand there all day ogling that man.

Then she realized he hadn't invited her to dinner, even with the obvious hint.

But he was going to do her yard. She'd accomplished her goal. Yet, she felt like she'd missed something in the process.

* * *

Gabrielle was running late as she sped home. She showered and was heading to her grandparents' when Lisa's car came to a screeching halt right in front of her. Gabrielle had to stand on her brakes to keep from hitting her. There couldn't be more than a foot between the cars when they finally stopped.

Gabrielle exploded from the car. "Are you crazy?"

Lisa hurried over to her. "You can't give my job away."

"Honey, you're AWOL. I need a dependable cleaning person. I can't do the cleaning and everything else that needs to be done. Regina's going to be cutting back on her hours to work at the clinic."

"But that's my job."

"Not anymore it's not. I can't show up to work when the mood hits me. I can't have guests waiting for the days I happen to feel like working or making beds. The B and B would be empty, and I wouldn't be able to pay the bills. Now move away so I can leave."

"Aunt Anna said I could always have a job there."

"Not when you aren't working." She reached for her door. "Can you please move your car? I have to go."

"You can't give my job away like that. How am I supposed to live?"

"You should have thought about that when you made the decision not to show up for work. If I have to work fifteen hours a day, if I have to clean every single room myself, I'm not putting up with your crap any longer. Now move your damn car."

Gabrielle got in her car and closed the door. Cranking the engine, she noticed Lisa backing her car out of the drive and peeling down the driveway. Everybody had taken Lisa's abuse for years, making excuses for her bad attitude. The world owed her, even Gabrielle. But Gabrielle wasn't paying that debt any longer.

* * *

Cornell glanced at his watch for what must have been the thousandth time. He looked out at the crowd in the dining room and outside. He told himself he was gauging how successful the event was and whether he should do this every Friday night during the summer. He could only fool himself for so long. He was looking for Gabrielle, and she was still suspiciously missing. Did she plan to stop by? She knew how important this day was.

Hold on. Since when did he depend on a woman for anything?

He closed the swinging door. The place was full. He had more orders to begin delivering Monday morning than he'd even dreamed. He didn't need Gabrielle. He appreciated the fact that his parents and brothers were supporting him.

Personally Yours was having a successful start. He wouldn't walk out there again looking for her.

Regina hoped Sam would be at the restaurant by the time she arrived. He was so quiet you never knew what he was thinking. She wished for once she knew what was going through his mind when they talked.

She'd dressed carefully in a low-cut dress that revealed just enough cleavage without making her look cheap. She even wore high-heeled sandals. As much as she hated them, they made her legs look nice—at least men had always said her legs looked good in them.

Was that smoke coming from under her hood? Her car started making those little stop-and-go jumps. "No. No." Big streams of smoke were billowing. Slowly she pulled her precious transportation to the side of the road. She couldn't afford to have a serious problem. She'd saved a little of the money Aunt Anna had given her, but it was for a rainy day, not to make costly repairs. She slid her shoes off her feet—

no sense in ruining her heels in the gravel—and donned a pair of old sneakers she'd put behind the passenger seat.

"What now?" She engaged the hood release. Her father changed her oil. She knew how to add coolant. But that was the extent of her mechanical knowledge. She grabbed her cell phone to call her brother. He wasn't answering. Just her luck. She called her second brother. He was still on the mainland. She was getting ready to call the garage when a truck pulled up behind her.

It was Sam.

"What's wrong?" he said, hanging out the door.

"I don't have a clue," she said.

Lumbering over, he gazed under the hood. He still wore his work clothes, so obviously he hadn't planned on going to dinner unless he was going dressed as he was. And she'd spent all that time applying makeup and choosing a dress. Her room was a mess of clothes that she had to hang up when she went home. What on earth made her go through all that trouble for him in the first place?

He lifted his head from beneath the hood. "You're going to need a tow truck. If you don't mind waiting for me to shower, we can go to the restaurant together. I'm running a little late."

Immediately she felt more favorable. "I don't mind." Happily she dialed the tow truck, and they waited twenty minutes for it to arrive, with her making a mostly one-sided conversation. She could handle that. She exchanged her sneakers for her heels and noticed him gazing at her legs and acting as if he didn't know she had a pair.

Regina knew she was confusing Sam, and she liked that.

The future maintenance bill slid to the back of her mind for the moment as they rode to the other side of the island. It was no more than five miles in a straight line from one side to the other. Of course, you'd have to navigate twists and turns, down one road and up the other before they made it.

But Regina had never seen the inside of Sam's house. And

since it was blocked from the road with gnarled trees, she really didn't know what the outside looked like.

Surreptitiously, she regarded him and he seemed at ease driving in silence.

"Do you keep your yard as beautiful as the B and B's?" she asked.

"Not quite. I have a greenhouse out back. Got some flowers growing around the place."

"Yours should be the finest on the island."

"After I take care of the others, I don't have much time for my own."

His garden shop wasn't on the water like the B&B. There was a quaint little sign on the main road and several feet back was the store. There was an acre or two of plants. In the winter, they were covered in plastic greenhouses.

Out of sight, across the street, he turned down a wooded lane. His house was a couple of hundred feet back from the road, just a hundred feet from the water's edge.

Regina gasped. "Your azaleas are beautiful. Your whole yard is magnificent." She hit him on the arm.

"Hey."

"Liar. You told me you didn't do much with your yard." Just like the B&B's, he had beds of flowers, grottos, and a fountain to die for.

He shrugged. "I do what I can."

"Men." She wished she had a yard half as magnificent as this.

She heard him opening the door. She was so engrossed in her surroundings, nothing else penetrated.

"How can you stand to be away so much?"

"Gotta work."

She was still gawking when he rounded the truck and opened her door. She climbed out, trying to take in everything.

"Wonder if you can do this to mine?"

"Sure. If you can wait ten years."

"I can't wait another minute."

He chuckled and Regina stared at him. She'd never heard him laugh before. But it sounded nice coming from him.

His house was four times larger than hers. "How many bedrooms?"

"Four."

The house stood on stilts the way most houses did on the island. Light spilled from every direction in the two-story great room with a glass wall facing the ocean. The glass was crisscrossed with wooden slats painted white. It was dusk and the sun's disappearing orange ball was a beautiful sight.

"Kitchen's that way if you want something to drink. Make yourself at home."

"Does that mean I can look around?"

"Knock yourself out," he said, and headed up the stairs.

But Regina focused on the room.

Two blue and white couches dominated the room, with a huge leather cocktail table separating them. A couple of boating pictures hung on the wall. But on the accent table were a number of beautiful photographs. Most were of his parents. He was in some of them. There were a couple of Aunt Anna and of her family functions. One at Aunt Anna's crab fry showing a table surrounded with teens. Regina's picture was in there. She picked up the one that focused on her.

When had he taken that? she wondered. There were so many crab fries. She never knew he even noticed her. Frowning, she set the picture down and explored the kitchen. She was thirsty.

The kitchen, which was right off the living area, was as airy as the great room, with white cabinets and speckled granite countertops. She opened the double-door refrigerator and tsked. That huge space and he had only a dozen eggs, bacon, beer and sodas. Regina shook her head. Her kitchen was tiny but the fridge was full. He obviously wasn't much of a cook.

Regina chose a Pepsi, then opened the sliding glass door and went onto the sprawling deck. It ran the entire length of the house. A mosquito bit her, and she headed straight for the screened-in gazebo and listened to the waves while she watched the sun disappear from the horizon.

What a wonderful place.

"What are you doing here?" Naomi asked Gabrielle.

"I tried to talk her into going to the grand opening, but she wouldn't hear of it," Wanda said. She was dressed in a nice pair of slacks and a blouse.

"I guess I'll fry fish for dinner. Your cousin went fishing today and brought by a dozen. I've already cleaned them."

"They'll keep for another night, Grandma. Take a night off for a change. My treat. Let's go to Cornell's place."

"I wouldn't darken that door with my presence, and neither should you. And by the way, young lady, I hear the two of you've been smooching and carrying on all over this island. Acting just shameful."

"You wouldn't even mention it if it were anybody but Cornell. And it was just a light peck," she lied.

"He shouldn't have put his lips on you, period."

"Oh, Grandma, you can't blame him for what his uncle did. Aunt Anna wasn't the easiest person to get along with."

"Don't speak ill of the dead, girl."

Hoyt came lumbering in from the other room. "Oh, Naomi, don't be such a grouch. You sound more and more like Anna every day," he said.

Naomi narrowed her eyes. "And your opinion is unbiased?"

"I never liked her. She never liked me, either. I could have dropped my dentures when she left the place to Gabrielle, although she was the logical solution. But when did that old bat take the logical route?"

Even Gabrielle was surprised her aunt had left it to her. Even though she'd cared for her, she didn't expect payment. Her aunt grumbled and complained about everything.

"Your grandsons are working there tonight, Grandma," Gabrielle said. "Lance and Chance will be disappointed if you don't show up."

Naomi sighed. "I guess I'll go, then. Have to support the children."

"That's my girl," Hoyt said to Naomi's eye roll.

"Humph."

Gabrielle smiled. Her grandmother doted on her grandchildren—all of them. It was one sure way to get her compliance.

The yard was full of cars. It seemed half the island turned up. In the end, her grandfather decided to drive so Gabrielle wouldn't have to bring them back home. Wanda rode with them. It was such a pleasant evening.

The building was old but cheerful with a fresh coat of white paint. Outside, tables were covered with red-checkered tablecloths. Little lanterns hung on trees and were set in the centers of tables.

Gabrielle and her grandparents spoke briefly to Cornell's family before they searched for seats.

The professors were at a table large enough to seat ten, and they beckoned Gabrielle over just as her grandparents arrived.

"I'm not sitting outside to be dinner for mosquitoes," Naomi said.

"The citronella candles should keep the mosquitoes away. And a nice breeze is blowing," her grandfather said. "Come on." He cupped Naomi's elbow and guided her along.

"Just take a moment to meet some of my guests," Gabrielle said.

The professors stood as they arrived.

"Isn't this delightful?" Mitchell said.

"Oh, just wonderful. I'd like you to meet my grandparents," Gabrielle said, and introduced everyone.

When they were all seated and had ordered their dinners,

the professor said, "We're writing a book on family history. My father's ancestor was one of the first who landed in 1607," he said.

"We have a long history here, too," Naomi said. "My ancestors arrived in 1607 and 1617." Rarely did she mention the ancestors who arrived with the first settlers.

"I discovered this island through my research," Mitchell said. "My family moved away after World War II, but they had records dating back to the 1600s. My father told me that one of his ancestors had fled this area in the mid-1800s and stole a golden bowl that was a family heirloom, just like the one they found in Jamestown. It was a sticking point for the family that she left with the bowl. They searched high and wide for her but were unable to find her. He told me the people from this island helped her escape, which is why I decided to spend a few months here gathering information."

From across the table, Gabrielle saw the suspicious shadow cross her grandmother's face and wondered what the professor had said to upset her.

"So you've come back hoping to get the bowl?" her grandmother asked.

"Oh, no, no. That bowl's probably long gone by now. I just wanted to know how she escaped; just gathering more information on her for my records."

Her grandmother nodded.

"Maybe you could get together and talk about it one day," Gabrielle said.

"I would love that. I hope Gabrielle will let me see old pictures. She told me she had boxes of them."

Gabrielle tuned out their conversation completely when she saw Lisa approach the table, looking around for a place to sit. Graham hopped out of his seat quickly and waved her over.

When she neared them, he said, "Join us."

"Not enough room," she said, her lips pinched.

Graham turned in a circle. "There's a place right there. I'll sit with you." Grabbing his plate and glass, as if it were a for-gone conclusion, he started to the other table. Lisa reluctantly followed him.

"The food's wonderful," he said. "But I already knew that. I miss seeing you. You okay?"

Lisa wondered what Gabrielle had told them. Obviously she hadn't told them she'd been fired. That bitch. As if she had the right.

Graham was looking at her all funny, like she'd grown two heads.

"I'm fine. I should be back soon." Gabrielle wasn't giving her job to any damn body. Lisa needed that job. So what if she needed a recuperating day now and then to pull herself to-gether. Everybody did. She'd just broken up with this guy she'd dated for a couple of weeks. Her nerves were just torn up. And Gabrielle just got on her last damn nerve having con-trol of everything and hogging it all for herself as if she couldn't share with the family.

Aunt Anna shouldn't have given that hussy anything. She didn't grow up on the island. She came back for a few months and winds up running the roost.

Lisa had worked at that B&B for years, and what did Aunt Anna leave her? A lousy twenty grand, that's all the thanks she got. So maybe in the last few months she'd been away. But her relationship with Carl had seemed promising. He'd told her he loved her. He even came home with her to attend Aunt Anna's funeral on account of she was so upset. She hadn't expected the old biddy to bite the dust that fast. She'd been hanging on like that for years. Lisa expected her to linger on a few more years.

Then to find out Gabrielle had worked herself into Aunt Anna's heart where Lisa should have been. Lisa knew deep down that Gabrielle had tricked Aunt Anna. That's how she ended up with the house and the B&B. It should have right-fully been Lisa's. She'd worked there all these years.

"Nobody puts the special touch on the rooms that you do," Graham was saying.

Lisa smiled. "I like for things to look pretty."

"They look very pretty when you finish. It's not just a job to you, is it?"

Lisa shook her head. She knew most people thought cleaning was a chore just to get through. But she liked going through the rooms. She liked looking in a room when she was finished and seeing how pretty it was. One of the things she liked best about the B&B was all the different scenes in the rooms. Some rooms were decorated in modern pieces, some in Victorian.

Graham leaned across the table and whispered, "I'm sorry Mitchell's room's so sloppy. I know it bothers you that you can't straighten up his stuff."

Lisa looked to the side. "That man. I don't know how he stands all that clutter. My aunt was like that. When I cleaned her house, if I moved one piece of paper out of place, she'd have a hissy fit. You can't get a room looking pretty that way."

Graham sighed. "I know. But I appreciate your work. The way you straighten a room is like a work of art."

Lisa felt her face heat up. Graham was such a nice guy. All his papers were tucked in the drawer like they were supposed to be. He wasn't a slob like Mitchell. His towels were placed neatly on the tub where she gathered them to be laundered. Now here was a man who appreciated a woman's hard work. She'd learned long ago that men in general treated cleaning like it was the woman's duty. They didn't consider the elbow grease a woman put into making the home a castle.

The B&B wasn't the only job on earth. She wasn't begging that bitch. She was going to the mainland first thing Monday morning and looking for a job. Somebody would hire her. She might just decide to become a secretary or something.

She couldn't type worth shit, but she could learn. She wasn't stupid.

CHAPTER 8

Never in his entire life had Sam met a woman who'd talked so much. At the restaurant he'd expected Regina to choose one of those large tables where a million people were seated. And he'd fully intended to eat his meal in peace while she entertained everyone, especially when she headed over to the table where her grandparents were seated.

Hoyt stood when they approached them.

"Hi, Grandma, Grandpa," Regina said. With a quick hug, she kissed them both on the cheeks. She greeted the rest of the people at the table while Sam stood off to the side, saying a quick, "Hey."

"I've got to make it to your place and buy some lime," Mr. Claxton said.

"You're late getting started," Mrs. Claxton admonished.

The older man dug his hands in his pockets. "Been busy."

"You don't need to be lifting those heavy bags," his wife said.

He frowned at his wife. "You just let me take care of the yard, dear."

"I could use some mulch," Wanda said.

"Well, if you and Mr. Claxton let me know what you need, I can drop it by," Sam said, pulling business cards from his wallet and passing one to each person. "My phone number's on there."

"How nice. I'll call you first thing tomorrow."

"Too bad you don't live near me," Mitchell bemoaned. "Would sure like to get you to give me some advice on my yard. Now that I'm retired, thought I'd spend more time sprucing it up."

Sam chuckled. "Feel free to talk to me anytime."

"I just might do that before I leave."

They yakked for nearly five minutes more before Regina surprised him by steering them toward a table for two in a cozy little area near a gnarled oak.

Everyone in the restaurant was shocked to see him show up with her—with anyone. They were craning their necks, tapping tablemates on the hand. He knew what they were saying. What was she doing with that nobody? Regina could do better than him.

Regina was the lively sort. She dated popular guys. Although lately he hadn't seen her with anyone special. He'd figured she was seeing one of those doctors or college students. Of course, she was in her late twenties, the same as he was.

He ignored them. Not surprising she'd yakked through the whole meal, only requiring him to make intermittent monosyllabic statements. Also surprisingly, her voice began to wear favorably on him. He found himself listening to her while she described how the doctor set a bone at one of her hospital observations.

He was glad he'd showered and dressed in a shirt and blazer for the occasion. She was feisty but a gentle little creature. She'd do well as a nurse, he thought.

"Are you going to work in the island clinic when you finish?" he asked.

"That's the plan."

"How much longer will you be in school?"

"One more year. Thank the Lord."

"I'm sure you'll be more gentle with your patients than the hag . . . ah, Mrs. Granger." The woman in question was sitting three tables over.

Regina smiled shyly. Was that a come-on? 'Cause she looked real cute doing it. It also effectively shut her up. Will wonders never cease? He didn't think anything could render her silent. She didn't like praise.

Chance came over, interrupting their easy repartee. "Can I get you some dessert?"

"Not for me. I'm full," Regina said.

"Sure you don't want to take some home?" Sam asked. When she shook her head, he asked for the check. He wanted to linger over coffee, listen to her talk a while longer, but he knew better. He'd been hanging out with his own silence too long.

After paying the bill, he guided her into his truck, wishing he'd taken the time to wash and wax it. She lived only ten minutes from the place, and much too quickly, he was parked in her yard.

"Would you like to come in for a soda or coffee?" she asked.

"Coffee keeps me up at night," he said.

"I've got decaf."

He shook his head. She'd had his head all cloudy lately, running out with glasses of juice and tea. Not for a second did he believe she was for real.

Sam would like nothing more than to come in, but he knew her game, and her kind only wanted to use guys like him. The island breeze flowing through the truck had finally cleared his fuzzy brain.

He wasn't going to get himself all worked up for Regina to drop him after he finished her yard. He might like her. She might be the prettiest woman on the island, but it wasn't worth the heartache.

He was doing this for Gabrielle and for Ms. Anna. He knew Anna picked out the house for her. If Anna were alive, she'd ask him to help Regina. Anna had done so much for him. Took a lost boy in when he was a teenager and made his life bearable.

"Got an early day tomorrow. I'll look your yard over sometime this weekend and give you some suggestions next week maybe."

He could barely see her nod in the dark.

It seemed as if the sun went out of her eyes. Did she really want him to come in? *Nah.* He was only fooling himself. It was all a game to her. He wasn't going to get himself all worked up about seeing her when he knew it would lead to nothing. She was still getting her flowers done, wasn't she? So she had nothing to look crestfallen about.

She reached for the door. "I guess I'll see you next week, then. Thanks for the ride—and for dinner."

"You're welcome." He walked her to the door and waited until she was safely inside and the lights turned on before he drove away.

"It was a pleasure meeting you, Mrs. Claxton. "I'm looking forward to speaking to you more about your family's history," Mitchell said.

"As am I. Gabrielle, where did your grandfather get to?"

"I'll find him." By her grandmother's tone, she could tell that she didn't trust Mitchell. Probably the mention of the bowl made her suspicious.

As she left, she heard Mitchell tell Graham he was ready to leave. Graham told Mitchell he'd walk back and handed over the car keys. He and Lisa were immediately engulfed in their conversation.

In the kitchen, Gabrielle dragged her grandfather from demonstrating something to Lance.

Gabrielle lingered to talk with friends after Mitchell and her grandparents left. Many of the B&B patrons had stopped by Lisa's table to speak to her. They genuinely liked her. Even her little one-room efficiency over her parent's garage was decorated beautifully. On the tiny deck, Lisa had included pots of colorful flowers.

Some people just had the homey flair. Gabrielle just wished Lisa was less antagonistic and more reliable. She really hated to fire her. And Lisa's father was moaning about renting the place out to a paying customer.

Then Cornell appeared. He'd shed his white coat. "Did you meet my parents?"

"We spoke."

"I wanted to introduce you, but it was pretty busy in back. They left before I could get a break."

"The locals are going to want you to turn this place into a restaurant," Gabrielle said.

"I don't think so. I might consider opening on Fridays until Labor Day."

"They will still stop by here left and right. The other places serve food their physicians are telling them to stay away from."

"You'd think I'd get more orders from the islanders."

"No, they feel they're supposed to cook at home. You're an upstart. Nice turnout."

His arm brushed hers, sending little shocks of pleasure through her. "Couldn't tell by this crowd." His gaze roved lazily over her. "Can you hang around for a while longer?"

"Sure. I'll even help."

"No, thanks," he said, throwing her a wicked grin. "But after I finish up, I'll take you riding on my bike."

Gabrielle laughed. "No way. I drove here in my nice safe car. I can drive home."

He slipped an arm around her, drew her close. "Time for you to live on the wild side, sweetheart."

"Are you safe?"

"Definitely not, but you'll have fun." She wondered if he was speaking about the bike or himself.

A middle-aged woman Gabrielle had seen around town a few times approached her.

"I read your ad in the grocery store. I'm looking for a part-time job. Right now I'm taking the ferry back and forth to the mainland to work, but working here would be more convenient. I'd like to spend more time with my children, and if you need me to work longer hours, I'll be available."

"Why don't you stop by my office tomorrow and complete an application?" Gabrielle said.

"I'd love to. I have references."

When the woman walked away, Gabrielle caught Lisa watching her with a frown. Things were looking up as far as Gabrielle was concerned. If this woman's references were acceptable, Gabrielle would be able to spend more time on her other responsibilities.

Unfortunately, she couldn't stop the smidgen of guilt eating at her gut.

Lisa drove Graham back to the B&B. He leaned over the seat to kiss her, but she pushed against his chest.

"What is it? You don't date white men?"

"That's not it; although, I've never dated a white guy before. I'm taking a break from relationships. I'm always tangling with the wrong kind of man."

"Whatever other men have done, I would never hurt you."

"You won't be here long, either. You're here just for a few weeks. Too temporary. Besides, my life's a mess. Gabrielle's getting on my last nerve, and I need to get my head on straight. I'm kind of still not over my last relationship."

"I've heard whispers . . ."

"All lies. I'm not as bad as people say I am."

"Of course you aren't. I think people don't take the time to know you. No matter what people say, you remember you have special gifts, too."

Lisa rolled down the window, lit up a cigarette. "You mind?"

Graham shook his head.

"I know you're bullshitting me. I'm the black sheep of the family. When the Big JC was handing out gifts, he forgot me."

"Don't you believe it—not for a moment. Making the B and B a comfortable home is a gift. Just because you aren't a scientist or a financier doesn't make you less important."

Lisa gazed at the big beautiful building. She liked talking to Graham. He never treated her like dirt. Always stopped to talk to her. But he didn't understand. Her family was always talking about how special Alyssa was because she went to college and got a degree in criminology before she was hired on at the police department. That was how she became an investigator so quickly over John, who'd worked there longer. They were awed with the fact that Regina was getting her masters in nursing. Sure Regina cleaned a few rooms to make ends meet, but soon she'd be working right alongside the doctor in the clinic. She'd be somebody. And Gabrielle had some kind of degree, too. People thought she was some hot stuff for leaving her high-paying job to come run the B&B, when the only reason Lisa didn't get the B&B was because she never went to college. Well, neither did Aunt Anna. And she ran it for decades. But they wouldn't consider Lisa just because she was the maid—without a college degree. She was sick to death of being looked down on. She could just smack Gabrielle for firing her like she was disposable.

Graham gathered her hand in his. "What're you thinking?"

Lisa inhaled and blew out smoke. It had gotten cooler but not cold yet.

"When you're a maid, people look through you like you're dirt. Important people stay here all the time. Taking an expensive vacation with their families. Even their children treat you like dirt. All high and mighty. Family's just as bad."

Graham reached over, took her chin in his hand, and turned her so that she looked him square in the eyes. "Don't ever let anybody make you believe you're nothing. You're somebody, Lisa Claxton. Now you say it."

Lisa turned away and gazed out the window.

"Say it!"

His shout made Lisa jump. "What's with you?"

"If it's the last thing I do, I'm going to make you see that you're somebody. You aren't nothing. I know how you feel."

"Pffft. You got your big college degree. You're a college professor."

"Lecturer. There's a big difference. You don't get the same benefits."

Lisa got mad. "Don't tell me people don't respect you, because I know they do. They know you're the one who's doing the writing on that project. The professor might sit around and talk all day, but you're the one working on that computer, putting things together. It's more yours than his."

"Do you know how much lecturers make? Not much."

"They can't take your degree from you. You can go anywhere and do anything. I don't have that. If I go to the mainland and get even another maid's job, I'm still nobody."

"You're somebody."

"My job at the B and B might not be much, but it's more than a job to me."

"You think I don't know that? It's your career. This old building is part of your heritage."

"Yeah. That's how I always felt about it." *Until now,* Lisa thought. Until Gabrielle fired her. She had no right to do that. No right at all. Lisa saw the woman talking to her tonight. She'd been complaining about having to take the ferry to Virginia Beach every day and how the big hotels didn't pay her squat and just about worked her to death. Lisa didn't want to even think about getting another job.

"I hope you come back soon. I miss you." Graham chuckled. "Even if you won't let me kiss you."

"We can be friends," Lisa said hopefully. "I like talking to you. You're a nice guy."

"If you ever need to talk to someone, I'm here, okay?"

"Thanks."

Graham extended a hand. "Friends. I won't try anything. Promise."

Lisa took his hand in hers. It was nice talking to someone who understood her and who she didn't have to worry about trying to get in her pants. She'd gotten in so much trouble with men lately. Graham had a college degree, too. And he respected her. This was a new experience for her.

"Friends," she finally said.

As Gabrielle hung on the back of Cornell's motorcycle, her arms clasped tightly around his waist, she wondered if he had planned this all along. Or if she'd gone and lost her mind. She couldn't deny the wind rushing against her was refreshing on this cool night. Beneath her helmet, her hair flowed out behind her. She wore one of his leather jackets, which was big enough for two of her to fit into. Good thing she'd worn slacks, she thought as they whisked past the ferry dock and flew through the village where her grandparents' house was located. Wonder what Naomi would think if she saw Gabrielle now? She didn't have to wonder. Naomi would shake her head at her stupidity for riding with that bad boy.

As they circled the island, Gabrielle let her mind roam freely. Her thoughts were anything but peaceful, though. She thought of Lisa. Lisa needed that job. But Gabrielle didn't know what to do. She couldn't make Lisa show up for work. She couldn't get her job done if she had to stop and do Lisa's.

And she wasn't putting up with Lisa's attitude. God knew she didn't want to fire her. But the busy season was coming up. They were fully booked every day from May through October.

They rounded a curve, and Gabrielle leaned more into Cornell, her breasts pressed against his back. Even in the wind, Gabrielle felt her body come to life. They were now riding along a straight patch, and Gabrielle leaned back as much as she could, but her body was still in contact with his.

Cornell felt her try to put some distance between them and leaned his body into a curve again. She tightened her arms around him. He liked that. Riding a bike cleared his mind, but riding with a woman on board stirred his juices. Just the thought of her thighs pressed against him had him thinking of himself being enclosed in those legs.

Things were moving much too fast or slow. Which, he couldn't say. He wanted her in his bed, but he didn't want complications. He wanted to celebrate the night's success with her, but he didn't want to need her. Didn't want to wait anxiously for her to arrive.

What a paradox.

Up ahead, Cornell saw their houses silhouetted in the dark. Not nearly ready for the evening to be over, he stopped near the beach behind her house and cut the headlights and the engine.

Gabrielle climbed off the bike, glad she'd survived her first motorcycle ride and truthfully wanting another. When her eyes adjusted to the darkness, she noticed the moon was bright in the sky and reflected on the rippling waves. It was just enough light for her to see Cornell as he climbed off the bike and engaged the kick plate so it wouldn't sink deeply into the sand.

"The ride wasn't so bad, was it?" he asked.

"It was fantastic."

Pulling off the helmet, she handed it to him, shaking out

her hair. After tucking the helmets away, he closed the distance between them, raked his hands through the long strands of hair, then rested it on her warm neck.

"Didn't your grandmother warn you about guys like me?"

He smelled of leather, the wind, and the sea breeze. "You know she did," Gabrielle said, feeling reckless.

He moved closer. "And are you naughty or nice?" There was something mysterious in his eyes, and her insides quivered.

"Depends," she said in a voice unlike her own.

"On what?"

She never got the chance to respond before his lips captured hers in a breathtaking kiss. The warmth was a contrast to the cool wind whipping on the beach. He nibbled at the corners of her mouth, ran his tongue slowly along the seam of her lips, then tasted her like he wanted to savor the experience. Slowly, he drew his hands down her arms.

Gabrielle could tell right then and there that he wasn't a love-her-and-leave-her kind of man. He slowly peeled the jacket off her, letting it drop to the ground. Her skin was so heated she didn't feel the cold. His fingertips drawing over her body had her feeling like a trail of heat was blazing through her. Desire spread to every fiber of her being.

Gabrielle guided his jacket off, and it followed the same path as her own. She should feel inhibited on this stretch of beach, but they were alone. This was their unique space.

She followed his lead and caressed his long lean body, never imagining she could derive so much pleasure from touching a man.

She trailed a hand down his chest, caressed his thighs, and captured his penis in her hand. He was swollen hard. She glided her hands back and forth. A deep moan escaped his lips, his manhood jerking in her hand. He caught her hand and moved it to his chest.

"Slow down, baby. I'm getting way ahead of you." He kissed her deep and hard. Gone was the gentle teasing.

"I'm not made of stone," he whispered roughly against her hair. "If you're going to stop me, you'd better stop me now."

"Who's asking you to?" was her prompt reply.

And then she was in his arms, her body pressed against his. This wasn't the gentle, easygoing man she was used to. This was the lion unleashed. All along she knew he was holding back. But this was what she wanted. She wanted the wild untamed part of him.

Before she knew it, her clothes were on the ground and she was standing before him naked in the moonlight. She shivered as his eyes gazed over her. She felt need so deep it reached her core.

"Cold?" he asked.

"A little." They were crazy. Mere feet away from the warmth of the house, they were making love on the beach. There was something magical about the night. There was something special about making love beneath the moon. There were always stories about the crazy things people did under the full moon.

He took a blanket out of some compartment and laid it on the ground. Then Gabrielle began to undress him slowly, caressing him as she did. Before she knew it, she was on the blanket. He kissed her thighs, and it felt like a flame lit inside her.

"Now," she whispered.

"Not yet. You're not ready yet."

She thought she would explode with need. But he took his time, and he built an intense yearning in her that she didn't know existed.

And then he was pulling on a condom. He pressed her knees apart and lowered himself onto her. He teased her before he slowly pushed inside. She clamped her legs tightly around him, clenching him deeply. They moved to a beat as old as time. She'd never, ever felt longing or need so intense. It seemed she was having an out-of-body experience. As pleasure increased, she wanted to hold on to it forever. Suddenly, her world stilled, and she cried out as she tumbled over into the most explosive orgasm of her life. Every muscle in her body tightened. With a long groan, he found his fulfillment. She wasn't ready to let him go, and she held on to him tightly.

It seemed a lifetime elapsed before she relaxed and opened her eyes.

He moved to the side, pulled his jacket over them, and cradled her head on his arm.

She trailed a finger down his chest and kissed him there.

"Cold?" he asked.

"Not now."

"You've got more layers than I ever dreamed," he said.

Nervously, she said, "I see the Big Dipper."

He leaned over her. "I see you."

She felt vulnerable. "What do you see?"

"The most gorgeous woman I've ever encountered. I see deeper than the surface. I see the wild Gabrielle who wants to come out and play. Forget about the baggage for a while."

She tried to push him away. "Give me a break."

But he wouldn't move. He captured her chin in his hand. "I do see you."

She closed her eyes briefly. When she opened them, the moon had cast a golden shadow over the water. The light reflecting off the full moon made golden sparkles in the sand. Something had changed in her.

It was a golden night.

Cornell pushed the bike to Gabrielle's house and left her at the door. He'd thought about staying the night, having her tucked against him, but he was still a little shaky with them as a couple.

He rode across the path to his own place with his mind on his hands caressing Gabrielle's soft curves. Maybe he should have stayed the night, after all. Whistling, he screeched to a halt. He'd almost run into the back of a car. Who the heck would be in his yard this time of the night? He moaned.

His mother's car.

Damn.

Sighing, he parked his bike in the detached garage behind the house. Inside he gathered a deep breath to confront his mother.

She waved to him and continued talking on her cell phone. By the conversation, it was obviously her closest friend. She was telling her about her horrible husband. When she saw Cornell, she hung up.

"That father of yours gets on my last nerve," she said. "Where have you been? You have sand on you. It's all in your hair."

"Hi, Mom." He kissed her on the cheek. "Are you all settled in? Need help with luggage?"

"No. No. I've been here for a couple of hours. I'm already unpacked in the guest room."

"Are you hungry?"

"I ate one of the dinners in your refrigerator. It was delicious. So was the grand opening. It's three in the morning. What in the world can you do on the island at this time of night? Even the bar is closed."

As much as he loved and respected his mother, Cornell was used to ignoring questions like that. Several times a year, his father and mother had one of their spats. At that time, she'd move in with one of her children.

"I'm telling you your daddy started acting like a fool the moment we got home. I told him I wasn't putting up with it. I need a break."

Cornell mentally made a list of tomorrow's schedule while his mother berated his father. It wouldn't do any good to intervene once she got wound up. He poured each of them a glass of wine before he sat and listened for a half hour before he got up and went to bed.

This was a good reminder of why he lived alone. He wouldn't want some woman badmouthing him like that every time he turned around. Bad enough Mrs. Claxton gave him a hard time. He could just see all Gabrielle's relatives wagging their tongues all over the island. All your business in the streets.

Damned if he was going to love the woman he lived across the street from for fifty years because he couldn't live with her. She wasn't the only woman with warm curves, even if her curves were the only ones front and center in his mind right now.

Things were going to be tense at his house for the week his mother would be there. His father always gave her a week before he threatened to throw out her clothes. Then she'd go home. And they'd make up.

Maybe his mother's appearance was a warning.

As much as he loved sex, as much as he'd like to have the trust and companionship, it wasn't worth all that drama.

Sam didn't immediately drive home. Actually, he was reluctant. He'd just think about Regina walking through his rooms. Touching things. He hadn't slept well at all lately with the way she was coming on to him and seriously messing with his mind.

He drove downtown to the bar, ordered a beer, and watched an old game playing on the tube. The bar was pretty full. But he stayed on his end of the bar and nobody bothered him—as usual. He was restless.

The noise was pretty loud. Too loud for him to think about a woman he'd lusted after since high school. It hadn't mattered that she was two years behind him or that she wouldn't give him the time of day. As soon as she turned those brown eyes on him, his tongue got all crossed up.

"Is that you, Sam?"

Sam focused on the waitress who used to hang with Regina in high school.

He'd lived on the island his entire life. Came to the bar often. She never gave him the time of day. He didn't dignify her question with an answer. Sam focused on the tube.

She came right over and got in his face. "Thought that was you."

Sam moved his drink to the side. "Yeah."

"Saw you at dinner tonight."

"Hmm. Is there anything I can do for you?"

"I'm closing tonight, but I sure would like to share a drink later on."

"Sorry. I'm leaving soon." Now, she saw him with Regina, yet she was asking him for a drink. He didn't think so.

She caressed the side of his face. "Anytime you're lonely, sugar, just **look** me up."

She had to be desperate. *He'd* have to be more than desperate **to look her up**—he'd have to be crazy.

"Hey," said the bar manager, who was also that evening's **bartender.** "Get the lead out. Got people waiting for drinks!"

"Just hold your drawers." She rubbed up against Sam. "Check you later, Sam."

She picked up her drinks from the bar and left.

Sam had had enough of the bar scene. Enough to drink, too. Her coming on to him just reminded him how much he wanted Regina.

He had a full day of work the next day, yet he knew he was going to toss and turn half the night. And dream about a nutmeg-complexioned beauty he wanted so much he could scream with need. He was going to do her yard, but he was going to put a stop to these drinks—and no more dates.

In the house, Sam dropped his keys on the foyer table and

grabbed a beer from the fridge since he hadn't finished his at the bar. He'd drank a quarter of the bottle and was in his bedroom when he realized something wasn't right.

It wasn't anything overt, just little things that were out of place that alerted Sam someone had been in his house. A cabinet door not completely closed. A drawer with his underwear caught.

He stopped and listened. Whoever was there was more than likely long gone. Still, setting the beer on the dresser, he took the baseball bat from the closet and made his way through every room. He checked the closets; then he walked around outside—and found nothing.

On the second trip through his house, he checked to see if anything had been stolen. He didn't keep valuables, except for a computer and a couple of TVs. None of them had been touched.

With nothing obviously disturbed, he couldn't even report the break-in. The islanders already thought he was strange. Now they'd add paranoid to the mix. He had good locks on his door. Whoever came in was a pro.

It didn't take a genius to realize anyone who had a connection with Anna was being systematically searched. Someone desperately wanted her golden bowl.

He'd have to talk to Gabrielle. Her home seemed to be the only one not broken into. Then again, if it was invaded, maybe she couldn't tell with all Anna's things around the place. Besides, Gabrielle wasn't that observant.

Damn it, he'd have to warn Regina, too.

CHAPTER 9

"Hey, Gabrielle," Sam said Sunday afternoon when he'd finally got a minute to make a phone call. "Just wanted to give you a heads-up that my place was searched Friday night while I was away."

"Did they steal anything?"

"Nope. Done by a real professional. Just thought you'd want to be on the lookout."

"Did you report it?"

"They didn't leave any evidence behind. I could tell because I know my place. I just want you to be careful. Probably connected to Mrs. Anna."

"This doesn't make sense, Sam."

"I know, but something weird's going on. Just want you to be careful," he repeated as if he wanted to get her off the phone. "I'm on my way to Regina's. I'll tell her."

"Thanks for warning me," she said, and hung up.

Sam had put off visiting Regina for as long as he could. Took him exactly seven minutes to reach her place from his. If he was lucky, she'd be gone and he could look the place over by himself and wouldn't have to see her at all.

Her car was in the yard. His luck was running for crap lately. His truck door slammed, and in seconds, she was at the window, then at the door running down the steps before he could get a good look around.

"Studying for exams?" he asked. He wouldn't look at her. Didn't need her breaking his concentration.

"How did you guess?"

"Got your glasses on." He glanced at her just as she snatched them off.

"Forgot."

"Look kinda cute in them." Now why the heck did he say that? Why did he look at her?

"Really?"

Hands on hips, Sam forced his gaze away from Regina and to her yard. He already knew what would work. He came by a couple times when she was working.

"I'm thinking you want it laid out so that you get lots of views from inside as well as outside. Even when winter sets in, you want the garden to keep its form." He could see her in the kitchen with a cup of coffee in the morning enjoying water gurgling from a small rock stream. The peace of the morning would get her off to a good working start. Dealing with folks, you needed some ammunition in your arsenal.

"Umm, I like that."

"We could repeat flower beds with hydrangeas, roses, and boxwood throughout the garden. We could build a pergola with a swing. You have a few trees that block the view of your place from other houses. A few well-placed plants can give you even more privacy."

"Sounds like heaven. What about my window boxes?"

"We'll restore those soon so we can get a few summer flowers in there. In this climate you can have blooms through fall."

He felt rather than saw her come to a stop right by his side. It was like she was blasting a furnace over to him.

"Can I afford all this?"

He stepped to the side, giving him some distance so he

could think. "I'll get your brothers and dad to build the window boxes and the pergola. Shouldn't cost much."

Her eyes turned glassy and a tear spilled over. Damn. Sam was so out of his element. He had to do something to break the tension. She'd come out wearing a short sleeve sweater that curved her generous breasts and hip-hugging jeans that revealed every curve. Some men were breast men, some were leg, some were butt. He was greedy. He loved all three on Regina.

"You get a grit in your eye?"

She got that look—the look she wore often around him, that she wanted to smack him upside the head. He could handle that.

"I need to talk to you about a couple of things," he said, knowing as much as he wanted to leave, he had to tell her about the break-in.

"Had dinner yet?"

"I'll pick up something from downtown."

"Mama fixed a plate for me. It's enough for four people. I can't eat it all. Come on and share." She didn't give him a chance to respond before she'd turned and traipsed to the house.

Whew. Sam wiped the sweat off his brow. Resigned, he followed her, watching the sway of her backside.

This wasn't good.

"What have you been doing down there?" Jade asked.

"Trying to find that damn bowl and jewels. Can't find crap. This thing is fucked up."

"Have you seen your partner yet?"

"Nope. Not one little peep. I'm getting worried."

"Me, too. This isn't like him. He was really pissed off with Roger for stealing from us. But that was months ago. I'm really getting worried."

"More likely he's getting tired of this screwed-up assignment. He's probably taken off."

"And leave everything behind? I don't think so. What about the gardener?"

"Zilch."

"You're going to have to find it and get out of there. I'm not feeling good about this assignment."

"I'm ready to get out right now."

"I'm not willing to give this job up, not when this is our biggest hit."

"Easy for you to say from your nice comfortable home. My butt is the one on the line here."

"Why don't you stop bitching and get the job done."

He disconnected. "Bitch."

Gabrielle was so pissed at Cornell she could sock him. After getting in her pants, he'd kept his distance, hadn't called—not once the entire weekend. She'd spotted a car across the street first thing Saturday morning. It had been there all weekend.

Even worse, she'd seen a woman coming and going from his house. Mostly she saw her back. Gabrielle wanted to give Cornell a peace of her mind. How dare he make love with her, then have another woman stay with him?

They'd been holed up in his house like cozy honeymooners. Never had anyone treated her so shabbily. She told herself maybe she shouldn't jump to conclusions. It could be his sister or some other relative. If that was the case, wouldn't he have called? After all, they did make love. Hadn't it meant anything to him?

You couldn't make yourself believe a lie forever.

Maybe it was just sex for him. Maybe she read more into it than he'd wanted it to be. It wasn't like they were . . . well, she thought they were at least dating. She didn't go to bed with just anyone.

Earlier that morning, she'd gone to church, then stopped by her grandparents' for early afternoon dinner before she drove to the B&B to spend a couple hours.

Now as she was prepared to drive into her yard, a ball skated by her and some asshole bounded after it. She stood on her brakes to keep from hitting him.

She hopped out of the car in the middle of the road.

"Are you crazy?"

All youth and cheerful exuberance, he ran to her with the football tucked under his arm.

"Crazy about you," he said around a beguiling smile.

He was old enough to know better, Gabrielle thought.

"Knock it off. She's off limits," Cornell said.

"She didn't say that." The younger man edged a step closer. Cornell grabbed a fistful of his sweatshirt and yanked him back.

"Hey!"

And then Cornell was standing in front of him, glaring at Gabrielle.

Ignoring him, Gabrielle got back in her car. Started to shut the door.

"Hey. Wait a minute."

She yanked the door closed and drove into her yard. When she got out, Cornell was beside her, looking like he could bend nails with his bare hands. The two guys from across the street were teasing and laughing.

"Why are you acting like this?" Cornell asked, low enough for the guys not to hear.

"Listen, if you just wanted a quickie, you should have been up front." If Lucky acted like Cornell, no wonder he and Aunt Anna never got along.

Cornell scrubbed his shoe in the dirt. "It wasn't like that."

"Explain it, then."

"When I got home Friday night, my mother was there." He glared at her as if she was the one who'd shown up uninvited. "She drives me freaking nuts."

"Listen, you don't owe me an explanation. I'm nobody to you." She was tired of everybody dumping on her. First Lisa and now him.

Frustrated, Cornell raked a hand over his head. "Lay off the dramatics, will you? I get enough of it from her."

"It's none of my business. Just go across the path and keep doing . . . whatever."

"I want you to meet my brothers."

"You could have introduced me to them."

They were across the path looking bored. "Hey, knuckle-heads. Come here."

Glaring at Cornell, Gabrielle stamped her feet.

While he waited for his brothers to cross the path, he said, "You look pretty. Been to church?"

Gabrielle nodded. "And to Grandma's for dinner."

His brothers finally reached them.

"Gabby, meet my brothers, Jamal and Marshall. Boys, Gabrielle Long."

They weren't boys at all, Gabrielle thought as she extended her hand. Younger than Cornell, but definitely men. "Pleasure to meet you," she said.

Jamal, the one who nearly ran her down before, captured her fingers and brought them to his lips, gallantly kissing the back of them. "The pleasure is all mine."

"What a charmer." But Gabrielle smiled at his foolishness.

Marshall stepped closer, leaned over, and kissed her on the cheek. "Anytime you get tired of older men, remember I'm the good-looking one."

"Get out of here," Cornell said.

Gabrielle laughed out loud as the men walked away. "Your brothers are charming."

"Is charm what it takes to keep you?"

"Who says I want to be kept?" He wasn't the only one who could play hard to get.

"We'll talk later," Cornell said. "My brothers will be leaving soon."

Gabrielle got the impression the conversation was for her benefit. She felt deep down it wasn't something he actually wanted to do but what he had to do.

"Forget it," Gabrielle said, and left him beside her car. She didn't have the time or inclination for games. He'd already shown her he wasn't serious. She knew how she felt when she was trying to break up with a coworker. It was uncomfortable. And she wanted to make it easier for Cornell. No hanging on because he didn't want to hurt her feelings or didn't know how to let her down easy. After all, they were neighbors. They worked together. Business was business. She wouldn't let pleasure interfere with it. She was right back to the place she'd been in Philly. Only this time she wasn't running.

She felt an uncomfortable kick in her chest. She just wished she could make her heart forget him as easily as she'd reasoned through the dilemma.

First thing Monday morning, Lisa took the ferry to the mainland. She dressed in a navy suit and white blouse. She trooped to what seemed like a million hotels along the beach and completed job applications. It had taken her forever to get to the hotels. When they revealed the salary, she was totally shocked.

There was no way in hell she could support herself on that amount. The B&B paid double that. She'd thought she was getting the going rate. It was true that when Aunt Anna's health started failing, Lisa had done chores other than cleaning. Maybe that was why she was given larger wages.

But working on the mainland, she had to pay more for gas and pay for the ferry ride every single day. That had to be subtracted from the meager amount they paid her. She was living in her parents' efficiency apartment now. She'd never be able to save for her own place at that rate.

It took an hour and a half to reach the hotels because she lived at the farthest point from the ferry. Damn, to work an eight-hour day, she'd have to put in eleven hours. She wouldn't have very much time left for herself.

Around noon, she ran into one of her high school friends who was job searching, too. Told her how they worked her on the last job. It had gotten worse in the last few years with all the cutbacks. They had to clean extra rooms. No way she could clean that many rooms in a day.

Lisa decided to try for a secretarial position. The application asked her how many words she could type a minute. She couldn't type at all. Just the little pecking she did on the computer. She had never taken a typing course. They asked her if she had any experience. Of course not, she thought. Then she tried for receptionist. She could do that.

Except the pay was also much less than what she was already making.

The last thing she wanted to do was go back to Gabrielle begging, she thought as she boarded the ferry. That hussy would hold it over her head for the rest of her freaking life.

It was Tuesday morning, and Gabrielle went to the B&B early. She hadn't seen Cornell since their confrontation.

Silas was working in the kitchen. She got a cup of coffee and went to her office for a few minutes. She was looking forward to interviewing housekeepers.

She really needed more than one. The shifts had to be covered seven days, more than a couple of part-time people could handle.

By midafternoon, Gabrielle and Regina were cleaning when Lisa came in all dressed up to work.

"You can just leave," Gabrielle told her.

"Grandma wants you, and these rooms need to be cleaned. What's it going to be?"

"Grandma can wait until after I finish."

"Something's going on over there," Lisa said.

"So why aren't you over there?"

"I don't handle family business. That's your and Alyssa's department, and since Zena the warrior isn't here—"

"Lisa, if you're lying to me—"

"I'm not a liar and you know it. She needs you now." Lisa took the stack of towels from Gabrielle and went into the bedroom.

Gabrielle stopped in her grandparents' yard. It looked like every police car on the island was at Wanda's house. Her grandparents, along with other neighbors, were standing in the yard. Her grandmother was crying, and her grandfather was awkwardly patting her shoulder.

Lord have mercy. Had Harvey Fisher finally killed Wanda? Gabrielle bolted out of the car and ran to her grandmother.

"What's going on?"

Her grandmother wiped the tears from her eyes with a wrinkled tissue. "It's Wanda. She passed away. She and I were supposed to work on the Founders Day program all day. When she didn't show up, I went to her house and used the spare key she gave me." Naomi moaned.

Gabrielle took her in her arms. Her grandfather looked relieved to relinquish the duty.

After pulling herself together, Naomi said, "I found her sitting in her recliner. She looked like she was sleeping, but her body was so cold."

Gabrielle hugged her grandmother again. "How horrible."

Naomi sighed. "A terrible thing. And she seemed so fit and

happy with her husband being away. She was looking forward to working with me."

Sheriff Harper Porterfield approached them. "Do you know her next of kin?"

"Her parents are dead," Naomi said. "She's an only child. We have to contact her husband. He works for the government and travels a lot. I'm sure there's some information in her house." Her grandmother wiped tears from her eyes again. "Wanda . . ." She cleared her throat. "Wanda didn't like to talk about him."

"Thank you, ma'am." Wanda's body was transported away. Yellow tape was strung up.

"Come on, Grandma. Let me fix you a cup of chamomile tea."

Her grandmother shook her head. "Nothing will soothe me. I can't believe it. She was just here yesterday sharing lunch with me. She attended church with us Sunday."

Wide imploring eyes regarded Gabrielle, but she wasn't seeing her. "I will never see my friend again."

Cornell was in a rotten mood. Gabrielle wasn't speaking to him, and his mother was driving him crazy. That day his mother had gone to the artist colony. He even worked longer hours to get away from her, and she had the nerve to say she should come to his place and help out.

Truth was, he missed Gabrielle. He'd really messed things up with her. But he didn't want to get too serious. Guess he wanted to be able to have his cake and eat it too. He didn't quite know how to handle a relationship with her. And until he did, it was best to stay away.

He still couldn't get over his brothers trying to play lovers with his woman.

His woman. That was the problem. He thought of Gabrielle as his. Didn't like the idea of her with another man, even his brothers. Even knowing they were kidding around. God, his mother had his head screwed up.

Three days had passed and they had not been able to contact Wanda's husband. There wasn't any reference in the house to a government office. There were no direct deposits from the government to his bank account or any check stubs. It was obvious he didn't work for the government. So where did he work?

Sheriff Porterfield liked this quiet little village. He sat behind his desk, facing trouble. He was trying to shuffle through papers and down a couple of doughnuts with his coffee before his space was invaded. Now the doughnuts were still in the box, his coffee cooling.

His job had been pretty easy so far. He was required to use few of the skills he had used on a daily basis in the city, although he knew how to handle an investigation—he was from Baltimore, after all. Plenty of crime there to keep his skills sharpened.

Wanda had had a heart attack. But the fact that Harvey Fisher was missing and the fact that Roger had died after spending time on the island were just too coincidental for Harper. Roger might not have died on the island, but Harper would bet his doughnuts his death was connected to the island. And he didn't like crime coming to his peaceful little place. Drug dealers, murderers, rapists weren't welcome on Paradise Island. He let them know quickly this wasn't the place they wanted to fool with. This place spoiled him. He liked things peaceful and safe.

He wished his investigator were here. Alyssa would love to dig her teeth into this. Her nose was like a hound dog's. She could smell trouble a mile away.

But right now he had to deal with Mrs. Claxton. She'd harassed him for a solid hour now. It was time he got her out of his office. He didn't like dealing with that woman on his best day.

She stood, wrapped the handle of her boat of a pocketbook on her arm. "I'm not pleased with the investigation, Sheriff."

"We're doing our best, Mrs. Claxton. Mrs. Fisher's fingerprints aren't on record anywhere." Harper stood, too. "As soon as I have anything, I'll be happy to share."

"Grandma, something isn't right about this," Gabrielle said. "There should be some information on these people."

"These people? These people? Wanda wasn't *these people*. She was my friend."

"I know, Grandma. I didn't mean any disrespect. But you have to agree. Look at your house. You have checkbooks, social security numbers, pictures, everything. They have nothing."

Naomi tilted her chin stubbornly. "Wanda was an honest woman and a good friend."

"But what do you really know about them? They came here less than two years ago. Wanda latched on to you, but did you really talk about her family?"

"She told me she was an only child and her parents had passed away shortly after she got married. She didn't have a happy childhood. That husband had given her a nervous condition. She suffered in that horrible marriage. I wish I had convinced her to leave him. He gave her that heart attack. All that stress and worry."

"Grandma, you might have to consider that they're criminals."

Naomi rounded on her. "Wanda wasn't a criminal. If you're going to talk like that, you can just go home. I don't need your help."

"Calm down before you give yourself a stroke. I'm not saying Wanda was, but her husband probably was. He was clearly abusive. She might have kept quiet out of fear."

"She was scared of him. But she wouldn't have harmed a fly."

Gabrielle let the subject drop. Wanda had been her grandmother's friend. Naomi wasn't ready to listen to disparaging information—even if it was the truth.

Wanda was dead. What good would it do, anyway?

"I'm going to hold a wake for her," Naomi said. "No telling when her husband will return. Sometimes he's away for a month or so. Wanda has made friends on the Founders Day committee and at church, and the ladies at church want to do something. Maybe I'll talk the pastor into holding a wake."

"I like that," Gabrielle said.

"It just isn't right that they can't find anyone. I'm donating pies but was so upset they all burned. Go with me to her house. I'm going to use the pies I baked for her. She can't eat them now, and I know she hasn't eaten all of them. I'll bake more for her husband later if he wants them," Naomi said. "On second thought, he can darn well do without. I didn't bake them for him in the first place. If Wanda got into anything bad, he forced her. I know she wouldn't have wanted to break the law. She wasn't like that."

"Are you sure we should be in her house? Are the police finished yet?"

"They've been through everything. What more do they hope to find?"

"Okay." It was better to go along to get along right now.

They walked next door. Naomi used her key to let them in. The house felt dark and desolate without Wanda's bubbly presence. Naomi ran a hand across the countertop where they had drunk so many cups of coffee and tea.

"Lord, Lord, Lord," she said. She shook her head. "She was such a good friend."

Gabrielle gazed at the picture of Naomi and Wanda. It was in a carved wooden frame and placed on the countertop as if Naomi had been her only friend. Maybe she had been.

Naomi nodded toward the photo. "She had to hide that picture when he was home. Didn't like her putting pictures around the place. Look at this. What kind of man doesn't want his wife to have pictures of loved ones around? There are no pictures of friends, or even her parents. None from her childhood. My house is filled with them. Even baby pictures."

Naomi sighed. "As much as I hate to think it, I have to agree with you, Gabrielle. That man was up to no good. And he probably even threatened Wanda's life. Why else would she have put up with a man like that? He was mean enough to do anything. To think of the kind of fear she lived with." Naomi shook her head. "No wonder she died of a heart attack. He's responsible. And I hope he rots in jail for the rest of his life."

"Try not to get yourself worked up," Gabrielle said. "It'll all work out. You always said the devil would get his due." Wanda had a chest freezer. Gabrielle wondered why she needed such a large freezer for two people. And especially since she was alone so often.

Gabrielle opened the freezer and reached for the first pie. Then she dropped it like it was a hot potato.

"Oh, my God!" *It can't be.* She shoved two of the pies aside and felt as if she was in the middle of a horror show.

"What is it, Gabrielle?"

"Call the police," she croaked out.

"Why? What in the world is going on, girl?" Naomi marched over, but Gabrielle quickly shut the freezer top.

"What's with you?" Naomi tried to get past Gabrielle, but Gabrielle held her hand firmly on the top, trying to catch her breath.

"It's Mr. Fisher," Gabrielle finally croaked out.

"What about him?"

"He's . . . he's . . ." Gabrielle gulped a breath. "He's in the freezer."

* * *

Gabrielle and Naomi were inside her grandparents' house when the sheriff knocked on the door. He had already asked her grandmother several questions.

"I just have one more question to ask you. When was the last time you saw Mr. Fisher alive?"

"Well, let's see," Naomi said. "It was the day she came over here. The day Alyssa left for Phoenix. Yes. That was the day. Well, I didn't actually see him. She told me she took him to the airport the next day."

"Thank you for your time, ma'am."

When the sheriff left, Naomi plopped down in her seat. "You don't think she killed him because I told her to take a skillet to his head, do you?"

"Of course not," Gabrielle said.

"She killed him. I mean, she seemed like the nicest person in the world. Remember that fresh meat smell that was in the house the day we took the pies over?"

Gabrielle's stomach roiled. "Yes . . ."

"It wasn't pork and beef. She must have . . ."

"Grandma, don't even think it. I'll never be able to eat again."

"You know it's the truth. She'd just finished cutting him to make him fit in the freezer."

Gabrielle couldn't get the picture of Mr. Fisher's frozen face out of her mind. The man stared right back at her, his eyes wide open. "I think it's going to be a long time before I can eat another of your peach pies." She was going to have nightmares for years.

"Every time I bake a pie, I'm going to think of it covering that man's face. I tell you it teaches you to treat people right. He must have just driven her plumb out of her mind. You never know people, do you? Or what they can be driven to do."

Naomi sat heavily in the kitchen chair. "She lived right next door. I went shopping with her. She came over every day and had tea or coffee with me. And even after she killed him, she served us cake. Remember? She served us devil's food cake that day. You think any blood got in that cake?"

"Grandma, you're driving me crazy." Gabrielle patted her grandmother's hand but felt so weak she found a seat before she fell on the floor herself. Wanda had used a carving knife to slice the cake. Was it the same knife she'd used to carve up her husband? Had there still been traces of blood on the knife?

"I told you that woman was strange," Hoyt said, walking into the kitchen for a glass of water.

"Everybody is strange to you," Naomi said tersely.

"She could have chopped you up as easily as she did her husband. I tell you it makes a man scared to close his eyes at night. That's probably when she did it. When he was in bed, sleeping peacefully."

"If you have nothing constructive to say, go talk to your boys," Naomi said.

Cornell had tried to keep his distance from Gabrielle, but after he heard about Mr. Fisher, he knew she must be distraught. He had to see her. At least that was the excuse he gave himself. The truth was, he missed her. Like he'd never missed a woman in his life. And that frightened the heck out of him.

He also gained a new appreciation for his mother's ranting. He was glad she was the kind to vent. He often saw Wanda's quiet presence around town. Always had a kind word and a sweet smile. That smile must have been harboring a whole lot of frustration. Cornell shivered. At least his father would know if his mother was coming after him with a cleaver. She would have shrieked the house down first. You had time to protect yourself. With women like Wanda Fisher you never knew what was coming your way.

Only thing was his mother drove everybody else crazy. Maybe leaving the house for a week was a good thing. Else she might go off the deep end.

Unfortunately, his mother wanted to go with him to Mrs. Claxton's.

He stood at the older woman's door. Gabrielle answered it.

"Hello, Mrs. Price."

"How are you, dear? It's just so awful."

"Yes, it is." She moved back so they could enter the house.

She didn't speak to Cornell. He couldn't blame her. But before he could speak, he saw her grandmother.

He gathered the older woman in his arm for a quick hug.

"Thanks for coming, Cornell."

"May I get you some tea or lemonade, Mrs. Price?" Gabrielle asked.

"Lemonade will be nice. I remember your aunt having a delicious recipe."

When Gabrielle left, Cornell followed her. She took the pitcher of lemonade out of the fridge and nearly dropped it when she saw him.

"Why did you follow me?"

"To talk to you. See how you are."

She stared at the floor. "And why the sudden interest?"

"I heard you found the body. I know you must be shaken up pretty badly."

"I'll deal with it, okay?" She took two glasses from the cabinet and poured the lemonade. Her hands shook slightly.

"Here. Put that down before you drop it."

"I can pour lemonade."

"I know. Just come here a minute."

"So you can run hot and cold on me? I don't need your kind in my life."

"Okay. Maybe I was a little floored Friday night. I handled

it badly. You got to me and my mother was at my house when I got there. Let me tell you, she drove me crazy. I'm always anti-women when I'm around her. But looking at your neighbor has given me a new perspective on her behavior."

She crossed her arms beneath her breasts, keeping well out of his reach. "Come again?"

He wanted to touch her. To soothe away her stress. "I acted like an ass. But you mean a lot to me. Took me a few days to clear up my head."

"I've got a lot on my plate right now. I don't need your baggage."

"Yeah. I know." He took a step toward her. "Just the same, I'm here."

"For this moment, anyway."

With a couple more steps, he dragged her into his arms. "Hey, give a brother some slack," he said, rocking her. She was so tense. He stroked her back. "I know this has been hard on you."

"You have no idea."

"But I can help."

CHAPTER 10

"You're here early."

Lisa looked up from her cleaning and smiled. She'd started on the top floor and was worried she'd miss seeing Graham.

"I have to leave early today. I'm going by my grandmother's to help her plan the wake for Mr. and Mrs. Fisher."

"What a macabre scene." Graham shook himself. "I thought this was a safe little island."

"It is," Lisa said anxiously. "They were outsiders. We barely knew them."

Graham chuckled. "You don't have to defend your town. I like it here." He crossed his arms and leaned against the door-jamb to watch her work.

Suddenly, Lisa was nervous. She liked cleaning his room most of all because he appreciated her work. She took extra time there, made sure his pillows were nice and plump. Made sure there wasn't a spec of dust on any surface and that the lace dresser scarves were straightened and without stains. She retracted the cord to the vacuum, gave the room another look-over to make sure she didn't miss a piece of lint or dirt, then smoothed a hand across the already made-up bed.

Graham remained in the doorway. "Would you like to go to the bar tonight? Or go to the mainland to take in a movie?"

"I . . ."

"Just as a friend. Nothing more."

"The bar, I guess. I don't know what time I'll leave my grandparents' place."

"I haven't taken the time to do any sightseeing here. Mitchell has kept me so busy. But I told him I wanted the weekend off. I need some time for myself."

"Good for you. I'll show you around town. And take you to the artist colony."

He smiled. "You just gave me something to look forward to."

His cell phone rang and he answered. After listening a moment, he picked up his laptop. "Duty calls. See you tonight."

Lisa inhaled deeply as he marched to the stairs. It was good to be back. Gabrielle hadn't been a bitch about her returning. She'd hired the other woman, but only part-time. They needed another cleaning person anyway, so she could *plan* some time off this time. And the important thing was that her job was still nice and safe.

Gabrielle had also asked Lisa to train the other woman, and she would train her on how to do the rooms correctly. Even if this place wasn't hers, she had a lot invested in it. She'd worked for Aunt Anna for years—much longer than that snotty Gabrielle. Aunt Anna had given her a lot of responsibility. She ordered housekeeping supplies and was in charge of the housekeeping staff. She even had to teach Gabrielle how to clean the rooms the way Aunt Anna liked. She'd never cleaned a hotel room in her life. So what did she know? Didn't even know how to run a B&B. Aunt Anna had taught her from her armchair. By then, Aunt Anna couldn't handle it any longer.

This was her place as much as it was Gabrielle's.

* * *

Gabrielle wiped a tired hand across her brow. She was in her office talking to a conference organizer about arranging a meeting on the island for the middle of May. Short lead time, but it would fill the B&B for five weekdays when they only had four rooms booked each day so far. But the catch was they needed a meeting room that would hold a larger group than the dining facilities.

"Unfortunately, I don't have a meeting room large enough to accommodate you," Gabrielle said. Her stomach ached at the potential of all that money going down the drain.

"The island *is* rather small," the woman said. "But my manager wants the meeting there."

"I may be able to arrange something close by," Gabrielle offered, hopeful.

"Is it large enough to accommodate one hundred people for one day? We will only need a room large enough for twenty-five for the rest of the week."

"May I call you back?"

"Of course. I'll be out of town for the next two days, but I'll call you when I return. In the meantime, please hold those bedrooms."

"I will. Thank you." Cornell's place was more than adequate, Gabrielle thought as she hung up. And after the renovation, it was modern and cheerful. He could also serve meals. The only catch was, she hated to call him. But this was business. Giving up the money for twenty rooms for five nights was out of the question. And in May the weather was comfortable. Some of those customers would want to stay over for the weekend.

She dialed the restaurant and found Cornell was making runs with one of his drivers. She left a message to have him call her.

After disconnecting, she realized she should have stressed her call was business related just in case he got the idea it was personal. She wasn't cramping his personal space. She wanted his premises.

Small conferences were a business angle they hadn't tackled before. Business was slow in winter. If she could work out a deal with Cornell, maybe she could keep the B&B full more days in the slow season.

Swiveling in her chair, she gazed out the window. She was lucky to have a view of the ocean. Even in winter the scene was breathtaking. Cornell offered gourmet-quality cuisine. Even with him expanding the kitchen to accommodate huge freezers and refrigerators, there was plenty of room left for a couple of sizeable meeting rooms, especially the main dining room area.

She'd write up a proposal to present to him.

Gabrielle sat at her desk for an hour writing up the proposal and answering phone calls. She glanced at the clock. She would have to leave soon to go by her grandmother's place. Naomi was grieving over Wanda's passing. Hoyt just made her angry with his "crazy woman" comments. Regina was holding down the fort as she did the laundry. And Lisa had taken care of the cleaning.

Lisa. She'd worked her way back in as if she hadn't been fired. And with the Wanda uproar, Gabrielle had no choice but to give her another chance. She wished she could depend on Lisa, leaving time for her to drum up more business, enough to keep a full-time staff year-round. There were enough companies in Hampton Roads to contact. But she didn't have to limit herself to the immediate area. She could send brochures to the onshore visitors center. She'd have to find a way to reach larger companies and make up new brochures that focused on businesses.

Gabrielle had finally returned his call. Cornell was fully prepared to woo her. He dropped by Sam's place for a bunch of flowers. The man picked them fresh from his garden, and his store manager arranged them beautifully and put them in a pretty vase. Cornell had to admit the arrangement was stunning. He only hoped Gabrielle would forgive him.

Besides, she'd called him. That alone should make the groveling easier.

He spoke to Regina at the front desk.

"Flowers for me?" she asked.

He chuckled. "Where's Gabrielle?" He hung on to the flowers. He was trying for gallantry.

"Gabrielle, is it?" She dialed a number. "Gabby, you have a delivery." She listened for a moment.

Cornell glanced around. The place seemed deserted.

"No. I can't take care of it. I'm busy," Regina was saying. Then she hung up and stood there quietly watching him.

"Well? Is she coming?"

Her eyebrows climbed. "Impatient, aren't we? She'll be right here."

A couple of minutes later, Gabrielle came rushing in. "Where's the delivery?"

Her cousin pointed toward Cornell. "There."

Gabrielle finally saw him and stopped dead.

Cornell thrust the arrangement at her, cleared his throat, and glanced at her cousin before he spoke, wishing she'd get lost. "These are for you," he said to Gabrielle.

She took the arrangement and inhaled. "They smell lovely. Let's go to my office."

"Gabrielle, can you sign off on this before you go?" Lisa asked.

"Sure." At the same time, she noticed Sam drive up in his truck and Regina disappear. Cornell stuck his head out of the door and waved.

"Hi, Sam," Gabrielle called out. Before she could form a sentence, Regina burst out of the door with a full glass of something in her hand, aiming straight for Sam. If Gabrielle had been in the way, she would have been knocked flat on her face.

"I came to invite you to dinner with my mother and me," Cornell said once they reached the office.

Her office was tucked in front of the building. It had a comfortable couch, a couple of Queen Anne chairs in front of the desk, and a nicely carved desk to match. And a breathtaking view of the ocean. Now he could imagine her gazing at the ocean while he was gazing in a pan on the stove. His office was a cluttered affair in one of the center rooms.

Gabrielle sniffed. "Listen, yesterday's call was business, not personal."

Cornell felt like a fool. Women had a way of doing that. "What business?"

Motioning him to a seat, she positioned herself behind her desk. It felt odd, this distance between them. He wanted to do something, anything to close the gap.

"I got a call from a group that wants to hold a meeting here in May. They need space for a hundred people. My place isn't large enough. But your restaurant is. Would you consider using it as meeting room space?"

Cornell turned it over in his mind. "I'm planning to have dinners there on Fridays from now until Labor Day. If the time doesn't conflict with that, I don't have a problem."

"If you could start your dinners after four, we may be able to work something out."

"Most people arrive late since they work on the mainland."

"I'm also thinking about advertising the B and B as a small conference facility if you'd be willing to let us use meeting space in your restaurant. I think both of us can make money from this since you will provide meals. It has the added advantage of keeping workers employed year-round."

"I don't have any objections to that."

"We need to work up costs." She handed him a folder.

"Here's a proposal I've written up. Why don't we set up a meeting next week to discuss it?"

"Okay." Slowly, Cornell opened the folder and flipped through the pages.

"Thank you," Gabrielle said. "Then we'll go ahead with the meeting in May." Gabrielle wrote some notes on a pad and tucked it into a folder. She was so impersonal. Any indication of warmth was missing.

"Is that all?" Cornell asked.

Gabrielle glanced up, still keeping a businesslike facade. "Yes." She dismissed him, but he refused to take the bait.

"My mother wants to have dinner with you."

Gabrielle remained silent.

Cornell sighed. "You gonna make me pay forever? Tell me what I have to do to kiss and make up."

"I'm not making you pay for anything."

Yeah, right. "Then are you coming?"

"Why should I?"

"Whew. You women really know how to work a situation, don't you?"

"Listen, I'm not cramping your style."

"I don't know where this is going to lead. I just know that for the moment, what we have feels right." Cornell couldn't believe he actually said those words. But they did feel right.

"What time would you like me to come?" she finally said.

"Around seven." He noticed that like before, she didn't offer him anything to drink. Sam was outside leisurely sipping on a cool drink while Cornell had worked his tail off all day and could use something wet. Things being the way they were, he guessed he was lucky Gabrielle was speaking to him at all.

"I'm fixing food for the wake. Your grandmother insists on a wake," he said.

"She wants closure."

"I know she's grieving, because she condescended to speak to me. I haven't heard 'that Price boy' lately."

That brought a chuckle out of Gabrielle.

"Gabby." He said the name as if tasting it. "I like the shortened version."

Gabrielle rolled her eyes.

"But you don't talk a lot. You expect a Gabby to talk a lot."

"I say what needs to be said."

The meeting was over. Standing safely behind her desk, she was ready to give him a brisk handshake and usher him from her office.

Frustration made his muscles tighten. Angrily he circled the desk and folded her in his arms. She looked up until her gaze met his. She fit against him so perfectly, they might have been made for each other. He felt the anger drain from him like a wave rolling out to sea.

Gabrielle told herself she didn't want this. Didn't want to be in his warm embrace. Didn't want to get herself involved with a man who was as mentally screwed up as she was. She wasn't expecting a marriage proposal. And she didn't expect to live in his back pocket.

But she wanted something. And then he was kissing her hungrily, pulling her body closer.

She wrapped her arms around his neck, pressed closer to him, felt his hands moving on her body. This was right.

But all too soon he stepped back. Her chest was heaving, and when she looked at him, so was his.

"Well."

"Yeah." She pressed her fingers against her lips.

"Is that enough to keep you warm until tonight?"

"Cornell."

"I'm burning up here." He tapped the end of her nose. "I'll pick you up at seven and walk you home after dinner."

"I live across the path, silly. I can get there on my own."

"Hey, humor a guy. See you at seven."

* * *

"She killed him."

"What are you talking about?" Jade asked, her voice clouded with sleep.

"It's damn near noon."

"Had a late night," Jade said. He heard the covers rustling in the background as she sat up.

"Harvey's dead."

"You've got to be kidding."

"Wanda killed him."

Jade barked out a laugh. "Wanda wouldn't swat a fly."

"Took a cleaver and went to work on him. Couldn't find him because he was in the freezer all this time." He would never have guessed the meek Wanda would have the nerve to strike out against her brawny, abusive husband. Gave him the creeps just thinking about it.

"Do you need my help down there?"

"I can handle it—if I can find the jewels. Thinking he might already have them stashed in that house somewhere. Just like him to put one over."

"You're getting paranoid. First Roger and now Harvey."

"Roger *was* cheating us."

"I know, I know. See what you can find. At least we only have to split our findings between the two of us."

"Provided I stay alive. The current survival rate doesn't sound promising." He hung up, started the motor, and drove through the downtown area. He parked four blocks from the Fisher's place. Donning sunglasses and a cap, he first did a few stretches while getting the lay of the land. When the coast was clear, he jogged toward their house. He jogged through a thick wooded patch before he came out in the woods in back of the house.

He wanted to search when there was still light outside and he could go through the things without a nosy passerby detecting a light. It was a good thing the woman kept a trail of huge trees and bushes from the woods to the house. A dog barked up the street. A kid passed on a bicycle, riding hell-bent to some place.

Gingerly, he made his way to the back door. With very little effort, he picked the lock. A child could pick the locks to this house. He made his way inside. It had a stale closed-in feeling. Not one dish was on the sink or on the countertop. She was a neat housekeeper. It should be easy to find what he was looking for. But it wasn't she who'd stored the bowl. The wife was totally clueless.

He just couldn't wrap his mind around the horror. Never in a million years would he have suspected that sweet old woman would kill Harvey.

They started out with four. Now it was down to two.

Harvey could have hidden the bowl and jewels anywhere. They might be in the back of a closet or somewhere in his office. Those were the first places he would look. Among tools or junk that would be overlooked by a novice and the police, who weren't aware they were dealing with thieves. They'd know soon enough, and he wanted to go through everything before they did. He shook his head. Men stored things in obscure places. He probably hadn't been able to find anything at the other houses because good ole Harvey had already found the valuables.

What do you wear for dinner with a friend's mother? She was even more nervous than the last time. *Friend* sounded so lame. Lover? Too crude, too unemotional. Making love should mean more than quenching a desire.

Gabrielle considered several outfits and discarded them all in turn. While she didn't want to overdo it, she didn't want to dress too casually, either. "Well, well, well." Her eye caught a dress that would serve dual purposes. Hot or staid, it depended on the perception.

That evening, before Gabrielle could walk across the path to Cornell's, her grandmother called to tell her someone had broken into Wanda's house. She phoned Cornell to cancel.

"I'll go with you," he said. "Dinner can wait."

The sheriff was talking to her grandmother in the yard when they arrived. "Roger and Fisher knew each other. We discovered that Fisher was an antiquities thief," he said.

"Oh, my God. The man living next door to my grandparents wanted my aunt's bowl."

"We didn't find it in the house. And if he had it, he would have left by now."

"What about Wanda? What was her role in the thefts?"

"She doesn't appear to have a record."

"But she had to know what her husband did for a living?"

"Not necessarily," Naomi said. "I've been able to deal with the fact that she murdered him. I know he was abusive. She was also very afraid of him. I think living with that kind of fear all the time twisted her mind."

"You think she killed Roger, too?"

"We haven't established a connection between Roger and Mrs. Fisher yet, except through her husband. The causes of death were vastly different," the sheriff said. "Although we now know Roger was murdered."

"You hear about husbands or wives killing each other on the news, but that kind of thing just doesn't usually happen here."

"At least they're all foreigners," Hoyt said. "None of them were islanders."

"We still haven't located Skeeter. We don't know if he's dead or alive." *Murdered.* Roger was murdered.

Hoyt's mouth tightened. "William talked to him the other day. Told him you're worried about him. He's alive and well, so quit your worrying."

"We also found a picture of the gold bowl in Fisher's possession," the sheriff continued. "But no bowl."

Gabrielle looked at Cornell. He rubbed her arm.

"You find that bowl yet?" Naomi asked.

Gabrielle shook her head. She couldn't feel worse than she did at that moment.

Regina had invited Sam to dinner. And wonder of wonders, over the iced tea she'd given him, he'd accepted. Well, maybe it was only because they were supposed to talk about what to buy first. But once she got him in her house, she was keeping him until she was ready to let him go.

She wasn't the best cook in the world—more like Gabrielle in that respect. She did enough to get by. Sam looked like a meat-and-potatoes man, so before Cornell had left the B&B, she'd asked him about the best cut of steak and how to prepare it. He'd told her to drop by his place and he'd have something for her. He'd seasoned the meat for her, bless his heart. Even gave her the already washed potatoes to grill, a salad, and something to snack on before dinner, and he didn't charge her a dime. He was a mighty nice man. Gabrielle was lucky she didn't have to work like Regina to get a date out of him.

She opened the grill cover and peeked. Her first time using it. The potatoes were almost ready. Cornell had told her to put the meat on the grill after Sam arrived. She liked that. Gave them a chance to talk.

She wore a sundress with just enough V to give him a peekaboo at her cleavage. Not too much to make her seem obvious.

The doorbell rang and Regina nearly jumped out of her skin. She pulled off her apron and smoothed her dress before she walked slowly to the door. She hoped she didn't smell like food. She ran to the bedroom to spritz on some perfume before she dashed to the door. The bell rang a second time.

She took a couple of deep breaths to still her beating heart and opened the door.

Sam looked good in his shirt and beige slacks. He handed her a bottle of wine and a bunch of flowers—as pretty as the arrangement Cornell had brought for Gabrielle—and a clipboard with some papers.

She took the flowers and wine, which was already chilled. "I made up some plans and estimates for you . . ."

"We'll get to that after dinner," she said. "Come out back with me while I grill the steaks."

"Want me to open the wine for you?"

She dug in the drawer for a corkscrew and handed it over. Then she selected two wineglasses. "Bring it outside with you, please," she said as she carried the platter of steaks and gently placed them on the grill.

He handed her a glass of wine, and she took her first sip.

"Nice evening," he said.

"Nice evening to eat outside. Not much of a view, but it'll happen."

He nodded and glanced at the little round table she'd covered with a pink tablecloth and two candles set in the center. She placed the flowers in the middle, moving the candles to either side.

The table did look good, she thought as she brought out a plate of appetizers.

She fed one to him. He looked stunned before he opened his mouth.

"Like it?" she asked.

He chewed, cleared his throat. "Delicious." He finished chewing and swallowed, then took another.

"You're a fabulous cook."

"Thank you. My mama made sure we learned the basics."

He shook his head. "This is a lot more than the basics."

"You're trying to get another meal out of me, aren't you?" she teased. She didn't dare give him a chance to respond. "It just might work. Women love men who appreciate their cooking skills."

Sam swallowed his wine and almost choked. Maybe she was coming on too strong. She'd better ease up a little. She turned her back to him, gathered her own glass, and sipped the wine before she peeked at the steaks. They were grilling just fine.

"Think I'll have much this summer?"

"Sure. In a couple years it'll be a showplace. You'll like it."

"Good. I just hope I can follow your instructions, that I don't kill the plants." She walked to the table, leaned over, and smelled the flowers. At the same time, she made sure she was facing him, giving him a view. When she stood, she noticed he hadn't looked away.

"I just love beautiful flowers. You're so thoughtful."

"I aim to please."

Sam knew he was in trouble. That woman had his blood boiling over. Damn, she smelled good, looked even better. She was so damn pretty. And the color of the dress complemented her medium-brown skin to perfection. He liked Regina a bit too much. He'd liked her for a long time. But she never gave him the time of day. He just didn't understand why she was coming on to him all of a sudden if it wasn't to get free services out of him. But he'd play along for a little while. When she found out she wasn't getting her flowers for free, he knew she'd stop the games.

But for tonight, he'd have to play her game. He sipped his wine for fortification. He'd make sure not to drink a second glass. He needed his wits about him.

Sam reached for another hors d'oeuvre. She sure could cook.

CHAPTER 11

"I won't feel comfortable until after the wake, but at least we can put some of this behind us. At least we know who they really were," Naomi said.

The fingerprint for Harvey Fisher identified him as Harlan Fleming. He was a known thief who worked with a man named Roger Peterson. Now the authorities knew Roger's last name was actually Peterson, not Moore. And Wanda's actual name was Wanda Fleming. She'd refused to change her first name. As far as they knew, she was never involved in her husband's criminal pursuits.

"She had to know something was going on," Hoyt said. "You can't live with a man and not know."

"Says who? Wanda was too intimidated to ask questions. Even if she knew, she wouldn't dare reveal it to him."

"Did she ever talk about the bowl?" Gabrielle asked.

"Not really. I broached the subject a few times, but she didn't focus on it. Only to say how nice it was that my roots went back so far."

Gabrielle kissed Naomi on the cheek and hugged her lightly. "Call me if you need me. I have to go."

Naomi smiled weakly and Gabrielle and Cornell left.

"Why did you ask about Wanda? Do you think her husband stole the bowl?" Cornell asked.

"I don't know," Gabrielle said, settling in the car. "Could she have killed him because he was going to steal the bowl?"

"Another angle is the thieves could have had a falling out. Fleming could have killed Roger Peterson."

"One wanted to keep all the money?"

"Something like that," Cornell said.

"So you think the bowl's gone? Why would Fleming have stayed? He stayed on two months after Roger died."

"We have to work under the assumption the bowl's still here. If you look at it, every place the bowl might be has been broken into. Everyone knew I visited Anna often. She raised Sam from the time his parents died when he was in high school."

"My house hasn't been broken into."

"You don't know that. You're so busy you wouldn't know if anything was out of place. Besides, it could have been checked when Anna was still alive. Like when you took her to a doctor's appointment. You were taking her all the time."

"I feel so responsible. I should have . . ."

"What could you have done? You couldn't take the bowl from Anna. She wouldn't have let you. Even I knew how stubborn she was. Which was why she and Uncle Lucky couldn't make it."

"Now it's all her fault."

"They were both to blame. He loved the woman, yet wouldn't do anything to keep her after the divorce."

"How do you know he loved her?"

"He told me. Actually, before your aunt died, she talked about how much she loved him. So I told her that he'd loved her, too. That he mentioned her often before he died. He was too stubborn to approach her."

"She changed after he died. It was like she had nothing more to live for. I'm glad you told her."

"Me, too, but what kind of love is that?"

Gabrielle shrugged. "People are complex. Look at the Fishers, ah, Flemings. Who would have thought they were harboring those kinds of secrets? Who would have thought Wanda would—"

"Look, we can't solve all this tonight. Don't get yourself all worked up."

"Too late."

"I want you to enjoy the dinner I spent hours preparing."

"Hours?"

"Well . . . it'll taste like hours. You're the first women I've brought home in years."

Gabrielle chuckled. "You've been a scoundrel that long, have you?"

He moaned. "Hey, you can't take every girl home to Mom. She'll start arranging wedding plans. You have to be selective."

"How many doesn't your mother know about?"

Gabrielle felt his gaze on her. "I see I'm going to have to change your opinion of me."

They took their time arriving at his house. As they walked the flowered path to his door, Gabrielle inhaled his woodsy soap. A fresh, clean, masculine scent. He wore jeans and a polo shirt.

His mother was indeed waiting anxiously for them. She wore a casual peach ankle-length dress with lovely beaded jewelry she probably purchased at the island's artist colony.

"How is your grandmother, dear?"

"She's holding up. She's determined to have that wake, though. The minister talked her into having it for both Fishers, although she just wanted it for Mrs. Fisher." Fleming didn't fit them.

"Oh, she made a big stink about that yesterday," Mrs. Price said. "She has no love for that man."

"I'll finish up dinner while you gossip," Cornell said.

"We don't gossip," Mrs. Price retorted. "We exchange information."

"What lovely jewelry," Gabrielle said.

"I got it yesterday. I've been working on sculptures at a friend's place on the other side of the island."

"Are any of your pieces here?"

"Yes. I brought several with me this time. The bowl on the table."

Gabrielle noticed several sculptures around the room that hadn't been there before. "Are the pieces on the side and cocktail tables yours?"

"Yes, all of them. This room needed color to brighten it up. This place was so obviously masculine. I couldn't stand it. I've asked Cornell a million times to choose some pieces from my collection, but he wouldn't. I even told him I'd shop with him if he'd just get *something*."

"Why wouldn't he?"

"I think he felt guilty. He had several pieces in his apartment in New York. When he decided to move here permanently, his girlfriend destroyed all of his artwork as well as his furniture in a fit of anger."

"Oh, my gosh. You see this stuff on TV, but you don't think people actually do it."

"She did. He knows how much I value my art."

"So he was reluctant to display more of your work. He doesn't want to be responsible for its destruction because your work is an integral part of you."

"I let my sons choose the pieces they loved. She destroyed the ones that were precious to him—and she knew it." She picked up one green piece with lines of white shooting through it. She set it back in place. "I don't blame him. I've taught him to treat women with respect. But you can't control what other people do."

"You're very gifted, Mrs. Price." The lively orange and green brightened the room's stark appearance.

"Enough of that. Let me get you something to snack on," Mrs. Price said. "You must be starved."

"Famished." Mrs. Price left the room, and Gabrielle examined the sculptures and was saddened at the loss of her precious pieces. No wonder it was difficult for Cornell to trust women.

At the bar, Lisa was bored to tears. Where was that waitress? In a minute she was going to get up and go to the bar for her own drink.

A couple of strangers had come by to hit on her, but she wasn't interested. She'd rather sit alone. And she was bone tired. Worked the whole damn week. If she took a day off like she wanted to, that Gabrielle would fire her ass. It was worse now that she'd hired that other woman. She acted as if working at the B&B was like getting a slice of heaven. The woman was so friendly, as much as Lisa wanted to hate her, she couldn't. Still, she didn't have to like the fact that somebody was there to take her place.

And her dad was nagging her to death about finding a place of her own. Trying to be so damn cheap. Wanting to know when she came home at night. Telling her she was staying out too late and crap. She was a grown woman.

"Can I get you a drink?"

About damn time. "A Long Island ice tea," she ordered, and glanced at her watch. The bar was full. Judging by how long it took the woman to take her order, it was going to take forever to get her drink.

She was pleasantly surprised when the waitress returned quickly with a tall glass.

"Thank you." Lisa paid and sipped. It felt good. She'd been nursing her drink for ten minutes when Graham slid into the booth across from her. Her mood lifted considerably.

"The old guard give you time off for good behavior?" she asked.

Graham shrugged. "He wanted to talk half the night, unfortunately. Had a hard time getting away."

"He acts like he owns you. Everyone gets time off. You need to put your foot down."

"Working with him is a real opportunity. I hope this project puts me on a tenure track at my college," he said, glancing around. "I don't want to be a lecturer for the rest of my career. It's really tough now. And this project, if we can blow it up big enough, could be my ticket." He pointed at her drink. "What're you drinking there?"

"Long Island iced tea. Want one?"

"No. I'll take water."

Lisa coughed out a laugh. "Don't tell me you don't drink. I'm not going to hang with a stick-in-the-mud."

He shrugged. "Sorry. Tonight, I'm here to enjoy your company and to unwind."

Lisa had nearly finished her drink, so he ordered another for her along with his mineral water.

"I wish guys on the island were as nice as you."

"You wish I was black, ah, African American, to be politically correct."

"Wouldn't hurt."

"See. I knew you had a thing against me."

"It's not that. I've begged off all dates right now. Like I said. I need to take care of myself for a change. I'm getting tired of being used and dumped."

He reached across the table, patting her hand. "You hold out until the right one comes along. Don't let them use you anymore."

"Don't get heavy on me."

"People don't encourage you much, do they?"

Lisa shrugged. "Doesn't matter." She had to swallow around the lump in her throat.

"It matters."

A tear slid from her eye. She never cried. Angrily she swiped it away. "You've gotta stop this."

"Okay," he said softly, but he didn't let her hand go.

The waitress returned with their drinks, and for a while they sat quietly listening to the music.

Someone played her favorite song on the jukebox. Lisa started twisting in the seat and snapping her fingers.

"I've gotta dance." She grabbed Graham's hand. "Come on. And don't embarrass me on the floor."

He threw her a panicked look. "Lisa . . . Lisa, I don't dance very well."

"All you gotta do is move with the music. Even white boys can do that."

Graham shook his head. "How many white boys have you dated?"

"None."

Lisa didn't know what to expect, hoped he wouldn't embarrass the heck out of her, 'cause she knew how some white guys danced, hands flying all over the place. If he was too bad, they could always sit. But when Graham started dancing, he moved with the beat. He definitely held his own.

Lisa swung close to him. "Thought you couldn't dance."

"I went to college."

"So that's what professors do on campus now. Maybe I should sign up for some courses."

"Not a bad idea," he said, and grabbed her hand, turned her in a circle, and broke into a swing.

"Whoa!" Lisa said, laughing, but she kept in the groove. She let herself go freely, and Graham stayed right with her—even tried some of her moves.

By the time they took their seats two songs later, Lisa was laughing and winded. Slipping into the booth, she swallowed her drink. Anywhere but on the island she wouldn't touch a drink once she left it. But the island was different. People weren't out to get you. Plus, only a couple outsiders were there, most of whom sat at the bar guzzling beer.

She hadn't felt this good in a long, long time, she thought as she gazed at Graham.

Graham leaned back in his seat, regarding her closely. "I needed that," he said. "Been here so long, thought I'd forgotten how."

"You still have some moves."

This friendship thing was real nice, Lisa thought. She didn't have to worry about him wanting to have sex with her and her having to fight him off.

Cornell helped Gabrielle don her jacket. He seemed to get edgier by the moment. What was wrong with him? Was he sorry he invited her?

"It was a pleasure seeing you again, Mrs. Price. Dinner was fabulous."

"You're going to have to thank the cook, then," Cornell said, and winked.

Embarrassed, Gabrielle felt her face heat up. At least his mother had walked away.

"Before you go, Gabrielle, I have something for you." Mrs. Price approached her with a package covered in tissue paper.

"Oh. Thank you." Gabrielle unwrapped the package to reveal a lovely delicate white and rose sculpture. "Oh, my gosh. Thank you so much. It's . . . absolutely beautiful." She hugged the older woman.

"Oh, you're the sweetest thing."

"Let's not get mushy now. Time to go." Cornell steered her toward the door.

"Good night, and thank you," Gabrielle said, holding tightly to her gift.

"You are very welcome, dear."

Mrs. Price barely got the words out of her mouth before Cornell guided Gabrielle out the door.

The night was cool and brisk.

"She likes you, you know. She's never given any of my dates a sculpture."

"She's nice." They walked to her house in comfortable silence, although Cornell seemed to spring with energy.

In her living room, she uncovered the sculpture and gently placed it on a sideboard.

"I have guests coming in soon for the crab feast," she said.

"Crab feast?"

"As soon as we get the first crabs of the season, we have a huge crab feast. Last year was the first time at the B and B, and the guests liked it so much they booked rooms a year in advance to experience it again. I was hoping you'd have it at the restaurant. It's on a Saturday when you're closed."

"You know, you're getting a lot out of me. How many bushels do I need to boil?"

"Grandma will fry them and you can boil some." She touched his arm. "She has a great fried crab recipe."

"That's wonderful, but I don't want to talk about crabs tonight." He moved closer. "I don't want to talk at all."

Gabrielle was thinking of Cornell when she heard the little bell ring at the front desk. He had her tied up in knots. Caressed her body enough to have her frustrated by the time he left. Said his mother was probably peeping through the curtains.

Please. With three sons, she didn't give his love life a second thought. Was glad he was involved. No, Cornell left because *Cornell* wasn't sure of his feelings, she thought as she went to the front desk.

"Good morning, Sheriff."

"Gabrielle, I'd like a word with you."

"Come back to my office. May I get you coffee or tea?"

Shaking his head, he said, "Nothing, thanks."

In a minute they were seated in her office with the door closed.

"John mentioned you were concerned about your aunt's golden bowl. That it's missing. He also said Peterson had tried to purchase it from her."

"That's what he said." Accustomed to "Moore" as Roger's last name, it was a bit of a jolt to hear him referred to as Peterson.

"We have some information. Both Fleming and Peterson were master thieves. Both are wanted for multimillion-dollar thefts. The value of the bowl is small compared to what they're usually after. Why do you think they're really here?" he asked. "There have been rumors that your aunt has stashed millions in that house, but most of the islanders think that's untrue. What do you think?"

"If she had millions, she would have paid for the renovations on the B and B. We had to get a loan. I've looked for that bowl. And I can't find it anywhere. There are a couple of places I still have to look."

"If a collector were to get all four bowls, the value might be worth stealing, but it's a long shot. And they'd have to steal the other three."

"One was recovered in the Jamestown dig. Aunt Anna had one. There are still two missing."

"They may already have the missing two. Maybe they received a commission to retrieve the last two. Private collectors are sometimes willing to pay a small fortune for artifacts. The one in Jamestown is well guarded."

"True."

"The fact that they're still here leads me to believe they haven't found your aunt's bowl," the sheriff said, shaking his head. "Something isn't right about this. For what it's worth, I don't believe they're after the bowl. I think it's a cover for what they're really after. Now, there's talk of the professors here doing research. Any way they could be involved?"

"Not that I know of. They're writing a book. Mitchell Talbot just retired from a prominent university. Graham Smith is a lecturer at some Midwest college. Mitchell gave me a copy of a previous book he wrote," Gabrielle said. "One of the bowls was in his family until the mid-1800s. He claims he just wants to see ours. He wants to see pictures of family members or any research from that era." Gabrielle thought about Wanda and her husband. "Roger started coming here shortly after the Fishers moved here. The professors arrived recently."

Harper scribbled in his little notebook. "I'll check them out. Make sure this book is on the up and up. There's one last thing. A distant cousin of Wanda's claimed the bodies. I mentioned the people here wanted to give them a wake, but she isn't interested. She's embarrassed about the whole affair."

"Grandma will be disappointed," Gabrielle said.

"I know. But the woman is Wanda's family."

After the sheriff left, Gabrielle called her grandmother, updating her on the news. Gabrielle was on the phone for half an hour until Naomi gave her parting shot. "We're still holding the wake!"

The next day around noon, the professors were working outside in the breeze. Gabrielle tried to hurry past without being noticed when Mitchell called her.

"Join us, Gabrielle. I want to show you a picture of the bowl that was in my family until one of my ancestors took it in 1843. I tell you, this thing has been a bone of contention with my family ever since."

Gabrielle glanced at the picture of the small painting.

"You see one of the descendents had an artist paint it. This is a photograph of the painting, which is all the memory we have of it. Of course, I saved the picture in a magazine of the one in Jamestown," he said.

"It's beautiful. Just like the bowl we have."

"I certainly would like to get a look at it."

"So would I," Gabrielle said, handing the picture back. As she peered at Mitchell's rapt face, she wanted to believe he was honest. She tried not to let the sheriff's distrust rub off on her. She remembered the dust on his computer. Obviously he wasn't using it. But Graham was always typing away on his computer. Even now it was on a table on the porch between their chairs. So the two were obviously working on the project.

"Sit and join us for a while. We've been working very hard since early this morning and thought we'd take a break."

The professor tended to forget that this was her place of business. But he was a paying customer and she'd humor him. She sat in one of the rockers. Besides, she was as curious about the family history as he was. Naomi thought he wanted to steal the bowl, but he seemed innocent enough. Besides, she reminded herself, he arrived months after Roger had been killed.

"I would love an opportunity to talk to your grandmother. The information on the bowl is a little sketchy. I wasn't aware the bowl we had at one time had been in the same collection as the one at Jamestown until I saw the article in the magazine. Then I began to research it."

"I know that I have an ancestor who escaped form Virginia Beach in the mid-1800s and moved to Philly," Gabrielle said. My dad has some documentation on her. I'll call him and see if he'll send it to me. It might help with your research. But my grandmother would have information on anyone who passed through this island."

"This is awesome, Professor. My goodness," Graham said.

"Yes, indeed. Your grandmother was telling me how she

escaped. She hid on the island, and they shipped her out through the Underground Railroad with runaway slaves."

"I imagine they searched all over for her," Graham said.

"Indeed they did. There was a hefty reward. So I don't understand why she wasn't caught."

"There were always rewards. And there were always those who risked escape in spite of rewards and the threat of death or worse. Freedom is precious," Gabrielle said.

"Indeed."

"It's always interesting to talk to you. Unfortunately, I have to get back to work." But before she could move, her grandmother drove into the yard.

Gabrielle started down the steps, but Mitchell nearly knocked her down trying to get to the car first.

"Mrs. Claxton. What a joy to see you. Come. Join us on the porch. We were just talking about family history."

Graham glanced at Gabrielle and shrugged.

Before they knew it, Mitchell had the door open and was helping Naomi take the pies for the daily meet and greet off the backseat. The pies were quickly delivered to the kitchen while Mitchell was pulling up a rocker for Naomi.

After asking Lisa to bring out a pitcher of tea, Gabrielle joined them.

"Thank you. Your iced tea is splendid," Mitchell said. "Don't know why my ancestor ever moved from the South. Or why they sold all that land in Virginia Beach. Just think how lucky they were to have it. Seems they sold it off piece by piece until all of it was gone."

"Wasn't there some documentation that quite a bit was sold after the Civil War?" Graham asked.

"Yes. And each generation whittled it down until there was nothing. How lucky your family is, Mrs. Claxton, to have held on to this island for almost four hundred years."

"The land belonged to us, from the very beginning," Naomi said. "Actually, the Indians were the first people to live here. They moved farther inland probably because of several years of ferocious storms. My ancestors didn't know that when they moved to the island, so they ended up settling there. We didn't get an opportunity to talk about your ancestors at the dinner. Where did you grow up?"

"I grew up in Colorado. My family left the Virginia Beach area a couple of years after the Civil War."

Naomi frowned. "After the Civil War?"

Mitchell nodded.

"But the bowl disappeared in the 1840s."

"That's correct."

"If your ancestors were on the island after that time, they weren't related to the original settlers."

"What are you talking about?"

"Mary owned the land, not her husband. When she married your ancestor, he made life so awful for her she was forced to escape. She gave up her land, her heritage, everything to get away from him. She'd had a baby, but he died during the winter. Her husband wanted an heir. She felt that he'd murder her eventually, especially after she produced an heir. As the story goes, their marriage was a nightmare from the beginning. Of course, you may be related to one of the founding families through another family member."

"How did you end up with your land?" Graham asked.

"Back in 1617, after the women escaped the pirates, they actually landed on this island before the ship sank," Naomi said.

When the ship hit something underneath and came to a complete stop, the women saw land off to the west. Knowing they had to find a place to dock before the ship sank, three of the ladies got into the boat and rowed to shore. It was November and cold. They didn't know how harsh the winter would be. When they made it to the island, the women set out on foot. Huge trees had been knocked over as if uprooted where they stood, as if a mightly wind had swept through the area. Many of the women didn't want to settle there. They'd hazard storm after storm from the sea. And it looked as if the island had been hit hard. But where would they go? The ship would sail no more.

So the women took the rowboats, and, starting out early that morning, they towed the provisions to shore—precious spices and seeds, flour, butter, even the silk, the Spanish doubloons, and a few jewels to be shared by all.

It took two days to get their provisions to shore. Then they had the chore of hauling it farther inland, away from the elements of the sea.

Other than a few deer, squirrels, a rogue wild pig or two, there was little meat to be had. But fish and provisions from the sea were plentiful.

They also found a freshwater stream about a mile from the shore. It offered the freshest water they had ever tasted. They also found a few edible greens. There were fruit trees, although very little fruit was available. A tree or two in the center of the island that the hurricane must have missed had a few on them. They dug a little hole in the ground to store some for winter.

Luckily, Abiola knew how to construct huts like the ones used in Africa with clay walls, and some of the women had watched their fathers build straw roofs. There were enough fallen new trees to support the walls. And quickly they constructed a couple of huts close together a hundred feet from the stream. By the first snow, they had roofs over their heads. Luckily there were enough trees left standing to shelter them from the worst of the ocean's breezes.

When spring finally came, it was a beautiful sight. Fresh plants began to emerge. Balmy breezes from the ocean kept the summer heat from blistering them. But they despaired that they would never see another living soul. They were in the middle of nowhere.

* * *

"They landed here, on Paradise Island. You see, at one time, there were many islands dotting these waters. But with erosion, one by one, they began to disappear, just as the beaches are disappearing now," Naomi said. "Luckily for us, this island still exists."

The island was a vacation spot where Gabrielle, as a child, and her parents visited grandparents, aunts and uncles, cousins. It was a place Gabrielle could play in the sand, on the beach. But generations of her ancestors had owned that land for nearly four hundred years. It was humbling that they held on to the land through war, through racism, through poverty, hurricanes, storms, and whatever else struck them.

Five families eventually settled on the island. Two were African and three were white. Some moved to Surry and Virginia Beach.

They ran businesses. Even the B&B was built right out of the Depression of the thirties.

Wow!

The amazing strength of her family never dawned on her before.

They were sitting on the back porch. Just beyond the trees was the little storage house. With the deaths and work, Gabrielle had been too busy to go through it. Soon she'd have to make time to search for the bowl.

Her ancestors had kept that damn bowl for nearly four hundred years. Damn if it was going to get lost on her watch, not without her trying like heck to find it.

Mitchell had fallen silent as he watched Naomi.

Graham pushed his glasses up on his nose. "Your tea is delicious," he said as eagerly as a puppy. "The best I've ever tasted. I'm so glad, in more ways than one, I was given the opportunity to work on this project."

* * *

Cornell could have kicked himself for inviting Gabrielle to dinner wtih his mother. Yes, she had a lush body. And his brain stopped functioning around her. But she wasn't his ideal black woman by any stretch of the imagination. She wasn't quiet and sweet. And now his mother couldn't stop talking about her. How dumb could he get?

Cornell's mother arrived at the restaurant around noon to have lunch with him. "I'm bored out of my senses," she said.

"I can put you to work here. One of my workers didn't show up."

"I'll be glad to help out. Why didn't you call me?"

He shrugged.

"Gabrielle seemed like a nice young lady. I like her."

"We're just friends, Mom," he said. "Don't call the preacher." Liar, liar.

"Oh. I'd like to think one of my boys was thinking of marriage. If not quite yet, at least a long-term relationship."

"Sorry to disappoint you. We're simply neighbors."

She threw him a knowing smile. "A mother can always hope, can't she? She's nothing like her aunt, you know."

"You could tell all that by one visit?"

She let that ride. "So what's going on? You came back late, and I fell asleep before you could tell me about this break-in."

"Someone broke into her grandparent's neighbor's house."

"The one who died?"

"That's the one."

"What did they steal?"

Cornell shrugged.

"Everything's usually so peaceful on the island."

"It's shameful," Naomi said to Gabrielle at the wake. "Her own cousin won't give them a decent send-off at the place Wanda loved most."

They were in the fellowship hall enjoying the fare the women had prepared for the wake. If nothing else, the islanders were enjoying the food. Naomi had found pictures of both the Fishers and had framed them before setting them on a table with two large peace lilies. The plants had nearly overshadowed the pictures before Naomi had found stands to prop the pictures on.

"She has a good turnout, and the reverend preached a good message about her," Gabrielle said. "That should count for something." There wasn't a spare chair in the room. There was also a lot of gossiping about the two, especially about Mr. Fisher's frozen body. But the islanders made sure not to say anything within Naomi's hearing.

"I'm grateful for that. Although her husband never set foot in a church. I have to give it to the pastor because he certainly had to work to find something decent to say about that man."

"He pulled it off," Gabrielle agreed, trying to find Cornell. She was ready to leave. "I think Wanda's cousin was embarrassed by this whole affair."

"Name a family that doesn't have a few skeletons in the closet," Naomi said.

"Grandma, maybe you should mingle."

"You're right. Get something to eat before you leave. You don't have to stay late. Hoyt will take me home."

Gabrielle glanced at the table laden with food. Naomi had baked pies since they were Wanda's favorite—and she certainly couldn't use the ones in Wanda's freezer. But Gabrielle couldn't wipe away the image of the pies on Mr. Fisher's frozen body. She hadn't been able to eat her grandmother's pies since that day. Truthfully, she couldn't eat a thing at the wake. So as soon as she could discreetly leave, she motioned Cornell over and made an escape.

CHAPTER 12

Gabrielle and Cornell checked out the storage building late one afternoon. Grateful there was a dusty light in the ceiling, she grabbed a stick by the door and swiped the cobwebs away as they moved forward.

"When they said she was a pack rat, they weren't kidding," Cornell said.

There was broken furniture that had been taken from the B&B over the years. If repaired, the pieces would be perfectly usable. Old furniture. Antique pieces.

"Some pieces are in perfect condition," Cornell said.

"But where in the heck would she hide anything in this mess?"

"Guess we'll start working on one side and keep going until we get through."

Pulling drawers out, Gabrielle said, "It'll take weeks."

"Not that long."

They searched for two hours. All the stored items seemed to be related to the B&B, including cabinets filled with registration and financial records dating back to 1940 when the B&B was built.

"Everything is here except the bowl," Gabrielle finally

said. Cornell had just shoved a dresser to the side so she could reach a bureau.

He smiled and swiped a finger down her nose.

Gabrielle's nose itched. "What was that about?"

"You had dust on your nose. Got it on your cheeks, too. Time for a bath."

"Your place or mine?" What made her say that?

"Your place," Cornell said. "We're too old for supervision."

And just like that, they were in the car and in her house in less than ten minutes. Hopping from foot to foot, slinging off clothes, they made a trail to her shower.

Warm water streamed over their bodies while they touched and kissed, and then he lifted her against the wall and he was inside her.

There was something sensuous about the feel of wet skin.

"I missed this," he said as he suckled on her nipple.

She groaned, slid her hands down his back, his chest. Wrapped her legs around his waist.

He moaned. "You're killing me, you know."

She kissed him on the chest. It wasn't the gentle or searching kiss of before, but of a woman who wanted him every bit as much as he wanted her.

He set her on her feet, slid down her body, and kissed her stomach, around her navel.

She shivered, glided her hands through his wet hair.

He gave her kiss after kiss after kiss.

"That's wonderful," Gabrielle said.

She slid her hands over his body, felt the corded muscles she watched many mornings as he ran along the beach.

For a moment they stood gazing at each other, enjoying every detail, and then they were together again.

After the first coupling, Cornell rubbed soap in his hands and washed her entire body, and she in turn bathed him. The simple act of bathing could be so seductive.

* * *

Gabrielle wore only a short nightgown and Cornell his slacks. They worked companionably in the kitchen as they prepared sandwiches.

Cornell grabbed her around the waist and kissed her neck. "You've got on too many clothes."

Gabrielle smiled. "Something can be done about that, you know."

"Oh, yeah?"

"You're insatiable."

They made love in the kitchen. When they finally sat to eat, Gabrielle asked, "Won't your mother be expecting you?"

"I don't think she's waiting up for me."

"Your car is just across the path. All she has to do is look outside the window."

"Guess I have to go home tonight. The one good thing is that her week is almost up. Dad will call soon, and she'll run back to the mainland."

Gabrielle laughed. "You're kidding, right?"

"Not at all."

"They're as crazy as Anna and Lucky."

"If not more."

Gabrielle smiled wistfully. "At least they stuck it out."

"They must love something about each other." He brushed her hair back from her face. More than once, he wanted to tell her how special she was, but he couldn't do that.

"I heard some fascinating information about the family from your grandmother," Graham said. "Mitchell became quite upset when Naomi said his family wasn't related to the first families who arrived 1607 in Jamestown, at least he wasn't connected to Elizabeth through blood. Seems her descendent, Mary, left the area before she bore any living children and made her way to Philly."

"I don't keep up with all that. It's enough to deal with the day-to-day stuff," Lisa said.

"It's a big deal for him. He's been saying for years how he hailed from four hundred years of ancestors here. Now it seems his ancestors were here less than two hundred years. Quite a comedown for him."

"At least you're getting a break while he's in a stew."

"I think I'd rather be working. First, he has to prove Mrs. Claxton wrong. Then he has to decide how we'll progress with this book."

Lisa shook her head. "The things you worry about. It's just a book. Can't go back and live all those years."

"The South literally lives in the past. We'll be living the Civil War for the next thousand years."

"You've got that right. Before I left, Gabrielle was going through the old storage shed. She probably thought Aunt Anna hid the bowl in there, but that's the last place she would have hidden it."

"Why?" Graham asked.

"She kept that thing close by. Someplace where she could take it out and look at it when she wanted to. She loved that old bowl. Used to let me hold it sometimes when I was a child."

"I'm looking forward to Founders Day. Maybe Gabrielle will find it by then. Since you knew your aunt so well, maybe you should help Gabrielle find it. It's your heritage, too. That bowl belongs to your family."

"Don't tell her that. Ms. Thing thinks she has the right to make all the decisions."

"You have to be assertive about your feelings. You have to become more involved in the family. Your aunt depended on you. Your grandmother depends on you, too."

"I don't know." Just like Aunt Anna, Naomi had Gabrielle hopping for her every time she turned around.

"What are you thinking?"

She shrugged. "Gabrielle hasn't had a vacation since she came here."

"You can look after things when she takes one."

"By myself? I don't think so." Not as tired as she was. "Tell you the truth, I need a break now, but if I take one, Gabrielle will give my job away. And they don't pay for squat at other hotels. I can't afford to let this job go."

"It's slower in winter, isn't it? You can take a nice long vacation then." With a twinkle in his eye, he elbowed her. "If you take it during a holiday, maybe we could go to Miami or Hawaii and spend the time on the beach."

"That's several months away. Besides, I could spend time on the beach right here if I get a summer vacation."

He smiled and shook his head. "Stop putting yourself down, Lisa. You're stronger than you think." He glanced toward the ocean. "Think I'll take a swim."

"The water's freezing out there."

"If you call this freezing, you should try the Pacific Ocean. You don't know what cold is."

"You're crazy." Lisa shivered just thinking about getting in that cold water. She always waited until June.

Late that afternoon, Gabrielle and Regina were cleaning the dining room. A small meeting had let out for the day.

"Lisa offered to help me find the bowl," Gabrielle said. "Said she worked for Aunt Anna a long time and might be able to find it."

"Do you trust her?" Regina asked.

Gabrielle sighed. "No."

"If she found it, she wouldn't give it to you."

"But she spent a lot of time with Aunt Anna."

"So did a lot of people. Lisa acts like you're the only one Aunt Anna left things to. I am so grateful she gave me the money to pay for my college tuition and enough to buy my little house."

"You deserved it."

"I don't know about that, but I welcomed it, anyway. Sam started on my garden the other day. It's already taking shape. He, my dad, and brothers are going to work on it this weekend. He said my yard has to be evened out. My eyes glazed over when he started talking about everything that needed to be done. I can't wait."

Gabrielle stared at her.

"What?"

"What happens after he finishes your yard?"

Regina gazed at the empty pitcher, felt a catch in her chest. "I don't know. He's not letting me close."

"You're my cousin and I love you," Gabrielle said quietly. "But I hate what you're doing. It's not right, Regina. He's a good guy. And you're using him."

Regina rolled her eyes. "Just get off your high horse, okay?" She knew she was snapping at Gabrielle because she felt guilty. "I like him, Gabrielle."

"Yeah, but what if he's falling in love with you? You're just going to break his heart. He's had enough loss in his life."

"He's a man, not a kid."

"Men hurt, too. But you don't care. You won't have to pick up the pieces when it's all over. You can just look out your window at your beautiful garden." Throwing Regina one last withering glance, Gabrielle snatched pitchers off the table and took them to the kitchen.

Regina carried her pitchers into the kitchen and put them in the sink. "Stay out of my business," she snapped too forcefully. Gabrielle's words were working on her conscience.

"It's not just your business."

Regina had to get some fresh air. Gabrielle could take the

happiest of news and turn it into a downer. But as she neared the door, she saw Sam's truck drive up. She wasn't ready to face him.

Regina didn't fetch a drink for Sam this time. She disappeared into the laundry room. There was always something to do in there.

Gabrielle waved at Sam and shook her head as her cousin disappeared. She poured a glass of lemonade and took it to him.

"How's it going, Sam?"

"Good." He glanced at the parking area and obviously saw Regina's car, then he looked toward the building. But he didn't mention Regina's name. It was already too late. Gabrielle's heart was breaking for Sam.

"I talked to the sheriff about the bowl."

"What did he say?"

After she told him, he said, "Maybe I should help you. I lived in the house a while. I might remember some of her places."

"Thanks. Lisa offered too. But . . . I don't know."

"Let me know. I'll be happy to help." Finished with the drink, he handed the glass back, directing another glance at the B&B.

Sadly, Gabrielle shook her head. "Well, I have to get back inside. See you later, Sam."

It was a couple of hours later when the professors sat on the porch catching the late afternoon breeze. They were chatting with some of the other guests. Mitchell had finally calmed down a bit about his heritage.

It was a comfortable afternoon, but the mosquitoes were biting like heck. Gabrielle went inside to spray on repellent before she joined them.

"How long has he been working for you?" the professor asked, nodding toward Sam.

"He's worked with my aunt since high school," Gabrielle

said. "He's the only one who's really done anything with the garden. Never has it been so beautiful."

The professor nodded. "One of the many joys of being here is your garden."

"To tell you the truth, I'm equally taken by it."

"Heard someone broke into your grandparents' neighbor's house. Your grandmother must be terribly upset."

"She is."

"If there's anything I can do, please let me know."

"How kind of you to offer, but I want you to enjoy your vacation." After all, he was paying her a bundle to stay there and shouldn't get involved with her personal family drama.

Sam was planting a tree in a space where the last one had blown down during the last Nor'easter.

When Sam finished with the tree, he went to a flowerbed that looked perfect to her. But with a gardener's eye, he obviously saw more than she did. He beckoned her over.

"Excuse me a moment," she said to the professors, and descended the steps to joined Sam. They were far enough away to have a private conversation.

"Someone's been digging in my flowers," he said. "Verbena and dahlias are planted here. They're difficult to grow."

"I haven't seen anyone around them. The children usually play in the designated areas. There aren't many here this time of year." She had a play area set up for them close enough to the adult area for proper supervision. Most of them liked to hang out on the beach, anyway.

"I'm thinking about erecting a fence around them."

"It's that serious?"

"It took years for me to get these things to grow properly. I don't want anyone messing around them."

"I'll have the employees keep an eye out. It could be an animal digging in them."

"They don't eat these." Sam took off his hat and wiped the back of his neck. "I'll give it a day or two and see what happens."

"Okay." Gabrielle was getting ready to leave when she saw Regina approaching them with a tall glass of tea. She knew the moment Sam saw her. It was like a light clicked on in his eye. Gabrielle closed her own eyes briefly. He was falling in love with Regina.

"Sam . . ."

"Yeah." He didn't take his focus from Regina.

Gabrielle shook her head. She'd never seen Sam enamored with a woman before. He kept everything inside. Was she interfering when she shouldn't? "Never mind," she finally said. She'd already said her piece. Obviously it had no effect on Regina. Gabrielle sighed. She had to get back to work. Regina didn't spare her a glance. Gabrielle wanted to shake some compassion into her.

"Got to say, that man's a dedicated gardener," Graham said when she climbed the stairs.

"He takes pride in this place. My aunt hired him when he was very young. She was like a mother to him. His parents died when he was in high school." Gabrielle didn't like to gossip, but everyone knew that much about Sam's background.

"I've got to say, that area has the prettiest flowers in the entire yard," the professor said. "And that's saying something when you have a garden like this."

Gabrielle glanced around. "I never noticed that, but you're right," Gabrielle said. A car with a Tennessee license plate drove into the yard. A new check-in. The door flew open and three children bolted out as if they were breaking from prison. Two harried parents slowly emerged after them. "I'll send out drinks," Gabrielle said, and left to greet her guests.

Gabrielle went home to rest a few minutes before returning to the B&B. One day she was going to have to find someone else to meet the guests so she wouldn't have to do it every day. She had just fixed herself a glass of iced tea and put her feet up on the hassock before the doorbell rang. Tiredly, she dragged her feet to the floor and answered it.

"My dad called Mom today," Cornell said, coming over the threshold with a huge smile.

"And?"

"She didn't want to leave with all the unsolved murders. I assured her everything would get solved without her."

Gabrielle chuckled.

"She left on the noon ferry," Cornell said with the smile of satisfaction that reminded her of a Cheshire cat. "I've got my house and my time to myself again, and I've got the whole evening free for you."

"Well, I don't. I have the meet and greet. You're preparing the snacks, remember?"

"Hmm. I remember. I have your idiot cousins delivering them." He pulled her close. "The hell with snacks. We have to celebrate. I want my snack now." Covering her lips with his, Cornell backed Gabrielle against the door and rubbed his hard body against hers. She tasted fabulous. He unbuttoned her blouse.

"Why do women's blouses have a thousand tiny buttons?" He grasped at them impatiently.

"I need a shower."

"Later." With the blouse finally undone, he dragged it off her shoulders. Her hand caught his T-shirt and tugged it over his head.

It took only seconds to toss their clothes aside. They slid to the floor, and before Gabrielle knew it, Cornell had donned a condom and was in her. He stayed there a second getting the feel of her as she enjoyed the length and strength of him.

She wrapped her legs around him tightly, pulled him deeper inside. He was as impatient and as needy as she as they moved to a harried pace.

He grasped her hips, sinking even deeper within. She

enjoyed every millimeter of him. They moved until first she and then he exploded with delight.

After their frantic lovemaking, Gabrielle had to shower quickly to make it to the B&B on time. Lovemaking or no, she still had to make sure everything was set up properly and to greet her guests.

The next morning, Gabrielle was surprised to see the sheriff at the B&B. He motioned her to a flowerbed. Regina, Lisa, and curious guests stood nearby and slowly moved closer to them. Sam was already working in the yard and approached them when one of the sheriff's employees started poking in the flowerbed.

"What're you doing here?" Sam said, rushing up to the flowerbed.

"We got an anonymous tip that something may be buried out here," the sheriff said.

"You're ruining my flowers," Sam said, outraged. "It took me forever to get them to grow like this."

Mitchell moved closer to them. "Why are you acting so strange about those flowers?" he asked. "You got something hidden out here?"

"What am I supposed to hide?"

Lisa stood beside Gabrielle. "You're acting mighty strange over some flowers. Why do you have to be acting so weird all the time?"

"Shut up, Lisa," Gabrielle said, and focused on the sheriff. "Is this really necessary?"

"Yes. The rest of you leave," the sheriff said. "This is police business. Move them back, John."

"Okay, folks, step back," the officer said, making a wall of his body.

Reluctantly, everybody moved away except the sheriff, Sam, Regina, and Gabrielle.

"Take the flowers if you must, but we're digging here whether you like it or not."

Sam moved to the shed and collected several buckets.

"Let me help you," Regina said.

Gabrielle started to offer her assistance, but Sam seemed to like working with Regina better. She held the bucket as he painstakingly moved each plant out, saving as much of the roots as possible.

Then the sheriff began to dig until his shovel hit something hard. Then he stooped and with gloved hands gingerly moved the soil aside.

"What the heck is this?" he asked. "We're going to have to get a forensics team in here."

"They're the bones of my dog. He died my senior year in high school. Ms. Anna let me bury him there," Sam said.

The sheriff began to uncover more of the animal. It was clearly the remains of an animal. Finally he dusted his hands and stood.

"Somebody's playing games," Harper said. "And I don't like it one bit."

"Who called you?" Gabrielle asked.

He gazed at the hole Sam was quickly filling up. "It was an anonymous tip."

Sam looked disgustedly at the sheriff. "I'm not going to be able to save this plant. It's too fragile for its roots to be disturbed." He glanced at the plant again. "Years' worth of work, gone up in smoke."

"There's nothing you can do?" Regina asked.

"I'm going to take it to my greenhouse and work with it. It doesn't like to be moved."

"I'm sorry about your plant, but it's a plant, not a baby for heaven's sake," the sheriff lamented.

"Wonder how somebody so insensitive got voted in as sheriff," Regina said. "Good thing an election year is coming up. When people are dying left and right, you're digging up dog bones."

Regina placed a hand on Sam's bunched shoulders. "It's okay," she said.

"I can take care of myself," he said to her. Then, taking his plant with him, he got in his truck and drove off.

For a moment Regina gazed after him. He was closing her out as if they didn't have a history. Maybe their relationship was new, but it was there.

"I have to leave, Gabrielle," Regina said.

"Go, go," Gabrielle said. "He needs someone."

Regina had gathered up a steaming kettle worth of anger by the time she reached Sam's place.

She hoped he was there and if he was that he'd let her in.

His truck was parked under a gnarled oak tree.

She heard the waves crashing against the shore as she made her way to the door to ring the doorbell. She received no answer. Finally she walked around the back of the house to knock on that door.

He had some kind of nerve refusing to let her in. She was going to bang on that door until she got a response. Even if he didn't want to date her, he could respect the fact that she cared about him.

Lord. She really cared for him, she thought, incredulous. This had started out as a way to get her yard done. She wasn't supposed to have feelings for him. She should have known this would happen. Despite what Gabrielle believed, she wasn't coldhearted. Sam had taken the loss of the flower pretty hard and her heart ached for him.

But as she turned the corner, she glanced at the green-house. Some of the glass panes were open, and she heard soft music coming from within. Some of the plants were so tall and thick that she couldn't see a human form. He was bending over a plant. And then he stood. His gloved hands were immersed in dark soil, gently placing the plant within. Then he patted the dirt around it and set the pot on a shelf.

Regina walked closer and knocked on the door—and

knocked and knocked. She pounded on the door several times before she captured his attention.

Sam glanced up with a surprised look on his face. Seconds ticked by while he watched her as if he were rooted to the ground. Obviously realizing he'd left her outside in the hot sun, he finally moved toward her, pulling off his gloves as he went.

Regina's heart tripped. She'd felt like a thousand fools driving up to his place. She was at a loss for words. She only knew this was exactly where she wanted to be. Was he equally thrilled to see her?

"You can just go. Don't worry. I'm still doing your yard."

"I'm not concerned about my yard." Regina approached him, but she really didn't know what to do, how to gauge him. "I'm sorry about your plant."

"It's my problem."

"I care, Sam."

"Sure you do." His voice was laced with enough sarcasm to poison.

"That's a mean thing to say."

Sam knew why she was there. He wasn't fool enough to think for a moment that she felt anything for him. As soon as he completed her yard, he wouldn't see the back of her backside fast enough. He wasn't doing the yard for her—it was for Anna, he reminded himself.

Then he felt her hand on his shoulder and shrugged it off. He couldn't depend on her. He couldn't depend on anybody.

"Let's go to the mainland, Sam. Walk the boardwalk along Virginia Beach."

"We've got plenty of beach and sand out here, if I wanted to walk in dirt. Besides, I've got too much work to do."

"You can take one day off."

Sam didn't know what it was like to take a day off. The only day he didn't work was Sunday. And he used that to clean up his house and catch up on paperwork.

"Call your assistant. Have her reschedule your appointments."

"What about you? You have classes and work."

"I'm studying for exams now. I've already taken my last class."

"I don't want to stand in the way of your studying. It's important."

"I'll make up for it when we get back."

Sam glared out the window. "Gabrielle needs all the help she can get."

"She can do without me for one day, for chrissakes. I'm taking this day off, Sam, whether you like it or not. Stop arguing with me."

He stood indecisive. "Why are you doing this?"

"Because I want to be with you."

He should tell her to get the heck away from him. He was weak. He was always alone. People like Gabrielle were nice to him; most just ignored him. While he didn't want to be alone to roam around his house, he wasn't in the mood to be around other people, either. He didn't understand himself. Even knowing she was just using him, he *wanted* to be with Regina.

He nodded. He didn't have to fall in love with her.

"Sam, why was that plant so important to you?"

"It doesn't matter."

"Of course it matters. Don't close me out the way you do everybody else. We're at least friends, if nothing more."

Sam shook his head.

"Talk to me, please."

With his hands against the wall, Sam sighed. "It was a gift from my mother. She gave it to me for my birthday just before she died. My parents were poor, and this plant was very expensive, but they sacrificed to buy it for me. They knew how much I loved to garden."

And then Sam felt her arms around him. Her lips grazed

his cheeks, and then their eyes met. He didn't want to touch her, but he found himself wrapping his arms around her waist, pulling her close to him. He'd loved her since high school. And for the first time, he had her in his arms—and he kissed her.

God, her lush soft curves fit perfectly in his hands. He kissed her cheek, trailed a line of kisses down her neck, across her chest. Her little moans drove him crazy. And she smelled delicious. Just made him want to have her for a meal.

"Regina," he whispered, then lifted his head to gaze down at her. Her eyes were soft, and the need in him was reflected in her eyes. She sprang on tiptoes to kiss him, and with her hands running enticingly over his body, he lost all control. He couldn't turn down the feast she offered him.

CHAPTER 13

It was May, and outside it was warm and cheerful. Gabrielle was on the phone talking to her mother.

"Your dad and I will be there for the crab fry, dear. How are things going at the B and B?"

"I'm sold out for the crab feast."

"I thought it was a brilliant thing you started last year. I'll help you, of course."

"Thanks, I could use all the help I can get."

"Have you had Aunt Anna's place fixed up?"

"Haven't had time yet. Probably won't start on renovations until the winter when it's slow."

"Your dad and I were a little concerned about the murder on the island. Your grandmother also mentioned break-ins."

"There have been a few, but nobody has been hurt."

"I thought I could stop worrying so much when you moved to the island. Looks like a mother can never rest."

"Don't worry about me. Cornell lives nearby. If I scream loud enough, he'll hear."

"And that's supposed to give me comfort?"

Gabrielle smiled. "It's a joke, Mom. He's okay. We're kind of seeing each other."

"Gabrielle, Cornell was always nice. I didn't have the same

prejudices as Mom, but he was wild. You can't deny that. He was a ladies' man. Loved his women."

God knows he did, Gabrielle thought. "I think he's changed. Matured."

"Nature doesn't change, honey. A lover is a lover."

Gabrielle was getting hot just thinking about the times in his arms. "I'm not sure this is something I want to discuss with my mother."

"Well, who would you discuss it with? Who would be more honest than your mother?"

"You're not exactly unbiased."

"Of course not. You're my daughter and I love you."

"I love you, too, Mom."

"Well, dog gone it, I miss you. We used to do a million things together."

Gabrielle missed her mother, too. They didn't have the usual mother-daughter skirmishes. Probably because Gabrielle was the only daughter. Her brother spent most of his time traveling. He breezed in once or twice a year. Still had the wanderlust in him. Her mother should understand that. She couldn't wait to shake the island sand from the soles of her feet. He'd inherited the gene from her.

To Naomi's dismay, her daughter had gotten pregnant when she was eighteen—the summer Gabrielle's father had come to the island doing genealogy research. One look and the man was in love. But he'd also swept her off her feet. Good thing they'd fallen in love. He was fresh out of college, but he married her and took her with him when he left. It wasn't easy back then for a mixed-race couple, and they'd spent the first fifteen years of their marriage overseas.

"Maybe we can go shopping together," Gabrielle said. "Or find a spa or something. We'll plan a whole day together while you're here." They ended the conversation and Gabrielle slowly placed the phone on the hook.

She was going to have to take a vacation soon. Maybe she and her mother could get away together. Or perhaps her mother could spend more time down there.

It was warm and just a bit windy outside. Next week, fishermen should be pulling crabs in.

The bell above the door tinkered. "Good morning, Gabrielle. It's wonderful to be back."

Gabrielle smiled at the woman who was attired in black jeans and a red V-neck sweater approaching the desk. "Ms. Rhodes. It's a pleasure to see you again."

"June, please," she said as Gabrielle handed her the registration form. "I have meetings in Virginia Beach this week, not every day, thank goodness, but a couple of days. I really didn't want to stay in a huge hotel, not when Paradise was just a ferry ride away. And the next week is my vacation. And believe me, I need it."

"We're glad to have you."

"Do you have my special room ready?"

"Yes, I do. You have the same room you stayed in before."

"Wonderful."

She signed in and Gabrielle handed her the key. "We'll have a crab feast just before you leave."

"I'm definitely looking forward to that."

When the woman had gone upstairs, Regina said, "She reminds me of Alyssa."

"I thought the same thing."

"Bet she could kick butt if she wanted to."

"I hope it isn't mine."

They both laughed.

"Did you calm Sam down?"

"Oh, yeah." A dreamy expression crossed Regina's face.

"He must have been pretty upset. Took you the whole day."

Regina pursed her lips. "We decided to play hooky."

"Sam?"

Regina nodded and walked off.

Sam needed a special woman. Someone who would get

him out of his shell. Someone who would treat him good. She had no doubt Sam would treat a woman well.

Gabrielle just wasn't sure if Regina was the one. Especially if she wasn't serious. But Sam was a grown man. What could she do?

Hoyt didn't know quite how to reach Naomi. Since Wanda died, their children and grandchildren came by regularly. She'd sit in the kitchen and talk to them. But at night she was quiet and restless. It was like she'd closed herself off from him. It didn't feel right. He'd rather have her fussing and complaining than be listless.

Sometimes that simpering Wanda got on his nerves, but Naomi had liked her. Women needed to let off steam with each other sometimes, he guessed, just like he liked to talk nonsense with his buddies.

Now, Naomi was sitting at the kitchen table, her full glass of tea forgotten.

"Can I get something for you, Naomi?" he asked. "I can run out and get you some chicken from the greasy spoon down the street if you want." She'd forgotten to fix supper again—for the second time that week.

"I'll get up and fix something in a little while."

"Why don't you take the night off?"

"And do what? Got nothing to do but cook."

He hated to see her like this. All hurting. He felt helpless. He didn't know how to reach her. Knew nothing he said would make the situation better.

"I wonder where it all went?" she finally said.

"All what went?"

"Us. I was just thinking about us. I don't know you anymore."

"Of course you know me. We've been married . . . now let's see." He had to count the years. "Round fifty some years now." Or was it fifty-four? The years passed so fast it was hard to keep up with them.

She shook her head. How can a man keep all those dates in his head?

"We share less now than we did years ago," she said sadly.

"I spend every night right here. We've had a whole life together."

"Why don't you go find something to do with yourself? You're just making me angry."

What did he do now? He looked at her helplessly. Honest to truth, he would never understand women. Even when he tried to be helpful, he only made things worse. A man wasn't meant to win where women were concerned.

"I'll run out for some supper," he said finally. "Anything you want in particular?"

"How many times have I told you to stay away from that fried food place? The doctor told you not to eat that stuff. Go on by Cornell's place and pick up something healthy. Get me baked chicken. Don't bring anything fried in here."

"You still fry food."

"Only because you pick over everything else. I just serve it now and then, not as a steady diet."

Hoyt shook his head. He should have kept his mouth shut while he was ahead.

"I'll be back soon."

"No, Mom," Cornell said impatiently later that afternoon, "we can't get away. Gabrielle's usually busy on Sunday afternoons. It's her busiest checkout day." His mom was probably already picking out the wedding china. He'd seen trouble the moment she'd handed Gabrielle the vase she'd made.

Cornell had already gotten calls from his aunts asking when the big date was, and when he was bringing her home.

Why was he hiding her? His mother must have hit the phones as soon as she'd gotten on the ferry.

He had a hard enough time wrapping his mind around the notion of taking a date home. It had been years. He'd never found the time to introduce the crazy one in New York to his family, which was a bone of contention with them. The time hadn't been right. This time, he couldn't avoid it. He lived too close to home.

"Honey, I've invited your aunts, grandparents. Everyone wants to meet her."

Cornell felt smothered. "Why didn't you ask me first?" He could see her little to-do list. Could see the menu already organized in the computer. The list of invitees for the brunch. He was probably the last to be notified.

"Well, I didn't think it was a big deal."

Yeah, right. "Then why are you making a big deal out of it?"

"Oh, for heaven's sake. It's just brunch. Everyone needs a day off."

"She usually has brunch at her grandparents'."

"It's just one Sunday out of the year for heaven's sake. I'm sure she won't mind. Unlike my disagreeable son. I don't understand why you won't introduce her to the family. Why are you hiding her away?"

"I'm not hiding her." He could see it now. People liked Gabrielle. His relatives would fall in love with her. Every time he went home, they'd ask when they were going to tie the knot. They already repeated like a broken record that he was the oldest. Told him it was time he put down roots. Every now and then his mother hinted at grandchildren.

"Well?" his mother asked.

Cornell didn't see a way out of it. His mother was the most tenacious person he knew. If he didn't comply, he wouldn't put it past her to call Gabrielle herself. She'd have picked up a brochure with the B&B's address and phone number before she left.

Damn it. What the heck was he thinking? He knew inviting Gabrielle to dinner was the last thing he should have done while his mother was there. But she was thinking he was ashamed of her, that he was hiding her from his family—and in a sense he was. He wasn't ashamed, but he was keeping her from family.

"I'm waiting."

Blowing out a long breath, he said, "I'll ask, but I'm not promising anything."

"That's all I asked, sweetheart. Try to be here by two," she said as if Gabrielle had already agreed.

Cornell wanted to hit something.

The twins had the bad fortune to come in right after he hung up. Cornell frowned as they headed his way with a stack of papers in their hands. Those boys were always smiling about something.

"We made up flyers," Chance said.

"Good for you." Cornell frowned. "For what?"

"The dance we talked about having here. Your place is big enough, and we can hang outside, too."

"You've got to be kidding." Souped-up cars and motorcycles passing his house all hours of the night. He wasn't going to spend his time off supervising teens. Bad enough working with them. "Heck no."

"The dinner worked out okay, didn't it? So will this. We always have to go into Norfolk because nothing's happening here," Lance said. "Then we have to get back before the last ferry."

"Works for me," Cornell said. Norfolk was miles away. He'd have the beach to himself. It was getting warm enough to snuggle up under a quilt with the cool breeze blowing through Gabrielle's hair and across their overheated skin. Whoa. Back to the matter at hand.

He knew how parties worked. The boys would invite a

bunch of friends who would tell their buddies. He'd end up with a crowd from Williamsburg to North Carolina.

"Yeah, Norfolk sounds extremely good to me."

"Come on, man. We never have anything here. We're too young to buy liquor at the bar."

"And you think I'll serve it here? Think again. I'm not serving liquor to a bunch of teens and have a big lawsuit as soon as some asshole drives drunk and hurts somebody. Not in this lifetime."

"Like you didn't drink at our age. I thought you were so smooth, man."

"I was headed for the military at eighteen, and what I did is none of your business."

"Ah, man."

Their faces were so crestfallen Cornell's heart began to thaw. Yeah, he was pissed off with his mother for roping him into brunch. For having to put up with the family folks every time he visited. No reason to take it out on the boys. He had been a teenager once.

Damn. There really wasn't very much entertainment for young people on the island. It wouldn't hurt for him to let them do something *one* night.

"If—and I'm saying a big if—I let you have something, it'll be for the island teens only and no liquor. And there has to be some supervision."

The boys' eyes lit up like Christmas lights. "We know how to act."

"No supervision, no party. Now, get to work." Cornell left his manager in charge and took the evening snacks to the B&B. He may as well ask her now.

When he arrived at the B&B, John Aldridge's car was parked in the yard. He and Gabrielle were standing outside talking while John leaned against the door with his arms crossed. The guy was clearly enchanted with Gabrielle. It was written all over his face.

Cornell wondered if they were discussing business or if the policeman was trying to finagle a date. If he didn't want her, John was waiting on the sidelines to step into his shoes. That just pissed him the heck off.

The jealousy that shot through Cornell was as shocking as it was unwelcome. He tried to hold on to his cool as he parked, and he exited his car as if he had all the time in the world. What he wanted to do was slam his fist in the grinning John's face. It wouldn't do to get locked up for being stupid.

"Evening," he said, and went over to stand by Gabrielle. She frowned as John spoke to her.

"John was just telling me about Mr. Fisher."

"In the last year, they stole a couple of priceless paintings, some jewels, and other stuff," John said.

"So you think Roger's death was a falling out among thieves?" Cornell asked, slightly mollified that John was discussing business and not contemplating sneaking a kiss from Gabrielle.

"Could be."

"Any idea where the rest of the team is?"

"We're looking into it. Any strangers who arrived in the last couple of years are suspect."

John's cell phone rang, and while he answered it, Cornell ran the recent information around in his mind.

Well, heck. That included Cornell. And John was looking at him as if he'd single-handedly stolen the bowl. The fact that he and Gabrielle were now in a relationship made him even more of a suspect.

"Gabby, there's one more thing I need to discuss with you," John said after he hung up. He glanced at Cornell. "You may want to discuss this in private."

"Cornell's okay."

"I talked with the bartender. He remembered seeing you the night Roger disappeared. We haven't been able to find anyone who's seen him since that night. According to the bartender, you left the bar with him."

"We went our separate ways. He drove his car and I drove mine. We just happened to leave at the same time. I always wondered why I didn't see him after that. Like I said, he left without saying a word. Left some of his belongings in the B and B. I gave you everything he left behind."

"Now with knowing Roger's background, they're looking more closely at his death and hoping they can find the rest of the ring. They're also hoping to get leads to where the stolen articles might be. I have to go. If you remember anything, give me a call."

Gabrielle nodded. "I will."

John touched Gabrielle's arm. "I might have more questions later."

Cornell wanted to break that hand.

"I'll be here," Gabrielle said.

Gabrielle waved to John as he drove away. When he was out of sight, she sighed like a deflated balloon.

"I don't have an alibi for that night. I might need one."

"There's no reason for them to think you're a suspect."

"You don't understand. That night is a total blank. I don't know what happened."

"We've already determined you couldn't have done it."

"Innocent people have been charged before."

"Give me a break. How much money do you think a police department is going to put into solving this?"

"One, possibly two, murders have been committed here. They have all the time to investigate."

"Roger's murder didn't occur here."

Gabrielle rubbed some warmth on her arms. Goose bumps had risen up, spreading a chill through her body.

Cornell hugged her. Then he said, "Come on. Help me get the snacks inside for your guests. They're waiting for you. You know how the professors always arrive on time."

"Cornell, I can't go to jail."

"You're not going to jail."

"I remember being angry enough to punch his lights out. What if I put thought to action?"

"You didn't kill him, Gabrielle. Don't make yourself crazy. Besides, you don't even know if he died that night. All this is speculation."

"It had to have been that night."

"It's more likely Harvey Fisher killed him, or whoever their other partner or partners might be. There is no honor among thieves. Now let's unload the food and entertain your guests. I came to spend time with you. After we leave here, we'll go to your house and see if we can figure out what to do the rest of the night."

Gabrielle's mind wasn't on new guests that evening. She was just going through the motions until she could get away. Perhaps it was a good thing she was busy. This way she wouldn't worry herself half to death.

"Gabrielle, you seem troubled."

Gabrielle smiled at Graham. "I'm fine."

"I saw the police car earlier. Is anything wrong?"

"No. Nothing. I see you have a few minutes away from the professor."

"He was making a long-distance phone call. He'll be down soon."

"You need a break. You work much too hard. I hope you have time to spend on the beach or go into Virginia Beach and Norfolk. There's too much to do for you to be cooped up here."

"I came here to work. I can't complain."

"I wish my cousin felt that way," Gabrielle mumbled too low for Graham to hear.

"Come again?"

Gabrielle shook her head and spotted the professor hopping jovially down the stairs. "Nothing. Here comes the professor. Enjoy your evening."

"I always do."

For days now, Mitchell had dragged Graham to the Virginia Beach courthouse to do research on his genealogy. He was trying his level best to prove Naomi Claxton wrong. Her ancestors may have been here since the beginning of time, but so had his, he'd moaned over and over. True, he'd used facts mostly written down and passed on through the generations. Each generation had recorded information about their ancestors. They couldn't be wrong.

And this nonsense that the man's second wife's name was also Mary made no sense.

"Ah, Mitchell?" Graham said quietly.

"What?"

Two days ago Graham had found the records of the "first" Mary's birth and her marriage. She was the daughter of a wealthy farmer who lived close to Virginia Beach. Graham was sure Mitchell was going to be very disappointed with his findings because now he'd found the record showing that this Mary had disappeared and been declared dead. Obviously her husband had been a powerful man to have his wife declared dead so soon. He also found information that their only child had died months before she left. Now he had the record of the man's second marriage to Mary Carpenter. Mary Carpenter had six children by him.

Graham had photocopied and recorded bits and pieces of information. Mitchell was going to have a fit when he discovered he wasn't a descendent of the 1607 arrivals in Virginia. He'd been touting that information for years. And it had gotten worse the closer 2007 came. Now it was here, and he had been part of the special celebration they held in Jamestown.

Graham glanced at him and shook his head. Mitchell was

going to be one disappointed man, and he regretted having to inform him. He hoped Mitchell didn't get the urge to kill the messenger. More than once Mitchell had wanted to wring Mrs. Claxton's neck.

Graham decided to hold back the information for now. It was almost time for them to leave, anyway.

More importantly, his mind had been on Gabrielle and the fact that she'd seen that guy named Roger before he'd died. He wanted to talk to Lisa to find out the island gossip.

He glanced at Mitchell, who was deeply engrossed in his work.

The older man grunted and looked up. His glasses had fallen down on his nose. His stringy hair, arranged to cover his bald spot, had fallen to the side, revealing the pink area. Mitchell needed to get some sun.

"Find something?"

"You said we were going to leave a little earlier today," Graham reminded him.

Frowning, Mitchell glanced at his watch. "That time already?"

"Yeah."

"Give me fifteen more minutes."

Graham sighed. "Sure." He wanted to spend a few minutes with Lisa before she left for the day.

He'd even gone to the bar the evening before, hoping she'd be hanging out there. She never showed up. He'd drunk his one glass of club soda and left.

Cornell paced in the dining room, came to a stop at the kitchen door, and gazed out to the ocean. He felt a noose tightening around his throat. He knew why. His family drove him crazy.

He glanced at Gabrielle, and some of the frustration went out of him. She rubbed her brow in concentration. He knew she was thinking of that damn bowl. She needed to get away from all the stress. The woman worked too much. Too bad none of her cousins could take over for her. Lisa was the logical person, if she could be trusted.

Cornell was going to have to think of something. Gabrielle would never think of taking a break just because she needed it. But she was the kind of woman who would go away if he needed a break.

She rubbed a soothing hand across his shoulder.

"What is it?" she asked.

"Do you realize we never get away from the island? Don't get me wrong. I like it fine enough. But we've been cooped up here forever. I feel caged in."

"Where do you want to go?"

"I don't care."

"You want to ride your bike?" she asked.

"Not necessarily. I just need to get away."

"Did anything happen?"

"Why does something have to happen? I like an occasional change of scenery. I don't take time from work. You don't take time from work. I like my job but I need—"

"Okay. Want to go to the mainland?"

"Can you get away?"

"Sure. If Grandma is free."

"I hate to involve your grandparents."

"She loves pitching in, trust me. Gives her a chance to do something other than worry about Grandpa. Besides, she used to do it for Aunt Anna when she was still working the B and B."

"Okay. Maybe we can take a short trip to Virginia Beach or take a flight to New York for a couple of days. In the meantime, my mom wants you to come to brunch on Sunday. Think we can get away and do something after? But first I have to ask you if you're available. If you aren't, I understand."

"If you said it with less enthusiasm, I'd have a real problem."

"She's got everybody coming over. Making a real deal out of it. The whole family. Like I said, she likes you."

"I like her, too. I get the feeling you're uncomfortable with me meeting your family. If so, I can beg off."

Cornell grunted. He was uncomfortable, but not because he was ashamed of her. "You don't know my family."

"They're probably like any other family. There is the camaraderie, the jokes between brothers and cousins, most of all there's love. They want to know you're doing okay. I always enjoy activities with my family."

"That's because you came from a normal family."

"That's a relative term. Whatever relationship your parents have worked out for themselves might not seem normal for you, but they can live with it."

"Hell on the kids, though."

"Was it really as bad as you let on?"

He shrugged. "Who knows?" Maybe he was feeling stressed out himself with this relationship business under the watchful eye of his family. It wasn't that he didn't want to be with Gabrielle, because he did. Being away from her was harder. It was just . . . Hell, he didn't know a damn thing. He had a funny feeling his boat was no longer docked. He was drifting out to sea.

CHAPTER 14

It was Friday night, and it seemed every teen on the island showed up at the restaurant. They'd started pouring in around nine-thirty. Cornell told them he was closing shop at one since some of them had curfews. He'd roped John and his brothers into being chaperons. His brothers had brought dates, of all things. Probably beat the kids necking. He put a stop to that immediately by giving them separate duties. No young ladies were turning up pregnant on his watch. Not at his place, anyway. What they did *after* might be another situation.

Sam had come over Thursday night to search Gabrielle's house for the bowl. The three of them had looked in unconventional places, with no luck. Before Sam had left, Cornell had tried to rope him into chaperoning, too, but Sam said he had plans. With any other person, you could ask about those plans. But Sam hadn't offered and Cornell hadn't asked.

Gabrielle had. Sam had ducked his head and mentioned Regina's name.

Cornell tapped Sam on the shoulder. "Man. You've got to be leery of those Claxton women," he teased.

"Don't I know it."

Gabrielle had hit Cornell on the arm, and Sam had actually smiled. Come to think of it, he'd never seen Sam smile before.

The man was much too serious. Comes from not having brothers, Cornell thought.

"I'll invite the two of you to dinner soon," Cornell had said.

Sam's eyes widened. "Sure . . . okay."

He and Sam used to go fishing sometimes. They were never close. Sam wasn't the kind to get close to anyone. But still, Cornell should have been more of a friend.

Now, placing a platter of fried catfish nuggets on the table, Cornell surveyed the buffet. The twins had collected a cover charge to cover the cost. It hadn't quite covered it all, but what the heck, they were teenagers. And it was something his uncle would have done. Cornell still missed Lucky. He felt good that he could keep the place going.

He finally saw Gabrielle being escorted in by his youngest brother and shook his head.

He felt a catch in his throat. Uncle Lucky had liked Gabrielle. He'd be happy they were together. And that Cornell had reopened the place.

John was stationed outside. There were a lot of woods behind the restaurant. And he'd made sure the kids either stayed in the backyard or inside. No sneaking off to the bushes. He knew how teens thought. He'd had some high times in those woods the summers he worked in his uncle's restaurant. Brought a smile to his face.

How did the old man stand it? Teens were enough to turn your hair gray. The twins were the first to arrive. Chance had a brown bag tucked under his arm.

"We're gonna fix the punch," he said.

"Already got that covered," Cornell said, nodding to a table pushed near the window.

"We were going to mix different flavors."

"Already done that. I went to cooking school. I know about flavoring punch." He took the bag from the boy's arm. "I'll take care of this.

"But . . ."

Cornell headed to his office. A peek in the bag revealed a bottle of tequila. And the night was just beginning. Cornell shook his head.

Cornell's arms were wrapped around Gabrielle as they moved in rhythm to a slow dance. As much as he enjoyed the feel of her, he couldn't completely take his eyes off the crowd. Already he'd caught the twins trying to spike the punch—twice. And during one of his recon trips he'd caught a couple getting ready to enjoy themselves in the backseat of a car. His brother, who was supposed to be guarding that area, had his girlfriend plastered on the hood of his car while he copped a feel.

While he understood the teenage needs, he didn't want it done on his property. With his uncle's reputation, the last thing he needed were gray-haired ladies marching on his establishment.

So when a man about thirty or so entered the party, he zeroed in on him immediately. The man was dressed in jeans and wore sunglasses, although the sun had disappeared hours ago. Cornell saw nothing but trouble.

He held Gabrielle tightly for a second, knowing he had to go and meet the trouble head-on. "As much as I hate to release you from my arms, I've got to get rid of this guy. Can't have him chasing seventeen-year-old girls." He knew how attractive an older guy looked to the young ladies.

Gabrielle turned and glanced toward the door.

"That's . . ." She squinted. "That's Skeeter."

"Doesn't look like him."

"I'm sure it is." She moved from his arms and started toward the man, who had taken off his shades and was gazing around the room as if he was looking for someone.

"Skeeter?" Gabrielle called out over the loud music. "Where have you been?"

"Hey, Gabrielle. Just getting back in town."

"Everyone's been worried about you. No one knew where you went."

"Had a few things to take care of out of town."

"Why so secretive?"

He shrugged.

"A lot has happened since you left. Do you remember Roger Moore?"

"Sure. I never hung with him much, just went fishing a couple of times with some other guys."

Did Gabrielle detect hesitation in his response?

"He's dead."

"What?" He was clearly surprised.

"No one has seen him since Valentine's when Aunt Anna died."

"No kidding?"

"And your grandfather and mine, along with the other two cronies, have been acting strange."

"What happened to Roger?"

"I don't know," Gabrielle said, watching him carefully, "but he's been linked to a robbery ring and drugs."

"No kidding."

"Did he ever mention family or anything to you on those fishing trips?"

"No."

He was lying, Cornell thought, but they weren't going to get much out of him that night.

"Welcome back, man," Cornell said.

"Thanks."

"This is a teen party. Adults aren't allowed. Sorry," Cornell said. "The place is open on weekdays. Feel free to come back then."

"Thought I could grab a bite before going home. Don't have a thing there to eat."

"Why don't you fix yourself a plate, compliments of the

house?" Cornell said. "I'll get you a carryout container. The buffet's in back."

Skeeter walked off.

"I wanted to ask him more questions," Gabrielle said.

"He's lying. You don't want him to get defensive. We'll do a little snooping after the party's over."

"He could be long gone by then."

"I don't think so. This is home. If he was hiding, he wouldn't have come here."

Cornell retrieved a container, and Gabrielle watched Skeeter pile food on his plate.

"This is going to be a long night."

As Regina walked out of the movie, she handed Sam's jacket back to him. It had been cooler than she thought in there. Of course, she wasn't dressing for the weather but for Sam. They were on the mainland. And he'd wrapped his arms around her shoulder like they were teens.

"Did you enjoy the show?" Regina asked. It was the latest Tyler Perry comedy.

"Yeah."

Regina glanced at him. Then he took her hand in his. A first for him. He usually kept his distance.

He looked very nice in black slacks, powder-blue shirt and navy blazer. She shook her head. She was so accustomed to seeing him in his work attire she forgot how attractive he was when he dressed up.

"Hungry?" he asked.

"Not after all that popcorn. I'm going to have to repent with a run in the morning."

"I'll run with you."

"You mean you're taking a Saturday off?"

"Yeah. After you planned the movie, I thought maybe we

could do something. How about going by a club before we go back to the island?"

"Okay."

"Sam? Sam? Is that really you?" Two beautiful women approached them.

He looked around and smiled.

"Hi," Sam said.

"You never go out when we invite you," one of the women said. Both looked to be around thirty. They wore designer from their handbags to their jeans and shoes. Their hair had that moneyed look.

"Always working," Sam said. "This is Regina." He didn't introduce her as a special friend or girlfriend. And Regina noticed he'd dropped her hand. Well . . . she captured his hand and smiled at the two women. He told her their names, but she didn't remember.

"Hi," they said. "We try to get Sam to get out to have fun. His company handles the garden at Green Oaks Country Club."

Green Oaks was mostly an African American country club in Virginia Beach.

One of the women tapped him on the arm. "You had us fooled. You told us you work all the time."

He glanced at Regina. "I usually do."

"Nice meeting you, Regina. We'll see you at the club, Sam." They walked off and Regina gazed after them.

"Special friends?"

He chuckled. "No."

Soon she was tucked into Sam's car, and they were driving to a club near the ferry. Regina glanced at Sam from the corner of her eye. Soft music played on the radio, lending an intimate air. Sam had gathered her hand in his again.

She had never looked at Sam as a suitor. He was just that quiet man who was always gardening. Although he never dated on the island, it was apparent he had suitors off the island.

"Want to tell me about your friends?" Regina asked.

"Nothing to tell. They're members of the country club. I see them sometimes when I'm there."

"Looks like they want you to become a member."

"I am. Do you want to go sometime? You used to play tennis. We could play there. They have a spa. We could make a day of it."

"I didn't know you played tennis."

"I started when Ms. Anna sent me away to school."

"Maybe I will. See if I can beat you."

He smiled at her as he pulled neatly into a parking space. "You could try."

"Are you challenging me?"

He turned the motor off. "Yeah. How about tomorrow morning in place of a run. That should work off that popcorn." And then he looked at her. And her heart turned over. It took her a moment before she responded.

"You're on. But afterward, you have to help me study for exams."

"I don't know anything about nursing."

"I have study sheets. You can call out questions while I answer."

He leaned over and pressed his lips against hers. "Be glad to."

Regina's heart turned over. She ran her hand over his shoulders as he gathered her close. She felt the powerful muscles beneath her fingertips.

He kissed her neck, the tips of her ears. He was nuzzling along her collarbone and down the V in her blouse.

Her hands left his back and slid down his side, along his thigh and then inside until she felt the bulge in his pants. She massaged back and forth.

He cupped her breast, running his thumb back and forth over the tip. A moan escaped her lips.

She nuzzled her face in his neck and undid the top

buttons on his shirt, slipped her hand inside, and felt the contrast of skin and hair.

He kissed her with pent-up need and desire.

She started to unzip his pants when suddenly the bright lights of a car pinned them and then it was gone. They came apart and stared at the light like a startled deer. Then the light was gone.

Sam captured her hand and briefly closed his eyes. "Good, Lord, what the heck are we doing right in the middle of the parking lot?" With obvious difficulty, he eased back from her.

"I think we should . . . should get that drink." Sam's voice was thick with need as he blew out a long breath. He brought her hand to his lips and kissed it.

"We don't have to," Regina said, swamped with desire.

"No, baby. Not here." He hugged her again, but gently caught her hands when they began to explore again.

It took a while for them to calm down enough to right their clothes and go into the club.

Gabrielle left the party a few minutes before Cornell and drove home to change into jeans and sneakers for their snooping. Everything was quiet.

Cornell had gotten a handful of the kids to help clean up the restaurant as promised. He'd warned the twins ahead of time that since they were getting the building for free, he wasn't going to pay a staff to clean.

Gabrielle made her way up to the bedroom and changed. She was pulling the last shoe on when she thought she heard a noise.

Heart pumping, she listened—and heard nothing. *Just the house settling,* she thought as she finished tying her shoe. Then she splashed water over her face and applied a moisturizer before she came downstairs.

Cornell was picking her up and hadn't yet arrived. She'd

thought for a long time that maybe she should take one of the pictures in her aunt's closet and have it framed. Maybe put it in the B&B dining room.

She opened the door to her aunt's room and was about to pop on the light when she came face-to-face with a creature from hell. It took a few seconds for her to realize the person wore a ski mask, black pants, and black turtleneck. She could see nothing of his face, not even the glint of his eyes. For a second they both were too shocked to move. It was when the black gloves reached out to her that she stumbled back and dashed toward the door, only to be pulled up short when he grabbed hold of her hair flying out behind her.

Gabrielle came to a tumbling halt against his chest. Her head screamed in pain. His gloved hang covered her mouth.

"Where is it?" His whispered breath rushed against her face.

"Wh-what?" Gabrielle asked.

He smacked her against the head. "The jewels, the bowl, the coins."

"I don-don't know." Gabrielle's teeth chattered so hard she thought she was going to bite her tongue off.

"Are you willing to die for them?"

"I don't know . . . really," she said. And then Gabrielle felt a knife against her throat. "Honestly. Aunt Anna didn't have jewels. Just the bowl."

"You're lying."

She felt the pressure of the knife relax. He started dragging her back toward her aunt's room. Suddenly the knife wasn't at her throat.

Gabrielle's brain started to function again. She'd checked her aunt's room a million times and had come up with zilch. If he got her there, he was going to kill her.

Gabrielle remembered something about stomping an attacker's foot. She lifted her foot and came down as hard as she could.

He yelled out and stumbled, giving Gabrielle a chance to break loose and run for dear life. She heard footsteps behind her, but she plunged ahead. When she reached the door, her shaking fingers fumbled on the lock.

Then he caught her again, tearing her from the door.

Gabrielle screamed.

"Gabby?" She heard Cornell's frantic voice from the outside. "Gabby?"

"Help! Help!" she managed to get out before a gloved hand covered her mouth.

She heard crashing against her door.

The man holding her swore, and suddenly she was free. She lunged for the door and opened it just as Cornell's shoulder hit her with the force of a linebacker, the breath rushing out of her.

They both sprawled on the floor.

"Gabby?"

All she could do was lie there and stare. She was dying. She knew it as sure as she couldn't breathe.

"Gabby? Gabby?"

She opened her mouth but only silence emerged.

He shook her. "Gabby?"

Finally she inhaled a deep breath, coughed, and breathed again. "A man," she finally croaked.

"What? Are you hurt?"

"God, you knocked the wind out of me."

"You okay?"

Slowly she sat up. "Now I am."

"What happened?"

"A man was in my aunt's room."

"Jesus. Looking for that stupid bowl?"

"He mentioned the bowl, coins, and jewels. My aunt didn't have all that stuff. She told me the ancestor had used them to buy the land and supply the farms when Abiola first married in the 1600s."

"Why does he think she has them?"

"I don't have a clue. Did she mention jewels to you?"

He rubbed his shoulder. "No."

"Are you okay?"

"Yeah." He flipped open the phone and dialed the police. "While we wait, let's go to her room and see what's there."

This time when Sam dropped Regina off, he came into the house. They had taken the midnight ferry and it was almost one.

"Want a nightcap?" she asked.

"Sure." He slid out of his jacket and draped it across the chair. She flipped on the TV, knowing the basketball game was still playing and Sam loved basketball. He'd caught snippets of it at the bar.

But when she slid on the couch beside him, his concentration veered from the game.

"Will you answer a question?" Regina asked.

"What?"

"Why are you so standoffish? Why didn't you ever mingle with kids in high school like the rest of us?"

"I wasn't popular."

"But you're a really nice guy. You didn't go out for sports or any extracurricular activities. I know Aunt Anna would have signed you up if you wanted to."

"She would have, but it was a tough time for me. I could barely put one foot in front of the other. And before I knew it, I had graduated. Anna sent me away to school. Said I needed to get to know new people."

"Did it work?"

"Yeah. I have some friends from school. We visit each other."

"I've never seen them."

"A friend of mine is coming to the crab festival next weekend."

"Will I get to meet him?"

"Him, his wife, and they have a couple kids. We usually stay at Virginia Beach."

She popped him on the shoulder. "You prefer Virginia Beach to here?"

He shrugged. "I was always uncomfortable entertaining here."

"Bring them here this time. I'll help you entertain."

"You have exams."

"My last exam is Tuesday."

"Guess I better hire someone to clean up my place."

"Your place is spotless."

"With guests coming, I want the place spruced up some to a woman's liking. What do I know about those special touches?"

"Lisa would be happy to do it."

"You're kidding."

"No, really. Lisa can make a room so pretty it sings. You may have to dish out a few dollars for her to buy a few items."

He shrugged. "I'm game."

His arm tightened around her shoulder. She wasn't thinking about the room or his friends, not even the crab festival when he pulled her to him and kissed her.

The police had come and left. They dusted for fingerprints, but since the man wore gloves, they didn't expect to find anything useful. It wouldn't be long before the calls would start coming. It was an island, after all. The news would soon be all over town. And really, Gabrielle didn't want to talk about it tonight. She'd have to tell her grandparents, then her uncles and aunts, then her cousins. She would have told the story at least twenty times before it was all over.

"Are you up to going by Skeeter's?" Cornell asked. "We don't have to. We can check him out another day."

"I don't think it was Skeeter, do you?"

"I don't know. What did you see?"

"Not much. It was dark. And he only spoke in a whisper." Gabrielle wanted to get out of the house. Chills were still dancing up her spine. Yet she didn't want to leave, just in case. But she couldn't stay at her home alone, either.

Cornell rubbed his shoulder.

"Maybe you should get your shoulder checked out."

"It'll be okay. I'm telling you, when this house was built, they were making doors that worked. You put your body against a door now, it'll crash in on the first hit. These doors would stand against a hurricane."

"They've had their share here," Gabrielle said. "Why don't I put a heat pack on it."

"Maybe when we get back," he said. "I don't think this character is coming back tonight. We'll just drop by Skeeter's for a few minutes. I'm staying with you tonight."

A giant boulder lifted from Gabrielle's chest. There was no way she could stay in the house alone.

Skeeter lived in an old hunting lodge that was sturdy enough, but the front porch was beginning to list to the side from age and storms. It had only two rooms. One room held the kitchen and sitting area, the other a small bedroom with a peg against the door to hold clothing since sometime in the last couple of decades when someone had installed an indoor bathroom in the only closet. It had taken up some of the bedroom space because a tiny shower had also been added.

Skeeter's car wasn't in the yard when they arrived. Cornell pulled his car out of sight into a hidden path that led to a stream. He cut the lights and they cracked the windows, but rolled them up when the mosquitoes started buzzing inside. Gabrielle was hitting at them on her arms.

"If you weren't so sweet, they wouldn't nibble on you. They don't bother me."

"Your jokes are not funny."

It was an hour later when Skeeter finally pulled into his driveway. He nearly hit the tree before his car came to a stop. He staggered out of the car. Skeeter had always had a drinking problem, which was the reason his relationship with Melinda hadn't lasted. She'd made it known she wasn't putting up with a drunk.

"I just remembered. I didn't hear a car take off after you broke in, and I didn't see one in my yard," Gabrielle said.

"He could have parked it farther down the road and hiked to it. Pretty foolish to park it nearby. Remember, Skeeter came by the restaurant tonight. He could have figured you would be away for a while."

"But Skeeter? He's an islander. Why would he do this?"

"We need to check out why Skeeter was away so long. He didn't answer that question."

"Now?"

"No time like the present."

Cornell started the motor and drove into the yard. When they knocked on the door, they didn't receive a response. They continued to knock.

"You think something's wrong?"

Cornell tried the door, but it was locked. Then they walked to the window.

The light was on inside. Skeeter had made it as far as the couch, where he'd collapsed. His chest rose and fell with his snores.

"That fool." He'd obviously passed out in a drunken stupor.

Lisa arrived at the B&B fifteen minutes early the next morning. In the past she never arrived early. Gabrielle was lucky if she showed up twenty minutes late.

"Heard about your break-in. Are you okay?"

"I'm fine."

"They say Cornell came in the nick of time."

Something was up. And Gabrielle wanted to know what. She had to be patient, because eventually Lisa would reveal her true nature. She just couldn't believe that Lisa was all that concerned about her.

Her grandfather also arrived before seven, looking her over critically. Her uncles had stopped by the house on their way to work. Offered her a room in their homes. Or they would send their sons over to protect her.

"I'm thinking it might not be a bad idea for you to move in with your grandmother and me for a while. Just until this thing blows over. Seems we have a crime wave wracking this island. I stopped by to talk to Harper this morning. I don't like it one bit."

"I'm fine. Several people have already offered protection."

"I don't know. I'll feel more comfortable with you under my roof."

"I'm not staying alone."

He glanced at her skeptically. "Everything working all right?" he asked as if he wanted to linger. Sometimes when Gabrielle had a small plumbing problem, her grandfather would make repairs.

"Just fine. How are you, Granddad?"

"Good, good. Something sure smells good in there. I guess I'll join you for breakfast if you have time."

"I'd love to have breakfast with you. You should have brought Grandma with you." Thank God Lisa was there to take up some of the slack.

After their food was on the table, Gabrielle asked, "So did you and Grandma have a fight?"

Hoyt set his fork down with a clatter. "What's with you women? Can't a man have breakfast with his granddaughter?"

"Yes, but you usually bring Grandma with you."

He grumbled and picked up his fork.

"I'm a good listener if you want to talk about it."

He just kept eating.

"Grandpa, haven't you and the men kept this secret long enough?"

"We've taken care of everything that needs to be taken care of."

"I'm not sure of that. John wants to question Jordan Ellis and Skeeter."

"Skeeter's on the island?"

"I think he arrived last night. He stopped by the restaurant."

He glanced at his watch.

"Talk to me, will you?"

"What's with you women? Naomi's going through my stuff. A man can't take a step any longer."

"She loves you. She wants to know everything is all right."

He pushed his plate back. "Everything's all right. I should have gone to the country store for breakfast. I don't know what made me think I could eat in peace here."

Gabrielle stood and walked out with him. "I didn't mean to make you angry."

"I'm not." He shook his head. "Call me if you need me. The boys and I'll be keeping an eye on your place today. And we'll keep an eye on things during the crab feast." He got in his truck and left.

Regina came into the front yard singing. "Hi, Gabby."

"Tell me something," Gabrielle said. "What is it about men that make them so stubborn?"

"You're asking me?"

"Why are you so happy today?"

"I don't tell secrets."

"Everybody's got secrets."

Mitchell and Graham came down a little later than usual for breakfast. Mitchell was clearly angry. Gabrielle glanced at Graham and he mouthed, "I'll talk to you later."

Mitchell got in his car without Graham for a change.

"What's wrong with Mitchell?" she asked, as Mitchell drove off.

"We discovered your grandmother was right. We did the research on his family and discovered they arrived here in the late seventeen hundreds."

"Well, I imagine they still arrived before the ancestors of most Americans. It's not that important."

"To him it is. He's a little put out with me for finding it. I delayed telling him for as long as I could. I know how caught up he is in this 1607 ancestry."

"I'm sure he wants his book to be accurate."

Graham shrugged. "Well, I heard about the break-in. Are you okay?"

"Just fine," she said for the umpteenth time that morning—and the morning wasn't even over yet.

He patted her hand. "I see it disturbs you to talk about it, so I won't bother you. I'm looking forward to the crab feast next weekend."

"So am I," she said grateful for the change of subject.

CHAPTER 15

Cornell's uncle punched him on the shoulder. "She's a looker," he said.

Cornell grunted. They were at the brunch. Gabrielle had appeased her grandmother by first going to church on the island and dragging Cornell along with her. He had to say, the preaching was good. Something he could relate to for a change.

The women were inside, more than likely taking Gabrielle through the third degree. If he wasn't sure she could hold her own and that his mother would protect her like a mother hen—she wasn't about to let this one escape—he wouldn't have left her.

After making his way outside, he found some of the men looking under the hoods of cars. His mother didn't keep liquor in the house. His uncle had snagged his second beer from the cooler in the trunk of his car and wrapped silver foil around the can to disguise it, just in case his mother poked her head outside.

"So they're going to have you tying the knot soon, hey, buddy?"

"We're just dating," Cornell assured him.

"They aren't going to be satisfied until you're as miserable as the rest of us."

"You're just a walking advertisement for marriage, aren't you?"

"No sense in going in blind."

The more beer his uncle drank, the more his tongue loosened.

They'd enjoyed a dinner that would rival their family's Christmas dinner. The moment he saw the table laden with food and cars parked as far as three blocks away, Cornell had started sweating. His mother had saved a place in the driveway for his Porsche—can't have the bride-to-be walking that far.

It was obvious he wasn't going to get the peace he desired talking to his uncle. He sought out his father.

"Glad you could make it, son. First good meal I've had in a while." He chuckled. "You're going to have to bring your young lady by more often. She seems nice."

"She is." He tried to gauge the time when he could discreetly leave.

"Your mother's in heaven."

Cornell felt himself heating up again. "I can tell."

"Don't be too hard on her. She built her life around her children and now you're all gone. It's hard for her to find her footing, so she dreams and worries of wives and grandchildren."

"She's a talented artist. She has plenty to keep her busy."

His dad shook his head. "Not the same."

"You still love her, don't you? After all these years. After all the crap you have to put up with."

"Of course I do. She puts up with me, too. I'm not perfect."

Cornell hadn't quite thought about it from that perspective. His thinking had been one-sided. He wouldn't come out smelling like roses all the time with his woman any more than she'd be Ms. Perfect for him 24-7.

"Whatever we've gone though, my life has been better sharing it with her. She needs her space now and then. I don't fault her going off for a week or so. When I call her, it's my way of saying I still love her. I miss her. It's time to come home."

"I never thought of it that way."

His dad shook his head. "Seems kind of crazy, doesn't it?"

Cornell shrugged. "If it works." Who was he to judge? He

and his dad talked for quite a while before his brothers roped him into a basketball game.

Cornell was feeling pretty mellow by the time he left with Gabrielle.

He parked on the ferry and they left their cars to stand at the bow, catching the fresh breeze as they rode toward the island.

"Your family's pretty nice."

He wrapped an arm around her. "Think so?"

"You had me thinking I'd be going up against the Spanish Inquisition."

"I think my mom threatened them. If they didn't love you, they'd never receive an invitation to her Christmas parties."

"Yeah, right."

"Hey, my mom's a powerful woman. She gets what she wants."

"Are you your mother's son? Do you get what you want?"

He gazed down into those fabulous hazel eyes and almost lost his train of thought. "Sometimes."

It was Monday morning and Graham noticed Mitchell was still sulking. Breakfast sat like lead on his stomach.

"Let's take a walk. I want to keep up my daily exercise."

Graham was already dressed in his Nike's and shorts. They started out walking toward the town. Mitchell was wavering about writing the book at all.

"We can still write the book," Graham said. "We have some valuable research."

"I have a family legacy to uphold. I'm writing a book on my family. Do you understand?"

"Mitchell . . ."

But the older man waved a dismissive hand.

Graham sighed. He knew Mitchell wasn't going to take the news well.

"Let's go." Mitchell had turned around before they reached their turning point, heading back to the B&B.

"What's going on?" Graham asked. "Why are we turning so soon?"

"I want to see the documentation."

Mitchell rushed them back to the hotel. Mitchell barely gave Graham enough time to take a shower before they were heading to the mainland.

An hour later they were searching through files.

"There." He gave Mitchell time to read the information on the first Mary. Then he turned to the documentation on the second wife.

"I can't believe it." Mitchell looked shell-shocked. Graham felt sorry for him. He'd placed so much pride on being part of the original settlers.

"There's only one thing to do," Mitchell said five minutes later.

"What?"

"I'm going to have to research Mary Carpenter."

"But I thought this book was going to be on the original settlers."

"I want to know my ancestors. It shouldn't take long."

Graham stifled a sigh. At the rate they were going, it was going to take forever to write this book—if they ever wrote it. He saw his route to tenure going down the drain. If Mitchell wasn't part of the original settlers, he wasn't very interested in completing the book. They had so much useful information. They'd spent untold hours on the project.

Deeply engrossed, Mitchell raked a hand through his thin hair.

Graham rarely drank, but right now he could use a stiff drink. He wondered if Lisa would meet him after work.

Cornell stayed with Gabrielle every night. They had tried to contact Skeeter again, but he'd disappeared again and hadn't returned to the island.

Usually after a couple of nights with a woman, Cornell was ready for his own space. After snuggling up with Gabrielle on a continuous basis, he still wasn't ready to return to his own place. And he was unwilling to analyze why.

Two weeks had passed since the teen party. It was Saturday. The B&B was packed. Gabrielle had to turn away as many prospective guests as she'd accepted. Some of the guests who had been there the year before had called saying they were spending the night in Virginia Beach but were taking the ferry over for the feast.

Mrs. Claxton had taken over Cornell's kitchen. Bushels and bushels of crabs waited for the hot grease and crab boil. Her secret batter was ready and waiting. Cornell had tried to get the recipe, but the sneaky woman had mixed the batter while he was distracted with one of the twins. He wouldn't be surprised if she'd engineered it.

Gabrielle's mother was preparing for the crab boil. Her dad left before daybreak to go fishing with her uncle. They were due back soon.

"This is such a busy month," Naomi said. "Especially after spending last weekend at the Jamestown 400th Anniversary celebration."

"That was quite a performance," Cornell said.

"Yes, it was. Hoyt usually builds a fire under huge black pots in my backyard. They've been in the family forever. I don't know from which century." Her hair was caught up in a bun on the back of her head, secured under a white cap. "You have a nice setup in your kitchen, Cornell. Air-conditioned, too. I like that. That grease hot enough yet?"

"It's ready," Cornell said. He noticed she hadn't called him "that Price boy" recently.

"All right. Let's do a test first. Make sure the batter's right."

The crabs sizzled in the grease. It might as well have been a dinner bell because all the workers drew near, waiting for the first batch to come out. Gabrielle had even called saying the workers at the B&B couldn't get away and asked him to send some over. He couldn't believe the fuss they made over a bunch of crabs.

"Chance, Lance, come over here and layer those paper towels to sop up the grease," Mrs. Claxton said.

The boys nearly tripped over each other getting the paper towels and layering them in place. Chance planted his feet firmly in place by the pan.

And then Mrs. Claxton lifted the first bunch of fried crabs from the hot grease. A collection of breaths held as she dumped them on the paper towels. Everyone knew they couldn't reach out until she gave the word. Taking a roll of towels, she tore off some sheets and dabbed the excess grease off the crabs.

"You know, I have a draining pan where the grease can drip from the crabs," Cornell offered.

"Doesn't sop up the excess grease," she said.

Cornell had to admit his mouth was watering like everyone else's.

"Is it ready yet?" Chance asked.

Mrs. Claxton frowned and patted once more. "They're ready."

Plates in hand, they seized the crabs like they hadn't eaten food for a week, then scattered to eat them. Shaking his head, Cornell took the single one left.

"Shall we share?" he asked Naomi.

"I need to have at least one taste to see if the batter's right."

"I have no doubt that it is. The only sound I hear is lips smacking."

The older woman actually laughed. She tore the crab in two, giving him half.

He expected it to be good, but Lord. He closed his eyes over the first taste. "You have to give me your recipe," he said. "I would become an instant millionaire."

"Family secret," Mrs. Claxton said.

It crossed Cornell's mind that if he married Gabrielle, he'd become a member of the family. He lost his smile. He was not ready for the big M.

* * *

"Are you all finished yet?" Lisa asked. "My rooms are done."

All of them had cleaned that morning, trying to get the rooms done as quickly as possible. All the guests were at the crab fest.

"I'm starving," Regina said.

"You go ahead," said Gabrielle. "I'll go when you return."

"Bye, y'all." Lisa was out the door in a flash.

"Sam went to the airport to pick up his friends," Regina said. "Their plane was late arriving. I want to wait for them, so if you want to leave now, go ahead."

Stunned, Gabrielle could only look at her cousin. "I can't believe it. Regina, do you actually have feelings for Sam?"

"It started out as wanting him to do my yard. And now . . . Gabrielle, he's everything I've ever wanted in a man. If somebody had knocked me upside the head and said, 'Girl, he's the one,' I would have told them they needed to visit a psychiatrist. I still can't believe I've fallen for him. I feel like somebody shot me with a stun gun."

Laughing, Gabrielle hugged her cousin. "I am so happy. I know he's out-of-this-world crazy for you."

"I don't know about that. We haven't discussed it. And as bold as I can be, I'm shy about bringing it up."

"If you wait for Sam, you'll be waiting forever." Gabrielle couldn't help the tears that sprang to her eyes.

"You can't stand here crying. Now go. Because when Sam arrives, I'm leaving."

"I'm going." Gabrielle took a birdbath and applied makeup before she drove the short distance to the restaurant.

The yard was packed with cars. As she entered the building, Alyssa and Melinda came in behind her.

"How was Arizona?" Gabrielle asked.

"Hot. Melinda's been filling me in on the island news. I

leave and all hell breaks loose. Not only that, I'm missing most of it."

"I'm so glad you're back. I need to talk to you later on."

"You'll have plenty of time. I'm spending the night with you."

"I don't think so."

"Oh, but I do. Nobody here can give you better protection."

Gabrielle liked the idea of being snuggled warmly in Cornell's arms. She didn't like the idea of being grilled by Alyssa half the night. She glanced at Cornell across the room, tall and handsome.

"I'll talk to you tomorrow." Right then the smell of fried crabs beckoned her.

In the morning paper, Roger's picture was projected across the front page.

Gabrielle set her cup of coffee down and read the article. She was full from the French toast Cornell had prepared for breakfast. He was reading the sports section. She slid her foot along his leg. He was nursing his java while he rubbed a hand up her thigh until the only thing she was concentrating on was making love with him again. She was seriously considering reading the article later and getting him back to bed until a statement captured her attention.

"Look at this. The paper says Skeeter had a fight with Roger on Valentine's night."

"We need to talk to him. Let's get dressed."

Before they could move, the phone rang.

"Your grandfather's at it again," Naomi said. "Those men have been hovering all morning. Hoyt's more agitated than ever. The four of them finally got in a car and drove away."

"He didn't say a word about where he was going?"

"I don't know what they're up to," Naomi said. "But I'm worried sick."

Before Gabrielle and Cornell could retreat to the bedroom,

Gabrielle got a call from John, telling her the men had confessed to murdering Roger Peterson.

Gabrielle got in her car and drove to the small station located on the center of the island. No way those men killed Roger. They didn't even know him.

"What are you up to?" she asked her grandfather. They hadn't been arrested yet.

"Go on back to your business," Hoyt said. "This is men's business."

Gabrielle's uncle was arriving with her grandmother. "A bunch of fools," Naomi said. "The older they get, the worse they get. You didn't even know that man, Hoyt. None of you did."

"Just go home," Hoyt said.

But within minutes, the other three wives arrived and John was trying to handle the biggest chaos the office had ever seen. With only a couple of officers on duty, including the sheriff, who wasn't in the station at the moment, the situation was quickly getting out of control.

The entire room was in an uproar when Harper and Alyssa rushed in. Usually their sizes alone were enough to intimidate, but when they were dealing with craggy old women bent on getting their husbands out of jail, they knew if they didn't control the situation, it would control them.

"What the heck is going on here?" Harper's booming voice reverberated around the room. The women rounded on him.

Everybody started talking at once until he held up a hand.

"Ladies, please take a seat. Someone will talk to you in a few minutes."

"But—"

"You've got three choices. Wait here, I can lock you up, or you can leave."

The room fell silent, and Harper and Alyssa went to Harper's office where the men were being held.

"What the heck?"

"Sheriff, I needed someplace large enough to hold all of them," John said.

Out in the hallway, Gabrielle paced back and forth, waiting for the sheriff to come out. She wondered why her grandfather and the men would confess to killing a man they didn't know—a man they had no contact with unless it was to save Skeeter.

She had to tell Alyssa what happened that night.

It was an hour before Alyssa and the sheriff came into the room. Harper didn't know what to think. He had been in this business long enough to know that these men didn't kill anyone. But they were involved somehow. They knew details that only someone involved would know—and they knew a lot more than the police.

He had no option but to lock them up. And he was going to have the entire island on his case.

It took him half an hour to clear the precinct of the women. One was left.

Gabrielle.

Gabrielle knew it was time for her to come forward. She pulled her cousin to the side. "I need to talk to you, Alyssa."

"Come in my office." She closed the door.

"I saw Roger the night he disappeared."

"Tell me what happened," she said, and Gabrielle did.

"It sounds as if he gave you a drug. It could have been a date rape drug. You can wake up without knowing what happened to you."

"That's what I thought."

"And you woke up in your house the next morning? Was there evidence of sexual activity?"

She shook her head.

"Are you sure, Gabby?"

"I'm sure. When you go without having sex for an entire year, you'll feel the difference when it happens. Trust me." She sighed. "I checked on Aunt Anna when I awakened. And she was dead. I thought Roger killed her for the bowl, but she died in her sleep—at least that's what I was told. So you can't lock up those men. They heard that John had questioned Skeeter."

"They know details about his death they shouldn't know, Gabrielle. The sheriff's locking them up because they won't reveal everything they know. If they didn't kill him, and I don't think they did, they saw him after he was killed. They know too much about his death. My guess is they're protecting someone."

"Granddad would never kill anyone."

"Someone did." Clearly weary, Alyssa wiped a hand across her brow. "Look, I don't like this any more than you do. He's my grandfather too for crissakes. Grandma is never going to speak to me again. And my dear old granddad is going to have a record, a man who's never been on the wrong side of the law in his entire life."

"I should have called you from the beginning," Gabrielle said.

"Yes, you should have."

Gabrielle was angry that Skeeter would let those old men go to jail to protect him. They all had wives and families.

She drove to Skeeter's place. The door was wide open, and he was pacing the floor when she approached the door.

Skeeter jumped when he saw her.

"Hey, Gabrielle. Nearly scared me to death."

"What happened the night you left?"

"What are you talking about?"

"Don't play dumb. I know something went down that night. What was it?"

He sighed. "I'm not supposed to talk about it."

"You've got four families in an uproar. The old men are sitting in jail trying to protect you."

"What?"

"They confessed to murdering Roger."

"They didn't murder anyone!"

"I know they didn't. They're protecting you."

"What?" Skeeter looked incredulous. "You think I murdered him?"

"Well, did you?"

"Hell, no."

"I don't know what to believe, Skeeter. Why did you leave?"

He swiped a hand across his face. "I was in a drug rehab program, okay?"

"Drug rehab?"

"Yeah. You know I always loved to drink. Then Roger turned me on to something stronger. Before I knew it, I was hooked."

"Did the old men know he'd provided you with drugs?"

"Yeah. My grandfather's been trying to get me off. He followed me one night and saw me buy it from Roger. He approached us. Threatened Roger. I was scared that Roger would kill him. Anyway, I'd missed work so much I was told I had to get myself together or they'd fire me."

"So what happened?"

"I told my grandfather. I just needed one more hit, you know, until I could stop. So I went to meet Roger. But he was dead when I got there. I didn't know my grandfather was following me. He pulled up with his shotgun. When he saw Roger, he told me to go back home until he contacted me."

William had served in the Korean War. Still considered himself the soldier.

"What happened after that?"

"The next day, my grandfather drove me to this rehab center in North Carolina. And I've been there ever since."

"But as soon as you returned, you got drunk."

"I didn't mean to drink, but I went to see Melinda and she wouldn't have anything to do with me. Said it was over. I love that woman. I couldn't take the fact that she'd left me for good."

"Skeeter, you've got to move forward. You can't hinge your recovery on someone else. You're supposed to start your job in a couple of weeks. If you go in drunk, you will lose your job for good."

"You think I don't know that?"

For some crazy reason, Gabrielle believed Skeeter's convoluted story. But it still left the unanswered question of who killed Roger. And how was she going to get those men out of trouble?

The men had claimed they'd killed Roger in self-defense, and since Roger had a record a mile long, they made bail later on that day.

Naomi made sure she was occupied in rolling up her hair when Hoyt came in the door. She heard him open the refrigerator, slamming cabinet doors. She knew he checked the oven and microwave next.

"Naomi!" he finally bellowed.

Naomi didn't respond.

"You in here?" he said.

Naomi still didn't respond. If he didn't talk to her, she didn't have to respond to him, either. It was a two-way street. She was sick to death of his mess.

"Where are you?"

She heard his footsteps coming down the hall.

"Didn't you hear me calling you? You need a hearing aid or something?"

"Does it look like I need a hearing aid?"

"Why didn't you answer me?"

"Why do I have to respond to you? Do you always answer to me when I ask you a question?"

Standing in the doorway, he regarded her a moment. "Thought you stopped your cycle years ago."

She wanted to just pop him one. "This has nothing to do with my cycle."

With a long sigh, he said, "What did I do now?"

"You don't know?"

He spread his hands wide. "If I knew, I wouldn't ask."

"You don't recall my asking you about fifty times what's going on with you and those men?"

He sighed tiredly. "I already told you it's nothing you need to worry about."

"Don't talk to me like I'm stupid. They locked you up. We have to hire a lawyer to defend you. That costs money. And we aren't rich."

Hoyt pulled off his cap and scratched his head.

"And where is the money from your private stash?"

His eyes widened, but he didn't answer her.

"You aren't going to answer me?"

"You had no business going through my stuff."

"If it's not my business, then whose business is it? You tell me that, Hoyt Claxton. Why don't you just pack your bags and move in with those crazy men you hang out with. You're a bunch of outlaws."

Hoyt signed tiredly. "Where's supper?"

"That's your final answer after being married for fifty-seven years?" When he remained stubbornly silent, Naomi presented him with her back and told him something she'd never told him in the years they'd been married. "Fix it yourself."

He called Jade to update her on their project.

Damn it, he just knew those old men had taken the jewels and bowl from Roger before they killed him. He wasn't going to get this close and end up with nothing. They were out of jail. They had it stashed somewhere.

But he had to be careful. Roger had ended up dead. He planned to live to enjoy his largess and Roger's portion, too.

"We've got to do something more drastic," Jade said. "I can't wait any longer. We've wasted enough time on this job."

"I'm not killing anyone," he said. "That wasn't part of the deal."

"Then you better find those jewels," Jade said, and hung up.

CHAPTER 16

Gabrielle rubbed her temples to ease her headache. She poured herself a cup of apple juice from the fridge and set it on the table.

"Hey." Cornell said, rubbing her shoulders. "Hard night?"

"I don't think I got a wink of sleep."

He pulled her close against him. "I missed you last night, sweetie."

Gabrielle smiled and patted his hand. "I missed you, too." But Alyssa had insisted on staying with Gabrielle. They'd talked half the night about their grandparents and Aunt Anna's bowl.

"So where's Alyssa?"

"She went to interview the old men. Skeeter has disappeared again. She suspects his grandfather is hiding him."

"Gabrielle, we need to talk."

"About what?"

"Us."

She felt a tug in her gut. "Getting tired of me already?"

"Nothing like that. You're the best thing to come into my life."

"That's a change," she said.

* * *

Regina had spent the afternoon with Sam and his friends. It was late when he took her home.

"Lisa did quite a job decorating your house," Regina said.

"Spent me out of house and home," Sam said, his voice filled with disgust. "Dragged me to a dozen stores to pick out pillows and trinkets for the tables. Had to buy a set of fine china, too, she said. Every time I complained, she told me to stop being cheap. Woman doesn't know the value of a dollar."

Regina laughed. "It was worth it."

Sam smiled. "Yeah. My friends like you."

"Are you surprised?" she asked.

He shook his head. "Everybody likes you."

"Including you?"

"Yeah." That single word poured reluctantly from his mouth. "Why are you still with me? I'm doing your yard. Your father's helping me. I would have done it anyway because of Anna."

"I want to be with you."

"But I know you came on to me because of the yard."

Regina blew out a long breath. "In the beginning it was just the yard, but then . . ." She touched his face tenderly. "Sam, you're the last person I would have thought I'd fall in love with."

Dumbstruck, Sam could only stare at her. He worked his mouth, but no words emerged. "In . . ." He cleared his throat. "In love with me?"

"Yeah."

"Jesus, Regina."

She chuckled. "Is it that bad?"

"I've been in love with you since high school."

Regina chuckled. "You can't be serious."

"Yeah."

"That was what? Ten, twelve years ago?"

"Something like that."

"And you're just getting around to telling me?"

"I know you didn't feel that way about me. Hell, you were

the most popular girl around school. You could do a lot better than me."

Regina laughed again. "I can't believe you. But you know what? I don't think I was ready for you back then."

"You weren't ready for me now."

"True. You don't let people inside your heart. You keep your distance. You're still keeping your distance. There's a lot I don't know about you."

"I've lived here all my life. You know everything there is to know."

"No, I don't. But we've got plenty of time to explore each other."

"Damn, Regina. You tell me this now?" His mouth seized hers ever so gently in a sudden opening of lips. He loved Regina's taste, loved the feel of her silky skin, her hips that she was always trying to hide. His hand stole down to caress her curves. While his mouth greedily devoured hers, he heard a gasp of pleasure escape from her throat. And to think that finally, after all these years, she cared for him. He wanted her with a passion that bordered on desperation, and he knew if he didn't let her go now, he'd stay the night. Reluctantly, he pulled back from her. Her mouth was soft, her eyes shining with need.

"I don't want to leave, but I need to be getting back," he said on a ragged breath. He started to get up, but Regina tugged him back.

"You have a curfew or something?"

"Feels like it," he said, but his eyes were on her lips and then his lips were on her. Feeling too good to let him go. Regina gathered him tightly in her arms. She wasn't giving him up.

He pressed her back onto the couch, and she felt the full weight of him for the very first time. Damn, it felt good. He pulled her shirt over her head and streamed kisses down her neck and downward until he pushed her bra aside and suckled at a nipple.

Regina moaned. Her fingers explored his body—his hips, his chest, his back. She moved her hands beneath his polo shirt to feel the texture of his hair and skin. She moved her hands lower, rubbed her hands against his penis.

He shuddered. She unsnapped and unzipped his pants, and then she had the full length of him in her hands.

He groaned and moved against her. "I . . . I . . ." She gripped his head in her hands and brought him back up to her, kissing him so deeply she thought he was going to take her breath away.

He wasn't getting away from her. Not tonight.

She pulled his shirt the rest of the way off and tossed it aside. She gripped his pants and slid them down his hips, hooking her feet in the waistband. He lifted his hips and she maneuvered his pants all the way down.

His hands fumbled with her pants. Felt in the front for the zipper. "Where is it?"

"On the side," she said.

He slid the zipper down and dragged the pants off her hips. "Where're my pants?"

Regina tried to drag him back.

"My pants?"

"Forget the pants," Regina snapped, frustration overriding common sense.

He searched frantically.

"Come back here. What are you doing?"

"Got 'em."

He kissed her again. "You with me?"

"Heck yes. I'm trying to get you to stay with me."

"Sure?"

"I'm going to kill you."

He chuckled, ripped the wrapper from the condom, and slid it on. "Next time you'll do that."

"Okay."

All laughter dissipated as he slowly slid into her. On a deep moan, her legs tightened around his hips. For a moment he didn't move. She wiggled beneath him. And then he was moving deep within her.

Regina felt like she was receiving a slice of heaven as he moved within her. She tightened her arms around him. Tightened her legs, lifted her hips to feel him even deeper. Sam gripped her hips in his hands. And suddenly she was on fire and cried out as the most explosive orgasm ever blew her into a million pieces.

Sam gripped her hair in his hand and gazed deeply into her eyes.

"Regina," he said roughly, straining against his own impending release. His eyes were so serious. And then his voice softened. "I love you," he said on a ragged breath. "I love you more than anything on earth." And then he was moving in her again until his roar split the air.

The next day was cool, and Jordan Ellis came roaring into the B&B's yard on his motorcycle. Gabrielle couldn't help thinking that he and Alyssa would be a match made in heaven.

Jordan was six-four, maybe even six-five. Alyssa was six feet even and proud of it.

"Gabby. How's it going?" Jordan asked.

"Okay."

"I'm looking for your sharp-tongued cousin."

"Which one?"

"Oh, you've got several? I meant Alyssa."

"She's back from her trip, but I don't know where she is. If I see her, I'll tell her you're looking."

He nodded. "Well, I guess I'll check out Cornell's place. Get something to eat."

"Actually, I'm on my way there. See you shortly."

He patted his motorcycle. "Hop on."

Gabrielle eyed the attractive machine, but she wasn't comfortable riding with anyone but Cornell. It was a sensual experience with him. "You go ahead. I'll be just a few minutes behind you."

He hopped back on his bike and took off down the road.

Gabrielle told Regina she was leaving for an hour. Regina had such a lovesick look on her face, Gabrielle had to shake her to get her attention.

"What?"

Gabrielle laughed. "What did you and Sam do last night? It's getting worse and worse with you."

"I'm not telling," she said, and started to walk off in a daze.

"Regina . . ." Gabrielle caught her arm. "Earth to Regina."

"Yes?"

"I'm going down the street. I'll be back in an hour."

"Okay."

Gabrielle didn't know if she could trust her B&B in this woman's hands, but she drove the short distance to Cornell's. Jordan's bike was parked outside, and he was already in the building.

When she went in, Jordan and Cornell were at a table talking. Gabrielle approached them. Cornell stood and kissed her lightly on the lips and she sat beside him.

"Where've you been, man?" Cornell asked Jordan.

"Working like hell. Needed a vacation. Got time to go fishing?"

"I'll take the time."

Jordan frowned. "Roger still around?"

"You haven't heard? They pulled his body out of Heron Lake."

Jordan sat erect in his chair. "You're kidding."

"Yeah. All kinds of crazy crap's been happening in the last couple of months."

"Including my grandparent's neighbors."

"Man, some of these women make you think twice about closing your eyes at night. You better make sure you're on her good side before you fall asleep." Cornell smiled at Gabrielle.

"What happened?"

"Mrs. Fisher was sick, man. She carved her husband up and stashed him in the freezer."

"Holy shit."

"Nobody knows how long he was in there because nobody ever saw him."

"How did they find out?"

"She died in her sleep. Heart attack or something," Cornell said.

"Grandma had given her some pies, which she stored in the freezer. She was going to use some for her wake."

"Opens the freezer and bam," Cornell said.

Jordan shook his head. "And this used to be a quiet little place. Did they find out who killed Roger?"

"Nope, still searching. He was involved in some theft ring."

"He was a sick SOB. Slipped something in Gabrielle's drink the last time I was here."

"You knew about that?" Gabrielle asked.

"Yeah. I was at the bar. I could see you zoning out when he slipped you out the door. I caught up with you before he got you in his car, smashed my fist in the SOB's face and took you home."

"So you took me home?"

"Yeah. Your aunt let us in. I told her what happened. She didn't tell you?"

"When I woke up the next morning, I found her dead in her bed." Gabrielle shook her head. "I couldn't remember a thing. The last thing I recalled was sitting at the bar with Roger. The next morning I woke up and Aunt Anna was dead."

"Jesus."

"The doctor said she died in her sleep from a heart attack. I was worried for a time that Roger had killed her trying to get the bowl. Did you see Roger after that?"

He shook his head. "I walked back to the bar to get my truck, then left town. Alyssa wouldn't see me. Sent her two dozen roses to get on her good side." He shrugged.

"Maybe she'll come around."

"Are you going to hang around for the Founders Day celebration?" Cornell asked.

"Yeah."

"They've got all kinds of things planned."

"Grandma's been working herself ragged on it. We usually show the bowl at the special ten-year anniversary. But this year . . ."

Cornell wrapped an arm around her shoulder. "It'll be okay."

The family gathered at their grandparents' house that evening. Naomi still wasn't speaking to Hoyt and he'd gone stubborn. He was rarely at the house anyway since he spent most of his time with his friends.

Gabrielle's uncles were on the back deck trying to figure out what to do to get the situation under control.

Gabrielle, Alyssa, Lisa, and Regina were crowded in the tiny kitchen with their grandmother preparing a snack. The older women were in the other room conversing. Obviously they'd been through it before and decided to keep a safe distance from the action.

"You stay married to a man all these years and this is what it comes down to," Naomi said.

"Makes you want to stay single forever," Alyssa said. "I know I'm not putting up with any mess from a man."

Lisa rolled her eyes. "Especially when you can whip his butt."

"I can whip yours, too."

"Children, children," Regina said, mixing the ingredients for the deviled eggs.

"She's been on a cloud all day," Gabrielle said, slicing ham to serve with crackers and cheese. "You just have to ignore her."

Alyssa rolled her eyes and sat down. She wasn't domestic by any stretch of the imagination.

"You're just jealous," Regina said. She took a plastic spoon and scooped up a little of the egg mixture and held it for Gabrielle to taste. "Enough Worcestershire?"

Gabrielle nodded. Regina filled the egg halves while Gabrielle topped the crackers with the ham and cheese.

"Hand me a couple of crackers, please," Alyssa asked. "I'm starving."

"What's happening with the investigation?"

"I can't talk about that." She got a plate and started piling it with food. Naomi had fried a chicken and made potato salad.

Alyssa's father came in the room, looked at all the women, and took a step back as if he'd ventured into a hornet's nest. Obviously he was the one the other men had sent to the slaughter.

He grabbed a cracker and munched on it. "Sure is good. Maybe I'll take a plate outside." The tallest in the family, he was six-five and towered over everyone else. But in the face of his mother's stare, he probably felt a foot shorter. He squared his shoulders.

"Mama, you and Dad need to patch this up. Daddy said you weren't speaking to him. You all been together too long to let this mess come between you."

"Did you talk to your daddy?" Naomi asked, darting a lethal glance at him.

"Yeah, but—"

"Was *I* the one sitting in jail?"

"No, but—"

"So why are you in my kitchen telling me what to do? I don't need your advice. Go on back outside with your boys. Tell your daddy to straighten up."

"I've already tried to talk to him. He's as stubborn as you are. Somebody has to be reasonable." He looked at the five women and shrugged, glad of a reason to escape. He'd forgotten to take his plate.

"I guess you told him," Alyssa said.

"Alyssa got her sharp tongue from you, Grandma," Lisa said.

Alyssa ignored Lisa and touched Gabrielle's arm. "Tell me about the professors."

"Not much to tell except they're working on a project about the first families and how they settled in this area." She told her about Naomi's announcement.

"Graham told me he found the documentation to corroborate what Grandma said," Lisa said.

"Mitchell's daughter checked into the hotel a couple of days ago," Gabrielle said. "She's here with a friend for the celebration."

"Grandma, you never actually told me the story of how Abiola met up with her husband and settled here." Nobody but Lisa would have the nerve to broach that subject with Naomi. Gabrielle stifled a sigh and waited for the lecture.

"If you girls got more involved with the family history, you'd know. I keep telling you to get involved in the Founders Day program."

"Lord, have mercy," Lisa muttered. "I wish I hadn't asked."

"When times get tough, and they always do, remember Abiola's story. You come from strength. Abiola wasn't a weakling. She did what she had to do to survive. And we're proof of that."

Lisa was clearly regretting her question by the time Naomi said, "Just sit down and I'll tell you the story. Otherwise I'll go to my grave with the information."

A little over a year after the women struggled to survive on the island, a group of men arrived. They were a hunting party hired to gather fresh meat for some of the settlers in Jamestown. They had gone fishing, and while they were out, a storm came up and washed them to the island. The men were as shocked to see the women as they were to see them. The women didn't know if the men were friendly or not, but

*they were glad to see other people, to know they weren't in
some strange place alone. They were even more glad to see
Englishmen who spoke their language. The men shared their
fish and caught meat for the table. The women used their
spices and cooking skills to prepare dishes fit for kings.*

*The men helped them patch up their huts and built more
substantial houses around the place. Work on the island was
nonstop. The women had worked from sunup to sundown to
survive.*

*Within a couple of days, people started pairing off. Before
the men left, they had chosen women to marry. The one
named George had chosen Abiola. A man called John had
chosen Elizabeth. The men took the meat back to the onshore
settlement, for by then, they'd worked off their indentured
status. By then the settlements had begun spreading out.*

*When they returned, several other men came with them.
Soon all the women were married. Some of them left the
island to settle in other places. Four families stayed on the
island. Abiola was sad to part company with Elizabeth, but
her husband wanted to live on the mainland.*

*The women used their riches to purchase the land and
equipment needed to settle and begin their livelihood.*

"So you're saying Abiola married one of those white
men?" Lisa asked.

"I thought you all knew that by now. There was no one else
to marry. According to the records, it wasn't until 1619 when
a boat of Africans arrived on the island. By then Abiola was
already married. They were indentured servants just like
many of the whites who settled in 1607. In seven years after
they'd worked to pay back their passage they were free to do
what they pleased."

"Hmm."

Naomi put a couple of deviled eggs on a plate. "Race
wasn't as big a deal back then as it is today or even later in the

seventeenth century. Class distinction was based on economics. As a culture, we've had advances and setbacks for as long as we've been here."

Lisa shook her head. "Somebody's always hating. But more important for now, what are you going to do about Granddad?"

"I'm not going to do a thing about him. He's the one who has some explaining to do," Naomi said. "And until he does, I have nothing to say."

"You're leaving?" Lisa asked Graham. A duffel bag was on the bed. He was folding shirts and placing them neatly inside.

"Not for a couple of days. Mitchell doesn't know what direction he's going in. He's going to stay on for a while to find his footing. When he decides what he's going to do with this project, I'll be back to help him. I've still got to get on that tenure track. And I still believe this book is the way."

"Oh, I hate to see you go," Lisa said.

Graham grinned. "I can't believe it. You'll miss me, huh?"

Lisa rolled her eyes. "Get real," she said, but she couldn't stop the disappointment.

"How long is it going to take you to finish up? We can spend the afternoon together."

"I'll get off at two."

"Meet me in the village? We'll take in the shops. And maybe go by the Founders Day site. They're working like heck setting everything up."

"Maybe we'll check out the artists' village," Lisa said. "They'll have stuff out early."

Graham grinned. "It's a date."

"Have you seen my father, Gabrielle?" Mitchell's daughter, Kelly Talbot, asked.

"Not since breakfast."

"He's so disappointed he isn't one of the original settlers, but knowing him, he'll find something else to capture his interest. He won't stay down for long."

"Good for him. So what are you up to today?"

"I'll probably go by the artist's village with June. Can't wait for the big day. June said the crabs were fabulous. Will they have them tomorrow?"

"They may have boiled crabs but not the fried."

"Next year I'll come early."

"Make your reservation soon. I'm almost full for the crab festival."

"Already?"

"Can you believe it?"

"Put me down for a room, please. The same one June and I are sharing now."

Gabrielle pulled out her book and logged the reservation. "Done. Enjoy your day."

As soon as Kelly left, Lisa rushed into the lobby. "I'm going to clean up in here, then I'm leaving."

"Why the rush?"

"I'm meeting Graham. He's leaving soon and we're going to spend the afternoon together."

Lisa had come in at six that morning to start on the rooms. She'd worked straight through to one.

"I'll get the lobby. Why don't you go? You didn't get a lunch break."

"I have time to get it before I leave."

"If you're sure. I won't dock your pay."

Lisa didn't take the time to respond. She straightened, vacuumed, dusted, and washed the glass in the door before she tore out of the building. Lisa had come a long way since their falling out.

"See you," Gabrielle called out. Lisa waved and ran to her car.

Regina left soon after Lisa. It was hours later before Gabrielle was almost ready to leave. Because of the celebration, she didn't have the meet and greet, but she set out snacks in the dining room for the guests. A few were milling around, and she socialized with them.

When the phone rang, she excused herself.

"Good evening, Paradise Bed and Breakfast," she said.

"Gabrielle Long?" a muffled voice asked.

"Speaking. How may I help you?"

"You can help me by bringing me the bowl and other antiques your aunt has hidden."

"What?"

"I have Lisa. And you'll get her back after I have the valuables."

"I don't—"

"You have until daybreak tomorrow to find and deliver it all or I'll kill Lisa."

"How do I know you have her?"

"One moment."

"Gabrielle?" Lisa's frightened voice came over the line.

"Are you okay?"

"So far."

"Lisa—"

"You have until daybreak," the voice said.

"I don't have—"

"I'll call you in the morning to give you the drop-off point." The person hung up.

Gabrielle called her grandmother to tell her about the kidnapping, then she ran out the door. On her way to her house, she called Alyssa.

"Girl, I can't just take off from work."

"It's an emergency." All these months she'd tried to find the bowl and couldn't. And that man mentioned other riches. What riches was he talking about? There was only the bowl. She needed to contact Sam since he'd lived with Aunt Anna.

* * *

Lisa shook her head. It was morning. She had to get up and get dressed for work. She tried to roll over in bed, felt herself caught by something. Her eyes snapped open. She looked around. She wasn't in bed. What in the world? She was in an old cabin tied to a chair. She pulled against the ropes. Her hands were going numb. Fear ran up her spine as she tried to figure out how she got in this predicament.

Now she remembered. She was supposed to meet Graham. The village shops had stocked extra items for Founders Day, and artists had set out their paintings and sculptures. There were specialty items like homemade soaps and jewelry. Many outside vendors were going to be at the event that weekend. She and Graham were going to cruise the stores a day ahead of time because things were going to be crowded tomorrow.

What day was it? Was it Founders Day? Had she slept the night away?

"Hello?" she called out.

No one answered. She must be in the middle of the woods. The cabin looked like it hadn't been used for ages.

Why was she tied up? What did they want? The last thing she remembered was talking to one of the hotel guests. Kelly Talbot, Mitchell's daughter, and June Marshall to be exact.

"Oh, God."

Lisa heard a voice behind her. "Hello?"

"Umm."

Lisa scooted her chair around until she was facing—Kelly. "What's going on?"

Kelly shook her head. "I don't know. You tell me."

Why would they kidnap the two of them? They had nothing in common.

"Who brought us here?" Lisa asked.

"I don't know."

She'd been as knocked out as Lisa had been.

"Where are we?"

Lisa glanced around the room. All the windows were caked with grime except for a tiny space someone had cleaned off on one of them. "I don't know." Was a serial killer on the island? They still hadn't figured out who'd killed Roger. Were they going to kill them?

Lisa started to shake all over. No telling what they'd do to her. What if Mrs. Fisher had been murdered? What if some serial killer had cut up Mr. Fisher and was going to do the same thing to Kelly and her?

Tears started rolling down Lisa's cheeks. *Lord have mercy.* Lisa looked up toward the ceiling. "Lord, if you get us out of this one, I promise to be good. No more going into work late. No more hassling Gabrielle about that damn bowl."

"What're you doing?" Kelly asked with a shaky voice.

"Hush up, I'm praying. It might have been a while since I've been to church, but I remember how to pray." She looked up at the ceiling again. "Lord, I'll stop cussing. I'll make it to church more often. No more shacking up with men. No more drinking. Oh, Lord, this can't be the end. Please, Lord! Don't let them chop me up."

"What are you talking about?" Kelly asked.

"They've been chopping up folks around here."

"Why didn't anyone tell me?"

Thinking about poor Mr. Fisher, Lisa's sobs came faster. Before she knew it, she was howling out loud, her body wracked with shudders. Then she heard Kelly crying beside her.

CHAPTER 17

Gabrielle scrubbed a shaky hand across her face. "The bowl has to be here somewhere," she said. Sam, Regina, Cornell, and a couple of cousins were there. Alyssa was talking to their grandfather and the other men, trying to piece together what was going on. Her uncles were on their way to the island. "I've gone through these rooms a million times."

In the end, her aunt had been pretty much confined to the house. The most logical place was her bedroom. But where on God's green earth could it be in there?

"Hey, Gabrielle!" Graham called out.

What was he doing there?

"Lisa didn't show up. I went back to the B and B and your grandmother said something happened to her."

"She's been kidnapped."

"Kid—come on. You've got to be kidding. Why and who would kidnap Lisa?"

"We don't know."

"What can I do to help?"

Gabrielle appreciated his concern. "You've been at the B and B for a while. Have you noticed anyone suspicious?"

He shook his head. "Just everyday people coming

and going. You don't think anyone from there is involved, do you?"

"I don't know. We have to get back to work."

"I don't want to get in the way. I'll go help your grandmother at the B and B."

"Thanks, Graham."

"Where the hell have you been?" Jade asked.

"Around. Why?"

"I need you over here."

"I can't come there yet," he said. "It'll look suspicious."

"Get your ass over here."

"Be reasonable. I'd be missed. I'm a fixture here. I have to show my face."

"I can just kill them and be done with it. They're about to drive me crazy with the racket they're making in there. I had to go outside."

"You can't kill them," he said, concerned for the women's safety for the first time. "You promised."

"It's up to you."

Frustrated, he rubbed the sweat from his brow. What did she do to the women? Jeez, why did he ever get involved with that sick bitch? Thank fate it was almost over and he'd never have to see her again. Didn't want to be in the same city with her.

He had his suspicions that Jade killed Roger. She'd dated the man, but Jade wasn't loyal to anyone but Jade. And if she'd killed Roger, she'd have no qualms about killing those women.

He turned his car in the direction of the ferry.

By the time Graham made it to the cabin, Lisa looked as if she'd been beaten to death and rung dry.

"Lisa?" He glared at Jade. "What the hell did you do to them?"

"I didn't do anything. They just lost their minds crying and carrying on as if I'd done something."

"Graham, you've got to save us," Lisa pleaded. "How did you know we were here? She's going to kill us. Help us, please."

Graham hugged Lisa as best he could with the ropes tied around her. He grabbed tissue from his pocket and wiped her eyes and nose.

"Okay, blow," he said, holding the tissue to her nose.

Lisa blew. "Graham, you've got to watch out for that woman. Help us."

The woman rolled her eyes. "Oh, please. What is this, the comedy show or what?"

"You scared the hell out of me. You know I can't be away from the B and B that long. It'll look suspicious."

"Graham, what's going on?" Lisa asked.

"Lover boy here has kidnapped you."

"June, Jade, which is it? Who are you?" Kelly asked. "What . . ."

June sauntered over to her friend and leaned over her chair. She kissed her long and hard. "Sweetheart, you didn't really think I'd fallen in love with you, did you? I needed information about your dear old dad. I needed an excuse to be here."

"I . . . I thought you loved me."

Graham sneered. "Guess you had to learn it the hard way. Jade doesn't love anyone."

"June?"

"The less you know the better, love." Jade left the woman's side.

Kelly began to sob softly. "How could you?"

"Graham, why did you kidnap us?" Lisa asked.

"I didn't want to. I didn't have a choice."

"Don't tell me you really have feelings for her," Jade

scoffed. "He wants your aunt's bullion and jewels. So just forget the romantic notions you had about him."

"But she didn't have bullion and jewels, only the bowl. And no one can find it."

"For your sake, sweet cheeks, you better hope somebody finds it."

"Graham?"

Graham sighed. "I'm sorry, Lisa. We had to do something to get it."

"You just pretended to be my friend? Why should I be surprised?" Sadly, Lisa shook her head. "You're just like all the others. You just use pretty words. You know how to get people to trust you, don't you? I'm such a fool."

"I didn't pretend. I care, Lisa."

"No, you don't. You were using me. You even asked me questions about that bowl. I've got to say, you're better at it than most. So what are you going to do now? Kill me after you get it?"

"I'm not going to kill you."

"You'll be on the run the rest of your life. You are going to kill me. You can't leave Kelly and me alive. We can identify you. I may have been stupid, but I'm not crazy."

"By the time they find you, we'll be long gone. They won't find us."

Somehow she wasn't reassured.

It was three in the morning. Daybreak would be here in a couple of hours. They'd torn Aunt Anna's house apart. Things were scattered all over the place. Goose bumps spread over Gabrielle's body. She and Lisa might fight like cats and dogs, but she wouldn't wish this on her. Lately she was beginning to like her cantankerous cousin. She hoped Lisa would live to fight with her another day.

Around eleven the previous evening, Mitchell had announced his daughter was missing, along with her friend. He was worried sick. Someone had seen a woman drive off with both of them.

Alyssa had reported the kidnapping, and the FBI had arrived hours ago. They had attached tracing equipment to Gabrielle's landline.

Cornell had made it all more tolerable. He hadn't left her side since he found out, and he'd been so supportive.

Regina shifted a mattress. "I wouldn't be surprised if Lisa didn't stage this thing herself. She's been after that bowl for years. Worried Aunt Anna to death until she turned a deaf ear. I know she hassled Gabrielle."

"You don't really think she'd do a thing like that, do you?" Gabrielle asked.

Regina shrugged. "If it was just her missing, I'd say yes. But Mitchell's daughter doesn't know her that well."

The FBI had told them to be visible about searching for the antiques. Sam and Cornell were still outside digging up every bush. There were holes all over the yard. Mitchell and Graham had joined them. Gabrielle was grateful the men were willing to help out. Graham had been a godsend, because her uncles and cousins were combing the island looking for the women.

Naomi and the women from the Missionary Circle had gone through the B&B and storage shed with a fine-toothed comb. The women had finally gone home, but Naomi had come to the house.

Gabrielle was leafing through some book on the shelf.

"I can see Aunt Anna laughing at us or trying to help us," Regina said.

"What was her favorite place?" Gabrielle asked. She was so weary, she was standing by sheer will power. "I know she loved to sit and watch the ocean."

"When Uncle Lucky's health declined, she would sit on that old bench in the backyard with him. The two of them would look out toward the rocks for hours," Regina said. "It was his favorite place when he got feeble."

"I wonder if it's under the bench," Gabrielle said.

"She wouldn't leave anything that valuable on someone else's property, especially a man she spent half her life fighting with."

"Even you said they made up when he was sick. Besides, we haven't been able to find it on *her* property," Gabrielle said. "What do we have to lose?"

The women ran outside and redirected the men's shoveling.

It took them fifteen minutes to find the bowl. There were a couple of gold bars and a bag full of gold doubloons.

"Oh, my God. I can't believe we found it," Gabrielle said.

"But no jewels," Regina said.

"I didn't expect to find this. Can you believe she had gold all this time?" Gabrielle said.

"These people expect jewels," Naomi said. "We don't have any. I've been praying all evening. Lord, I hope they don't kill those girls."

Gabrielle took the things they found into the house and spread them out on the kitchen table. "We just have to give them what we have."

"You can't give it to them," one of the FBI agents said. "They aren't necessarily going to release the women once they get these."

Naomi inspected the findings. "Our bowl had a design on it that isn't on this bowl. This isn't our original bowl."

"What are you talking about?" Gabrielle asked. "You think this is a fake?" It had been a while since Gabrielle had seen the bowl, but it looked authentic to her.

"No. This is the bowl Mary sold for the money for passage to Philadelphia and to make a new start."

"The kidnappers don't know that," Gabrielle said. "It's still a bowl from that era."

One of the agents glanced at his watch. "Someone should

be calling soon. It's time to clear out." Most of the people scurried out. Sam and Regina, and Gabrielle and Cornell were the only ones allowed to stay. Of course Alyssa was there representing the police department.

There was nothing worse than having to wait. Seconds seemed like minutes and minutes like hours. Gabrielle paced until Cornell pulled her into a seat and sat beside her. He smoothed her hair back and held her tightly in his arms. She welcomed his embrace.

"Lisa? Lisa, are you awake?" Kelly asked softly. June was sleeping somewhere in another room, and if they spoke too loudly, she'd hear.

"Who can sleep?" They'd scooted their chairs back-to-back hours ago and had rubbed their fingers and arms raw trying to untie each other. The knots were so tight they would have to be cut.

"I heard something."

"It's just a mouse scurrying across the floor. Probably smelling the food June was eating earlier."

"Will it attack us?"

"They're more afraid of us than we are of them. Besides, you're bigger than it is."

"It's so quiet," Kelly said. "And it's so dark."

"Not completely. Can't you make out things in the moon-light? I see a sliver of moon through the window."

"I'm from the city, and it looks dark to me. And I hear all those creepy things outside."

"Don't worry about that." Lisa remembered her grand-mother's recital of Abiola's story. Grandma kept telling Lisa she was strong, but she felt as weak as a baby kitten.

"We have to get out of here," Lisa said finally. "They can't leave us alive. We can identify them."

Kelly drew in a ragged breath. "I thought June loved me. My dad doesn't even know about that part of my life."

"Whatever you are, he's going to want you alive."

"He'll be disappointed if he finds out. If I'm dead, it won't matter, will it?"

"Don't talk like that. You're his only child. He'll be heartbroken if anything happens to you. Besides, he was a teacher. All kinds of students have been in his classes." Lisa wasn't comfortable with the conversation. She let people live the way they wanted to. Lord knew she wasn't perfect. She had no room to look down her nose at anyone.

"Let's try to get loose," she said.

Gabrielle's phone rang at four.

"Hello?"

"Thought I told you not to involve the FBI? I should kill Lisa because you didn't follow instructions."

"I didn't call the FBI." At least that much was true. Alyssa had called them.

"They aren't going to be able to help, anyway. Do you have everything?"

"Yes."

"Put the whole lot in a black garbage bag and take the next ferry to the mainland. Head West on 64."

"Then what?" Gabrielle asked.

"I'll call. If I see one FBI agent, I'll kill Lisa. And don't send a replacement like your cousin. I'll know." Then Gabrielle only heard a buzz in her ear. Hanging up the phone, Gabrielle relayed the message, then searched for a black garbage bag.

Cornell stuffed the bag with the things the FBI had collected. A gold-painted brick, a cheap gold bowl someone found in a department store, and old costume jewelry. Gabrielle hoped they knew what they were doing.

"Be careful. You drop that bag off and leave," Cornell said. "I wish I could go in your place."

Gabrielle was so worn out with worry and lack of sleep she couldn't manage a smile to ease his concern. Then he kissed her and for a few seconds held her gently in the comfort of his arms.

"Be careful, Gabrielle. I love you."

For a moment, her gaze touched his. "What a time to tell me."

"Just wanted you to know."

Gabrielle smoothed the frown from his brow, and then she was in her car driving to the ferry. The FBI had given her a second cell phone to use to call them. They also had homing devices in her car and in the bag.

It was a brisk morning, and the ferry was nearly deserted. She knew that on the other side of the island, islanders were preparing for the Founders Day celebration and soon ferry loads of cars would invade them.

Once her car was parked on the ferry, she couldn't stand the confinement. She got out and bought a cup of coffee and made her way to the railing. It was so dark, she couldn't see the seagulls as they flew in sync with the ferry moving across the ocean.

Cornell loved her. She couldn't believe someone with such a warped opinion of marriage was in love with her. Not that he'd asked her to marry him, only that he loved her. At least that was something. Because God knew she'd fallen in love with him long ago.

She didn't have time to dwell on that right now. Not with Lisa's life on the line.

As slowly as time moved earlier, it was moving at warp speed now. Before she knew it, she was leaving the ferry and driving toward 64.

Jade took a last draw on her cigarette and tossed it away. She pulled on her scuba gear. These people were really something.

She knew they'd get the FBI involved. But the good thing about Hampton Roads was you never knew which way a criminal would hit you. She was going to use water. It was going to be almost impossible for them to track her. She'd taken a couple of weeks to plan this.

She could just feel all that money coming in. She'd waited so long for this. This bounty would more than make up for what that traitor Roger had stolen from her. She didn't give a shit about what he'd stolen from the others, but nobody cheated her. And that prissy Graham didn't deserve to breathe. He was so naive. Did he really think she'd let those women go so they could describe her to a sketch artist and she'd have to look over her shoulder for the rest of her life? She could just see it now, walking into the post office only to see her face displayed on the wall.

She did not plan to leave the good old USA. The only way she could stay put was to leave no witnesses. What Graham didn't understand was that he was a witness, too. If the Feds got to him, he'd give her up before he took a deep breath. With him out of the way, there was more for her to spend. She'd already killed Roger.

She rubbed her hands together. Oh, yes. Victory was just around the corner.

Gabrielle's phone rang again. She had made it to 64, but at least she was going in the opposite direction of the traffic. It was a nice weekend and people were coming to town for the beach.

"Did you follow my instructions?"

What did this idiot expect her to say? "Of course."

"That remains to be seen. Of course, your cousin's life depends on it."

"Where do I go next?" Gabrielle asked.

She was given directions to the James River and hung up

when she heard the buzz in her ear. The area wasn't a place she knew well.

Gabrielle's phone rang again. Puzzled, she glanced at the number. Cornell. She pressed the TALK button. "You aren't supposed to call me."

"I know, but I'm worried sick. Where are you headed?"

"To the James River." She told him exactly where. "What are you doing?"

"Just getting off the ferry."

"What?"

"I took the one after you and the agents. I wasn't hanging around wringing my hands."

"Who's taking care of your booth at the celebration?"

"I've delegated."

"Mr. Hands-on?"

He chuckled. "I won't hold you. Just call me after they make contact so I can stay close by. Be safe, sweetheart."

Feeling less alone, Gabrielle disconnected and continued on.

"We made it." Lisa and Kelly had scooted their chairs against the wall. June had left and Graham hadn't made it back to the cabin yet.

"I don't see how this is going to work," Kelly said.

"It's better than nothing."

"Okay, let's go." They hit the chairs against the wall as hard as they could.

"Ouch. That hurts," Kelly said. "My chair didn't break."

"Let's try again. On three. One. Two. Three." They knocked again, but the damn things held. "These chairs are older than I am. They should shatter in pieces."

"They made them sturdier in those days," Kelly said.

"Let's keep knocking." They knocked so long, sweat ran down their faces. But finally the legs gave way and they only had the backs attached.

"I need to catch a breath," Kelly said.

"Just take a couple of minutes. We have to get out of here."

Gabrielle was near the James River. In that location there was only one way in. The FBI cars couldn't get too close without being spotted. She listened to further directions.

"Get out of the car, take the garbage bag, and walk toward the river," the voice said.

Gabrielle was afraid to take the second phone with her just in case the person frisked her. Grabbing the bag, she left the car and walked. It seemed to take forever. But the person stayed on the phone.

"Do you see the boat?"

"Yes."

"Get in it and start the motor. Keep that phone pressed against your ear."

Gabrielle climbed into the motorboat and started the engine.

"Put the coat and hat on."

Gabrielle did as she was told. If any of the agents saw the boat, they wouldn't know it was her. The homing device would tell them where she was going, but she knew they'd lost sight of her. There were lots of small fishing boats in the water.

She was on her own.

"Head to the opposite shore."

Gabrielle had driven several minutes before the voice said, "See the buoy in front of you? Attach the bag to it, then head back in the opposite direction."

"Wait a minute. It's supposed to be a fair exchange. I'm not leaving the bag unless you turn over the women."

"No way. You've got FBI all over the place. I'm not giving them up until I'm safe."

"I don't trust you, either. Fair exchange or no deal."

"Then they're both dead. Your call."

Gabrielle waited a moment. But what could she do? "Okay," she said finally.

"Smart move. As soon as you secure the bag, drive back to shore and leave the boat where you found it."

Oh, God. What chance did the women have now? There was only junk in the bag. At least it left room for bargaining again if the thief really wanted the artifacts. She had to hope they really wanted them. She made it to the buoy and secured the bag. She waited a minute before she took off in the opposite direction. It was still dark, and the bag was soon out of her sight. Oh, my God. Had she made the wrong move?

Gabrielle finally disconnected from the caller. What did it matter now? She called Alyssa and told her what had happened. Then she called Cornell.

Jade retrieved the bag and swam a mile away before she came up near shore. She sat on the bank and opened the bag. Damn, her hands were shaking. Finally. Finally she had what they'd worked so long to achieve. She gently poured the items on the ground and with a small flashlight, she got her first glimpse of the items.

"Son of a bitch!" They were going to be sorry. Did they really think she didn't know the difference? She'd seen the real bowl in Jamestown. And this costume shit wouldn't begin to pass for antique jewelry. Even she knew the difference between some painted brick and the real thing. They would pay.

She tossed the stuff back into the bag and secured it. There were boats close by. But she'd noticed earlier when she was waiting for Gabrielle that two men on one boat had been drinking. She'd listened to their conversation and knew the fishing trip was more to get away from their wives. They were laid back and drunk from a bottle of whiskey. She swam close to their boat and eased the bag onboard, then silently swam beneath the water and on to where her car was parked.

Precious Lisa was a dead woman.

A plane hovered overhead. A Coast Guard boat shone a beam of light on the little boat bobbing in the water.

"This is the U.S. Coast Guard. Put your hands up."

Two men shot up in the boat with their hands reaching for the sky.

One of them said, "We're being kidnapped by space invaders."

The other warbled and fell overboard.

Two divers dove into the water to save him and brought him aboard their boat.

It didn't take long for them to figure out the black garbage bag had been tossed into a hapless drunk's boat.

Jade came to a screeching halt in front of the cabin, took her gun out, opened the door, and marched into the cabin. A lantern gave off a little light inside. The women were standing against the wall. They were still tied, but broken pieces of the chair littered the floor.

"What the hell happened?"

"You get the goods?" Graham asked.

"Hell, no. The bag was full of junk. They're probably interrogating a couple of drunks as we speak." She waved the gun toward the women. "One of them is going to die."

"Wait a minute, Jade," Graham said. "We agreed to steal, not kill anyone."

"That was before they tried to cheat me. We can't go back. This setup was hard enough. I'm not going to get anything out of close to two years of work. So they're dying." She cocked the gun.

The women started screaming.

Graham spread his arms in front of the women as if to protect them. "Calm down, Jade, and think. We can still get our goods. We still have the women. We have something to bargain with."

"Move aside, Graham."

"I can't do that."

"Then you can die with them."

Before she could react, Graham rushed into her like a linebacker and knocked her to the floor. Her gun went off. But before she could push him aside, the women were on her. She saw a foot coming at her a second before pain exploded in her head. "No!"

"Get the gun, Kelly," Lisa called out. She kicked Jade until she was unconscious.

"Oh, God. There's blood all over the place," Kelly said.

Lisa bent to check on Graham.

Graham was dead. Lisa and Kelly had run out of the cabin and found their way to the road, fearing Jade would come to and come after them.

A passerby had stopped to help them.

Jade had ceased to be a problem. Lisa had done a pretty good job rendering her immobile. She was in a Norfolk hospital in a coma.

Lisa's jumpy stomach wouldn't settle as she and Kelly rode home with Gabrielle later that day. All bruised and sore, she felt as if she'd lived the longest twenty-four hours of her life.

Gabrielle reached over and patted her hand. "How are you holding up?"

"I'm breathing," she said. Gabrielle had nearly squeezed the life out of her when she'd picked her up from the hospital, surprising Lisa speechless that she cared so much.

Gabrielle rubbed her hand. "That's saying a lot."

"Yeah. I could sure use a smoke right now or a stiff drink. I'm hitting the bar as soon as I get a nap."

"Don't have any on me. Sorry."

"You were always a goody-goody. You look like hell."

"Haven't had any sleep."

"She put her life on the line for us," Kelly said. "That's something. Besides, I thought you promised the Lord you'd quit drinking if we got out of the mess. You were real religious back at the cabin."

"You had to remind me, didn't you?" Lisa faced Gabrielle whose eyes were focused on the road. "I could hardly believe you'd do anything to save me. Especially with all the trouble I gave you."

"We're family, Lisa."

Being beholden to Gabrielle wasn't exactly the position she wanted to be in, but damn, she was alive! She felt like kissing the ground. "Thanks, Gabrielle. Guess you found the bowl."

"Elizabeth's bowl, anyway and some doubloons. You'll see."

"That old bat has been hording those riches all these years."

"Before you ask, no, we aren't selling them. We're going to have to decide what to do, but I think it would be good to have them displayed at a museum. Maybe at some university."

Lisa blew out a long breath. "Nobody but you and Alyssa would think of something like that." When Gabrielle started to speak, Lisa held up her hand. "I'm not complaining. I'm going with the program."

"Now, I know it's going to snow in May." They all laughed, releasing some of the tension.

When they arrived at their grandparents' house, Naomi was the first one out of the house, followed by the professor.

Lisa thrust open the door and ran into her grandmother's open arms. When Naomi's comforting arms closed tightly around her, Lisa felt the tears running down her face. She felt like she'd cried a river.

"I was strong, Grandma," she said, but she knew her rubbery legs were going to give out any moment.

"I know you were, child." Naomi leaned back and wiped tears from her own eyes, examining Lisa, making sure she was in one piece. "I know you were. You come from strength."

"Guess you knew what you were talking about."

"Of course. I'm your grandmother."

"I remembered Abiola and I thought of what she did when the pirates captured her. How she made a new life here."

"She was a survivor. That's why I told you about her. You can do anything you set you mind to."

It was all a lie, Lisa thought. "I'm always trusting the wrong man. Always getting into trouble. That's the story of my life," she said. "Graham was so nice to me, but he was only using me. I couldn't pick a good guy if my life depended on it."

Using gentle strokes, Naomi smoothed Lisa's hair back from her face. "Focus on the important things. You're alive and you're here."

A lump clogged Lisa's throat. "And Graham died to save us."

"He didn't have to do that. There was some good in him."

Gabrielle stood to the side watching the homecoming as everyone poured out of her grandmother's house to greet both Lisa and Kelly. Gabrielle wiped her own eyes. Mitchell was holding tightly to Kelly. They were both sobbing.

Gabrielle felt like the old folks were imparting wisdom and suddenly everything people had said about knowing your family history made sense. When times were tough, you needed the strength from the past to realize things can be better in the present and future, and that you can survive.

Cornell and Gabrielle stood a half-mile down the shore from the Founders Day festivities. They really weren't in the mood for celebrating, but the fireworks were about to begin and Gabrielle had wanted to see them.

After the ladies were returned to the island, the island doctor had checked them out. Family and friends had made a big production over them before they went to bed. Naomi even condescended to speak to Hoyt. It was anybody's guess how long that would last. At least the men and Skeeter were in the clear, as Jade had killed Roger.

The professor announced that he'd have to spend more time on the island doing research. Graham's research was questionable and he'd have to do it all over again.

After the hoopla had died down, Gabrielle had tried to sleep, but she only managed a couple of hours with Cornell's arms wrapped securely around her.

"Well, at least Grandma got to display a bowl," Gabrielle said.

"There's still the question of what happened to the original one."

"God only knows where that thing is. We tore my place apart and couldn't find it."

Cornell shifted to the other foot. "I was thinking it makes no sense for you to go back there, not when you can stay at my place."

Fireworks suddenly lit up the night sky, reflecting pinpoints of light on the water.

"I love the fireworks here. Always have," Gabrielle said.

Cornell wasn't focused on the fireworks but on Gabrielle. He glanced at the fireworks then. He had to agree the colorful lights dancing in the air were spectacular.

"Did you mean it when you said you loved me?" Gabrielle asked.

"Every word." Another flash of light hit the horizon. "You know what this reminds me of?" Cornell asked.

"No, what?"

"The first night we made love on the beach. It felt like I was seeing fireworks then."

"That was sex."

"No, baby. It was more than sex. Much more." He watched the play of lights for a few moments. "I didn't want to talk about this tonight. I didn't want this to get mixed up with all that happened today."

Gabrielle glanced at him. "What?"

"I know I'm not God's gift to women, and I'm kind of messed up with my ideas about marriage and love, but I do love you. I promise to be faithful and true to you."

"I love you, too," Gabrielle said.

"And I want to marry you. Will you marry me?"

Gabrielle felt like an explosion had hit her head-on. "Well, you know we can't get away from my crazy family," was all she could think to say.

"At least we have something in common," Cornell said. "Is that a yes?"

"Definitely."

With the next explosion, Cornell picked up Gabrielle and swung her in a circle. Her shrieks rent the air as pinpoints of light flashed across her laughing face. That was a picture Cornell wanted to see for years to come.

Dear Reader,

I hope you enjoyed your time with Gabrielle and Cornell, and the many quirky secondary characters. *Golden Night* is the first novel in my "Quest for the Golden Bowl" trilogy. It celebrates the early families who settled in Virginia and their descendents. Our lives are so busy we forget the strength of our ancestors. Sometimes their strength helps us to achieve our goals. So don't forget to sit down with your older relatives and record your family's history. Most would love to tell you stories about their lives and the stories that were told to them about earlier generations.

In the next novel in the series we will visit with Jordan and Alyssa. It promises to bring you fascinating twists and turns, and lots of intrigue, and it will definitely turn up the volume on sultry sizzling heat.

Please accept my heartfelt thanks for your support and for so many kind and uplifting letters and e-mails.

Don't forget to visit my website *www.CandicePoarch.net* for reader questions, recipes, prize drawings, and other interesting tidbits.

You may write to me at: P.O. Box 291, Springfield, VA 22150.

With Warm Regards,
Candice Poarch

ABOUT THE AUTHOR

Candice Poarch is a nationally best-selling author of 16 novels. She was reared in Stony Creek, Virginia, and currently lives in Northern Virginia, with her husband and three children. A former computer systems manager, she has made writing her full-time career. Candice is a graduate of Virginia State University and holds a Bachelor of Science degree in physics.